"According to Mr. Snyder's buddy, I'm your old man."

Tara scoffed at Jack's words. "You're not my man at all." She caught the gleam in his eyes and frowned at him. "You're teasing me."

"Guilty," he said. "But I am at your disposal for the next few weeks. You can do what you want with me."

"I'm not going to ask you to have sex with me, if that's what you mean."

"It wasn't," he said, his grin spreading. "I was talking about helping you refinish that piece of furniture."

"Sorry."

"No apology necessary." He brushed a strand of hair from her face. "I'm flattered that you look at me and think about sex."

She wondered how this conversation had spiraled out of control so quickly. So what if Jack was handsome and charming and likable? She should have acknowledged the growing attraction between them and taken better steps to prevent it. "You weren't listening. I said no sex."

"It's okay with me if we start out slow."

Dear Reader,

Websites of missing persons are filled with images of people who have disappeared, never to be seen again by their loved ones. Way too many of these missing persons are children.

The Truth About Tara grew out of a what-if. As in, what if a woman looked eerily like an age progression photo of a missing child, but didn't want to know if she'd been abducted? What if she was desperate not to be the face on the milk carton?

Out of those questions, the character of Tara Greer was born. Milk cartons don't typically depict the photos of the missing anymore, so Jack DiMarco comes to the Eastern Shore of Virginia to check out a tip for his private investigator sister.

I took a research trip to the Eastern Shore to check out the setting for this book. It's lovely and serene, a peninusla of land surrounded by salt marshes, the Chesapeake Bay and the Atlantic Ocean. It makes perfect sense that Tara would love her life there. I hope you enjoy "visiting" the Eastern Shore as much as I did.

So is Tara a missing person? You'll have to read the book to find out!

Until next time,

Darlene Gardner

P.S. Visit me on the web at www.darlenegardner.com.

The Truth About Tara

DARLENE GARDNER

HARLEQUIN®

entertain, enrich, inspire™

If you purchased this book without a cover you should be aware that this book is stolen property. It was reported as "unsold and destroyed" to the publisher, and neither the author nor the publisher has received any payment for this "stripped book."

PLEASE RECYCLE
THIS PRODUCT IS RECYCLABLE

Recycling programs for this product may not exist in your area.

ISBN-13: 978-0-373-60727-3

THE TRUTH ABOUT TARA

Copyright © 2012 by Darlene Hrobak Gardner

All rights reserved. Except for use in any review, the reproduction or utilization of this work in whole or in part in any form by any electronic, mechanical or other means, now known or hereafter invented, including xerography, photocopying and recording, or in any information storage or retrieval system, is forbidden without the written permission of the publisher, Harlequin Enterprises Limited, 225 Duncan Mill Road, Don Mills, Ontario, Canada M3B 3K9.

This is a work of fiction. Names, characters, places and incidents are either the product of the author's imagination or are used fictitiously, and any resemblance to actual persons, living or dead, business establishments, events or locales is entirely coincidental.

This edition published by arrangement with Harlequin Books S.A.

For questions and comments about the quality of this book please contact us at Customer_eCare@Harlequin.ca.

® and TM are trademarks of Harlequin Enterprises Limited or its corporate affiliates. Trademarks indicated with ® are registered in the United States Patent and Trademark Office, the Canadian Trade Marks Office and in other countries.

www.Harlequin.com

Printed in U.S.A.

ABOUT THE AUTHOR

While working as a newspaper sportswriter, Darlene Gardner realized she'd rather make up quotes than rely on an athlete to say something interesting. So she quit her job and concentrated on a fiction career that landed her at Harlequin/Silhouette Books, where she wrote for the Temptation, Duets and Intimate Moments lines before finding a home at Superromance. Please visit Darlene on the web at www.darlenegardner.com.

Books by Darlene Gardner

HARLEQUIN SUPERROMANCE

1316—MILLION TO ONE
1360—A TIME TO FORGIVE
1396—A TIME TO COME HOME
1431—THE OTHER WOMAN'S SON
1490—ANYTHING FOR HER CHILDREN
1544—THE HERO'S SIN*
1562—THE STRANGER'S SIN*
1580—THE SECRET SIN*
1636—AN HONORABLE MAN*
1666—THAT RUNAWAY SUMMER*
1714—TWICE THE CHANCE
1745—THE CHRISTMAS GIFT

*Return to Indigo Springs

Other titles by this author available in ebook format.

To my nieces Marlee and Reva
for helping me with the scenes where the
Down Syndrome children appear.
They're both longtime volunteers at a camp
for children with mental disabilities.

And to the families of the missing.
May the lost be found.

CHAPTER ONE

THAT WHITE PICKUP WAS as conspicuous as the evening sunset over the Chesapeake Bay.

It took its time in coming, too. For the past block, since Tara Greer had crossed the empty street to walk along the sidewalk, the pickup had rolled along at a speed roughly equivalent to her pace.

In ten or fifteen more minutes, children who walked to school from the bordering neighborhood would start appearing. So would the school buses that transported students from the rural areas of the Eastern Shore that fed into the elementary school.

For now, however, Tara was virtually alone.

Tara glanced back over her shoulder, hearing the slow thud of her heartbeat over the rumble of the truck engine. She couldn't tell much about the driver except that he was male and had thick dark hair. The pickup didn't have a front license plate, so it wasn't registered in Virginia.

Even though it was early June, when tourists seeking peace and quiet were starting to show up in the area, something about the pickup seemed off. The Eastern Shore was geographically removed from the rest of Virginia, sandwiched by the Chesapeake and the Atlantic Ocean, seventy miles north to south but only fifteen miles at its widest point. Wawpaney was about three or four miles inland from the bay, a community of a few hundred without even a bed-and-breakfast. Strangers stuck out.

The school was in sight. Tara walked faster down the uneven sidewalk shaded by leafy oak trees and tall pines. It was barely past eight in the morning, but there would be people, safety if the guy tried anything.

The truck drew even with her, slowing down for the space of a few heartbeats before continuing past her. Tara chided herself for being silly. This was Wawpaney, not the mean streets of a big city. The town's Native American name meant daybreak, the most peaceful time of day. Nothing bad happened here.

No sooner did she have the thought than the driver swung the pickup over to the curb and shut off the ignition. The sigh of relief caught in Tara's throat.

The man who hopped out of the truck was tall, lean and probably in his early thirties. He looked normal enough, but so did lots of prison inmates.

Through an opening between the trees, the man

was momentarily bathed in sunlight that magnified his appearance. He had a square jaw and a nose that was on the long side, a combination that lent him an air of gravity. Or maybe he looked serious because he wasn't smiling.

If he smiled, he'd be handsome. But if he smiled, she'd be even more freaked out.

She veered off the sidewalk, intending to run to the other side of the street. She gave silent thanks that as a physical education teacher she wore tennis shoes to school.

"Wait! Please!" The man's voice was low pitched and pleasing to the ear. "I just need to ask you something."

Tara froze on the dew-damp grass of the swell between the sidewalk and the street, considering once again that she might have overreacted. She drew in a deep breath of bay-scented air, reminding herself it wasn't like her to be skittish.

The man was walking toward her, getting closer with every step. He wore jeans and a light-colored shirt with the sleeves rolled up, projecting a casual coolness instead of sinister purpose. Probably a tourist who'd lost his way. He got to within a body's length of her.

"Do you need directions somewhere?" she asked.

"No," he replied.

She retreated a step closer to the curb, then

stopped and squared her shoulders. She wasn't sure how, but now that she could see the man up close she knew he meant her no harm. Stepping onto the sidewalk, she crossed her arms over her chest. "Then you *were* following me."

"It's not what you think," he said hurriedly. "I was driving over to the school, hoping to talk to you. And then suddenly, there you were."

She should have been alarmed, but his eyes, a velvety-brown shade, seemed kind. His voice was so low it was almost soothing.

"Why would you want to talk to me?" she asked. "I've never seen you before in my life."

If she had, she'd remember.

"My name's Jack DiMarco. I'm visiting from Kentucky." His accent was soft, evident only in the slight rounding of his vowels. He rubbed a hand over his mouth and shook his head. "I'm not sure how to say this."

"How to say what?"

He opened his mouth, closed it then withdrew a piece of paper from the back pocket of his jeans and unfolded it.

"Maybe this will help you understand," he said, holding the paper out to her.

Tara had a premonition that she didn't want to see whatever was on the paper. She didn't know what had gotten into her this morning. She wasn't normally so anxious. Careful not to touch him,

Tara took the paper. On it was the photo image of a young woman with golden-brown hair, a high forehead, wide-set eyes and an oval face with a rounded chin.

Tara's free hand flew to her mouth. "This looks like me."

"I think so, too," the man—Jack—said. "Except for the hair. Yours is more reddish-brown."

It made no sense. Why would this stranger have a drawing of her? She waved the paper at him. "Where did you get this?"

"It's a computer-generated photo done by a forensic artist," he said. "My sister pushed for an updated version of it. She's a private investigator."

Tara caught only the first part of his answer because she was reexamining the photo. Underneath it in large block type was the name Hayley Cooper. The smaller print below the name blurred as she belatedly recalled his last two words. Her chin came up. "You're a private investigator?"

"I'm not," he said. "My sister is. Since I was coming to the Eastern Shore, anyway, she asked me to check out a lead on one of her cases to see if it was worth pursuing."

"What case?"

"A missing-person case."

Tara's shoulders relaxed. She breathed in air that carried the familiar smell of salt water and late-spring blooms. Without reading the rest of the print, she extended the sheet of paper back to him. "There's been a mistake. I'm not Hayley Cooper and I'm not missing."

"You don't understand." He nodded down at the piece of paper. "That's an age progression. It's an approximation of what the missing person would look like today."

Tara's stomach tightened as the tension returned. She remembered a magazine article a few years back about Jaycee Dugard, a missing child who'd been found after being held against her will for eighteen years. The magazine had run Jaycee's current photo and her age-progression one side by side. They'd looked remarkably alike.

"What does this have to do with me?" Tara asked.

"Maybe nothing." He rubbed the back of his neck. "Here's the deal. My sister is investigating the case of a three-year-old who was abducted twenty-eight years ago from a shopping mall in a little town outside Louisville."

"And?" Tara prompted.

His mouth twisted. "Is there any chance you could be her?"

It felt as if all the blood rushed from Tara's head. She fought not to sway. The stranger was watching her carefully, as though she were a specimen under a microscope.

"That's crazy," Tara said.

"You're about the right age," he said. "Hayley would be thirty-one in a few weeks."

"I'm thirty-two." Tara needed time to gather her composure while she assessed how to handle the situation. The next few moments could be crucial. "What led you to me?"

"I'm not exactly sure," he said. "That photo I showed you, my sister made sure it was posted on all the missing-persons websites. She's gotten dozens of tips, too many to physically track down every one herself."

Tara wanted to find out more about the websites, but it was more important to convince the stranger he was wrong about her.

"I've lived in Wawpaney my whole life," Tara said. "I've never even been to the Midwest."

He tilted his head. "Are you sure? Most people don't have memories from their first few years."

Tara had only one, although it had never made any sense. She'd gotten good at banishing the memory, if that were truly what it was. It had been years since she'd awakened abruptly from a deep sleep with her body shaking and tears dampening her cheeks.

"I'm sure I wasn't abducted." She managed to laugh. "The neighbors would have been awfully suspicious if a three-year-old suddenly joined the family."

Before he could respond, she added, "Besides,

I've seen baby photos of myself. You have, too, right?"

A corner of his mouth kicked up. He seemed to relax. "I'm from a family of six," he said. "My mom takes so many photos she should have bought stock in Kodak."

"My mother, too." Tara was relieved the hand that still held out the paper to him wasn't shaking. This time he took it.

"Sorry to have bothered you," he said. "My sister warned me the lead probably wouldn't pan out. Most of them go nowhere. But you've gotta admit, that photo looks an awful lot like you."

"I'm sure age progression isn't an exact science." Tara needed to get away from him as soon as she possibly could. "If you'll excuse me, I've got to get to school. Class is starting soon."

"Of course." He seemed about to say more, but she didn't give him a chance, passing by him and continuing on the cracked, narrow sidewalk to Wawpaney Elementary.

She was fortunate that Jack DiMarco wasn't the private investigator in his family. Otherwise, it might not have been so easy to convince him she wasn't the grown-up version of Hayley Cooper. She forced herself to act normally and walk at a measured clip, resisting the urge to glance back to see if he was still studying her.

She couldn't afford to do anything that would make him suspect that most of what she'd just told him were lies.

MOST DINERS THAT LOOKED like old railroad cars were actually cleverly designed fakes. Or so Jack had heard. The place with the silver exterior where he stopped for breakfast just outside Wawpaney, though, had to be an exception.

The inside was long and narrow, with a counter lined with stools running the length of one side of the diner. Opposite the counter were booths with windows that overlooked the parking lot. It seemed as though the floor rumbled when Jack stepped inside, as though the railroad car still had some miles left in it. That could have been his runaway imagination, though.

He took a seat at the end of the counter and looked over a plastic menu with fingerprint smudges— it ran the gamut from breakfast to dinner. Home-cooked entrées, tried-and-true favorites and dishes with fresh ingredients populated the menu. The scent of bacon and eggs filled the air.

The place was nearly full, although it probably held no more than thirty or thirty-five customers. Conversational voices blended together to create a continuous hum.

Jack looked up from the menu, surprised that a waitress was standing across the counter from him, waiting. Her curly black hair framed a round, friendly face. She was so short they were almost at eye level, although he was sitting down.

"Sorry," he said. "I didn't notice you there."

"You must be a tourist." She balanced one hand on her hip. "The locals all know the menu by heart."

"The food must be good here," he said.

"The best, especially the fresh seafood and homemade desserts. The lemon meringue pie is to die for," she said. "But our breakfasts are nothing to sneeze at, either. Where you from?"

"Kentucky," he said.

"You don't sound it."

"Lexington, not Appalachia," he said. "It's pretty urban, with lots of transplants."

"What brings you here?"

"Road trip," he said.

"Business or pleasure?"

His waitress asked so many questions, she reminded him of his two sisters, who never hesitated to poke around in his business.

"Both," he said, hastening to ask a question of his own before she could fire off another one. "Tell me, do you know anything about Tangier Island?"

"Sure," she said. "Never been myself, but I hear it's real tranquil, though maybe not so much as it used to be on account of tourism. No cars—just bikes and golf carts."

Tangier sounded like the kind of place people with high-stress jobs and expendable cash vacationed. No wonder Robert Reese had chosen it.

"Any idea how to get there?" Jack asked.

"Easiest way is the ferry in Onancock, which is up the coast a ways along the Chesapeake," she explained. "Or you could always charter a boat. It's not a long trip. Tangier's only ten or so miles off the coast."

"Thanks," he said. "I appreciate the information."

"Have you decided on breakfast?" she asked.

"What do you suggest?"

"You can't go wrong with the creamed chipped beef or the sausage gravy biscuit. They come with either grits or home fries."

What the hell, Jack thought. When on the Eastern Shore of Virginia, eat as the natives do. "I'll have the creamed beef with grits. And coffee."

"Black?"

"Two creams, two sugars."

She flashed him a grin. "Interesting."

"Why is that interesting?" he asked.

She leaned over the counter. "It means you have a sweet side."

He thought of the glare he'd adopted as the top relief pitcher for the Owensboro Mud Dogs, a minor league baseball team in his home state that for many was the last stop before reaching the big time. Jack had gotten called up to the majors late in the season twice over the course of his career, both for brief stints. His goal was to make the third time stick.

"Not everyone would agree with that," Jack said.

"Then they're not looking hard enough." She raised her dark brows and left the counter to take another order.

His phone rang for the second time that morning. He checked the display. Not Annalise this time. His other sister, Maria, the private investigator. Jack had grown up with his older two sisters and younger brother in a rambling house on the outskirts of Lexington with parents who didn't always give them what they wanted but provided them with everything they needed. The perfect family, other people called them.

The two stools closest to him were empty, but the rest of the diner was filling up fast, providing him an excuse not to answer. If he didn't, however, one of his sisters would keep calling until they got him. They might even enlist the help of his mother. He clicked through to the call. "Hey, Maria."

"Jack! I'm so glad I caught you. Are you okay?"

Almost thirty-two years old and they still checked up on him, proving his family wasn't perfect. Privacy was pretty much impossible. Considering what had happened to their younger brother, though, it was understandable.

"Hold on a minute," he told her. To the waitress who was bringing his coffee over to the counter, he said, "I'll be back in a few."

"Where are you?" Maria asked on the other end of the line. Patience had never been her strong suit.

He exited the restaurant into the bright sun of the morning before answering his sister's question. "At a diner on the Eastern Shore."

"You're there already? You didn't drive straight through, did you?"

"No, I didn't," he said. "I just got a really early start this morning."

The high-pitched giggle of a little boy carried through the gravel parking lot. The man with him lifted the boy and tossed him in the air a few inches before catching him and swinging him to the ground. A deep, pulsing throb started in Jack's shoulder, only partially due to yesterday's eight-hour drive and the too-hard mattress at the hotel just outside Richmond.

"Annalise said you didn't answer your cell this morning," she said.

"Some states have laws against using the phone while you're driving." Jack didn't know if Virginia was one of them, but it was as good an excuse as any.

"Just as long as you're okay." Maria's pause lasted a few seconds. "You are okay, right?"

He was getting tired of answering that question. He scuffed his foot in the gravel. "I'm fine. You and Annalise don't need to keep tabs on me, you know."

"You can't blame us for being worried," she said. "We know what a blow it was when the orthopedist told you that you couldn't pitch again."

Those hadn't been his exact words. After performing a second surgery in a six-year span on Jack's right shoulder, the doctor had said he doubted Jack would ever be able to throw a fastball in the nineties again.

Maria didn't wait for Jack to respond. "And then when you announced you were taking off, well, what were we supposed to do?"

Jack took a deep breath and got a whiff of the bacon cooking inside the diner. "Accept that I need some time alone."

"Of course you do," Maria said. "You've never wanted to be anything but a pro baseball player, but you're not getting any younger. You need to figure out what to do with the rest of your life."

Jack had fallen in love with baseball at his first T-ball game when his ball soared to the outfield. Even though he now realized the ball had gone only about sixty feet, he'd felt as powerful as Babe Ruth. Later he'd gotten that same feeling when he took the mound. He'd had his future mapped out since he was a kid. He wasn't about to change his mind now. He wasn't going to share the particulars with Maria, either.

"Hey," he said. "I checked out that lead for you."

"Already? I thought you just got to Virginia this morning."

"She wasn't hard to find in a place as small as Wawpaney," he said, even though it had been a shock to see a woman matching the age-progression photo walking on the sidewalk toward the school. "But she wasn't your missing person."

"You're sure about that?"

Jack had experienced a moment's doubt that the woman was being entirely truthful, but it made no sense for her to lie. It was human nature to want to know where you came from. She obviously already knew. Add to that her reddish-colored hair, her age and her comment about baby photos and Jack was convinced.

"It's not Hayley," Jack maintained.

He heard what sounded like a sigh. "I didn't really expect her to be."

"Any luck with the other leads?"

"Not so far. I've checked out more than half of them and they're all dead ends. But as I told Hayley's mother from the start, finding her daughter is the longest of long shots."

Jack leaned against the sun-warmed passenger door of his pickup. Five years ago Maria had left the Fayette County sheriff's office to become a private investigator and had never looked back. "Then why take the case?"

"She said not a day goes by that she doesn't think of her missing daughter," Maria said. "She doesn't care if the odds of finding Hayley are one in a million, as long as that one chance exists."

Jack reached into his back pocket, withdrew the paper with the age-progression photo and unfolded it. Unlike an actual photograph, where personality could shine through, the computer-generated likeness seemed flat and lifeless.

What would it be like to know nothing about the person your loved one had become? Or if they were even alive at all?

"Why look for her now?" he asked. "It's been almost thirty years. The trail must be ice-cold."

"Lots of reasons. Her husband is making noises about moving to be near their grandchildren, but it's probably mostly because she just had a scare with breast cancer."

"Is the father on board with the search?"

"Interesting that you ask. She didn't tell him she was hiring me. Apparently their marriage barely survived the tragedy the first time."

Jack felt for the couple, but their plight didn't concern him now that he'd eliminated the pretty Wawpaney Elementary schoolteacher as a victim. He had pressing problems of his own.

"Wait a minute," Maria said abruptly. "How did

we start talking about the case? I wasn't through asking about you."

"Some other time," he said. "I came outside the diner to talk to you. My food's probably ready by now."

"At least you're eating," she said.

"Bye, Maria." He ended the call and was back at the counter at about the same time the waitress arrived with his Southern breakfast. The paper with the age-progression photo was still in his right hand. He set it on the counter.

"Here you go." The waitress placed a plate of steaming food in front of him. She started to walk away, then paused, a curious expression on her face. She pointed to the paper. He'd refolded it so that the top half of the woman's face was visible. "Is that Tara Greer?"

The waitress didn't wait for his answer. She picked up the paper, shook it out and stared down at it. "Why, yes, it is. Why do you have a drawing of Tara?"

The anonymous person who'd given Jack's sister the tip hadn't provided the name of the woman who looked like Hayley Cooper, only the information that she taught physical education at Wawpaney Elementary. Jack probably should have thought to ask the woman he'd stopped her name. If he didn't follow up on the waitress's remark, his sister might disown him.

"Tara's the teacher who works at Wawpaney Elementary, right?" he asked.

"That's right," the waitress said. "She teaches PE."

At least he'd stopped the right woman, although even he could deduce she was a PE teacher from her shorts and Wawpaney Elementary T-shirt. The athletic clothes called attention to her toned arms and legs and the general glow of health surrounding her. He'd thought she looked fantastic.

Jack nodded at the sketch. "That isn't Tara."

The waitress took another look before she put the paper back down. "I'm a little farsighted, but that sure looks like her to me."

Jack thought of all the other false leads that his sister was chasing down. "Turns out lots of people look like this woman."

The waitress tilted her head. "Is that the reason you're on the Eastern Shore? Because you're searching for the woman in the photo?"

"Not even close." Jack folded the paper and put it back into his pocket. The waitress regarded him expectantly, waiting for him to expand on his reply.

It wouldn't hurt to tell her at least part of the truth, Jack thought.

He dredged up his favorite line from the inspirational poem he'd hung in his locker after his first shoulder surgery, the one about sticking to the fight when you're hardest hit.

"I'm here because I still believe in myself," he said.

The orthopedist in Owensboro had written him off, but Jack hadn't lasted almost ten years in the minor leagues by giving up when the going got tough.

Quitting had never been an option before.

It wasn't now, either.

LAUGHTER AND EXUBERANT shouts rang out from the field adjacent to Wawpaney Elementary. Sixteen kindergartners, eight to a side, swarmed around the soccer ball. Tara referred to the phenomenon as the clump. No matter how many times she explained spacing to the children, they abandoned the knowledge in favor of running to where the action was.

Tara watched from the sideline, leaving the whistle hanging from the lanyard around her neck. With summer vacation only hours away, she decided in favor of fun and exercise over the fine points of playing soccer. She opted against telling them to tone it down, too. They probably wouldn't be able to, anyway.

Especially Bryan, who did everything with gusto. He was only five, just a few years older than Hayley Cooper had been when she'd been snatched from the mall, yet he had a stronger personality than most adults.

All of the children were distinct.

Dwayne could run faster than his classmates. Ashley was more interested in the flight of a shorebird than the game. Jorge was half a head shorter than everybody else but made up for it by trying the hardest.

Observing the children made what the stranger had suggested this morning even more preposterous. Surely any one of her students would know if they'd been taken against their will from a shopping mall only two short years before. They'd know if their mother wasn't really their mother—even if, like Tara, they'd never seen a baby photo of themselves.

"Tara!" Mary Dee Larson, the kindergarten teacher who was Tara's best friend on the staff, approached from the direction of the sprawling brick school. She wasn't any taller than five foot two, but her short, quick steps ate up the ground. Tara had avoided her since earlier that morning when Mary Dee alerted her that she expected to get the scoop on the hot guy she'd seen Tara talking to. Mary Dee wouldn't interrupt Tara's PE class to talk men, though. She wouldn't be walking so fast, either.

"Your mom's waiting for you in the school office." Mary Dee was slightly out of breath, concern pinching her sharp features. "She says it's an emergency."

Tara's heart sped up. Her mother called and left

urgent messages at least once or twice a week. However, she rarely stopped by the school. "Did she say what kind of emergency?"

Mary Dee shook her head, rustling her silky black hair. "I didn't ask. I just volunteered to come get you and keep an eye on your class."

"Thanks." Tara took off at a jog, her head emptying of the questions about her childhood she'd intended to ask her mother. They seemed unimportant now.

She burst through the double doors and hurried along the wide empty hall, the soles of her tennis shoes squeaking on the tile floor. A colorful Enjoy Your Summer! banner hung on the wall outside the office. Beside it stood Tara's mother.

She was dressed in the same flowing print dress she'd worn that morning to her job at the bakery. With flyaway long blond hair she couldn't manage to tame, her mom never looked quite pulled together. She seemed even less so now, with her lipstick worn off and her hands fluttering.

"Tara, honey!" Her mother rushed forward to meet Tara, the skirt of her dress flowing behind her. Though she'd spoken only two words, her North Carolina drawl came through loud and clear. In her wedged sandals, she was still a good four inches shorter than Tara. "I know you're busy, but I just had to come on over here and see you."

Her mom seemed physically fine, eliminating

one of Tara's worries. On the heels of it came another.

"Did something happen to Danny?" Tara asked, referring to the ten-year-old who was her mother's latest foster child. Her mom had hooked up with the program the same year Tara went off to college, which was already a dozen years ago.

"Why ever would you think something like that?" Her mother sounded truly stumped. "Danny's fine as can be."

Tara felt her pulse rate slow down. "Then what is it?"

Her mother tapped her index finger against her lips, the way she did when she was thinking about how to phrase something. *What would Mom consider an emergency?* Tara wondered.

"Wait a minute. Why aren't you at work?"

"Would you believe Mr. Calvert said no when I asked for time off this summer to be around for Danny?" her mother asked, her tone conversational. "What could I do but quit?"

Tara let out a surprised, involuntary breath. "But you loved that job."

"I liked it," her mother corrected. "I never will put work before family. Danny needs me, the same way you did when you were younger."

While Tara was growing up, her mother had switched jobs as often as some women changed hairstyles. Her mom had once walked away from the reception desk of a dental office because she couldn't get permission to leave early to attend Tara's high school volleyball game. Another time she'd quit her job at the grocery store to go on a school field trip to the National Wildlife Refuge.

Tara swallowed a sigh. "I wish you'd talked it over with me first. I already told you I could help out with Danny this summer."

"Then what I did wasn't so awful, now was it?" Her mother grabbed Tara's upper arm and squeezed. *Finally,* Tara thought. Her mother was ready to reveal the reason she'd come to the school. "It's about that summer day camp where I want to send Danny."

"The one in Cape Charles that's just starting out?"

"That's the one." Her mother clapped her hands. "I volunteered to help and got a break on Danny's tuition!"

Tara would bet anything there was more to the story. If all her mother had to report was good news, she would have waited until Tara arrived home from school.

"What aren't you telling me?" Tara asked.

Her mom sucked in a breath through her teeth. "I volunteered you, too."

"You what?"

"Before you say anything else, hear me out." Her mother talked so fast her words tripped over each other. "You know how hard it is to find a camp for children like Danny. This one's a gift from God, being that it's new and fifteen miles away in Cape Charles. There are only ten children signed up, but they still need lots of volunteer counselors. With your background, why, you're perfect. So I filled out the paperwork for both of us."

Tara could have predicted the next answer, but asked the question, anyway. "When is this camp?"

"It starts Monday and goes for two weeks. But you don't have to be there all day, every day." Her mother worried her bottom lip with her teeth. "Orientation's at seven o'clock tonight. Now you see why I had to rush on over here and tell you?"

Tara sighed. "You could have told me before today."

"I know, honey. I should have," her mom said. "I was so excited for Danny when I heard about the camp that I didn't think. And you will be able to get time off here and there to do all those other things you do."

Tara worked at some businesses in the summer on an as-needed basis to help out friends and keep busy, but in order to volunteer at the camp she'd have to cancel the kayaking trip she'd impulsively booked. But then, Tara hadn't shared her plans with her mother yet.

"Oh, please, Tara." Her mother laid a hand on Tara's arm. "Say you're not mad."

Tara should have been more irritated than she was. She might have been if the trip had excited her more. But the bottom line was that her mom's kind heart was in the right place.

"How can I be angry?" Tara asked. "Like you said, you're only thinking of Danny."

Her mom's lips curved upward, relief evident in her smile. She touched Tara's hand, her blue eyes sparkling. "I am so darn lucky to have a daughter as wonderful as you."

Tara was the one who was lucky.

After losing her husband and her oldest child when Tara was a baby, her mom had showered all her love and attention on Tara.

Not for a single second of her childhood had Tara doubted she was loved. Mom had been there every step of the way: volunteering to be home-room mother, sitting in the stands at her athletic events, chairing the all-night grad party commit-tee, chaperoning the prom.

And because a handsome stranger had spun a wild tale, Tara had been prepared to ask her mother for proof that they belonged together.

So what if beneath the hair dye Tara's natu-ral color was the same golden-brown as Hayley Cooper's would be? And there could be plenty of explanations for why Tara had never seen baby photos of herself.

As for the flashes Tara sometimes got of a

woman shaking her and yelling that she should stop crying, the woman could be anybody. Or nobody. Maybe she was simply the stuff of nightmares.

"I love you, too, Mom," Tara said.

Her mother beamed and ran a gentle hand over Tara's cheek the way she'd done so many times before.

You don't want to believe your mother could have abducted a child, a little voice inside Tara's head insisted.

True enough.

It was a moot point. As far as Tara was concerned, the absurd matter was closed.

The only person who had ever raised the possibility that Tara hadn't been born a Greer was a stranger passing through town. When Jack DiMarco left Wawpaney, he'd taken the question with him.

CHAPTER TWO

TANGIER ISLAND WAS A THROWBACK, a tiny slice of land in the Chesapeake Bay with nothing near it but crab shanties on stilts and miles of water. The teacher in Wawpaney who looked so much like the age progression of Hayley Cooper seemed very far away. So did civilization as Jack had come to know it. If not for the tour guides who greeted the ferry from Onancock, Jack imagined Tangier hadn't changed much in hundreds of years. The guides stood in front of golf carts, which according to the ferry captain was the main method of transportation on the island aside from walking. The boat had been about a third full, which apparently was typical for a weekday before summer kicked in. The other passengers, all of them dragging suitcases, went directly to carts. Jack hung back.

"Ten dollars for a tour of the island," a short middle-aged woman, wearing a straw hat, called to Jack. She had the same formal English accent as the ferry captain, which supposedly didn't sound much different than the way Tangier residents had spoken in the 1600s.

"How much to take me to the Marsh Harbor B and B?" Jack asked.

"The same." The woman smiled at him, revealing a gold front tooth. She swept a hand toward her golf cart.

Why not? Jack thought. He hopped in, resting his large cardboard folder on his lap.

"Do you have any bags?" the woman asked.

Jack tapped the folder. "This is all I need."

The woman nodded and joined Jack in the cart, pressing her foot down on the accelerator. The canopy over the cart provided welcome relief from the blazing June sun that made the day feel warmer than eighty degrees.

The cart crawled ahead more slowly than the posted fifteen-miles-per-hour speed limit down a quiet, narrow street leading away from the dock. People wandered from shop to shop. None of them seemed to be in a hurry.

"This is Main Street," the guide said, pride evident in her voice. A few restaurants shared space with a place to rent bikes and a smattering of gift shops, one of which proclaimed Tangier The Soft Crab Capital of the World. There wasn't a fast-food chain or department store in sight. In the distance, a church steeple pointed to the sky.

"Legend has it that Tangier Island was settled in the middle of the 1680s by the Crockett family. No relation to Davy," she said in her accented

English. "This was after Captain John Smith discovered Tangier in 1608. Not counting the tourists, we have about seven hundred residents, most of them watermen."

After a few blocks, she veered the golf cart off the main thoroughfare onto an equally narrow street. She chatted about the island's eclectic mix of styles while they passed Victorian cottages that were next door to double-wide trailers. A few homes had weathered gravestones in their front yards.

Jack breathed in the earthy smell of the marsh. He wasn't in Tangier as a tourist, but the guide had aroused his curiosity. "How big is the island?"

"Three miles long, one-and-a-half miles wide." She turned the golf cart down another street that had a partial view of the bay. "We have room for some churches, a few grocery stores, a school, a health center and not much else. Even in the high season, we're not crowded. Exactly how we like it."

She pulled up in front of a large yellow clapboard house with turn-of-the-century Victorian architecture and a steeply pitched white roof. A wide porch wrapped around the house.

"Here we are," she said.

If Jack had known exactly how close the dock was to the B and B, he would have skipped the golf cart and set off on foot. But then, he would have missed the nuggets of information about Tangier.

He pulled out his wallet and withdrew enough money for her fee plus a healthy tip. "Thanks for the ride."

"I hope you have a wonderful time here on our little piece of paradise," she said, puttering away with a wave of her hand.

The house had none of the trappings of tourism except the Marsh Harbor B and B sign suspended from one of the porch railings. Jack climbed the three wooden steps leading to the front door, stopping abruptly when he noticed a gently swaying hammock occupied by a man with white hair. Could it be? Jack narrowed his eyes. Yes, it was Robert Reese.

Although they'd never been introduced, Jack recognized the other man from his website photo. Not many guys sported a full head of prematurely white hair before they were forty years old.

Jack strode forward, the soles of his sturdy sport sandals clapping against the wooden slats of the porch. "Dr. Reese?"

The man rested his book against his stomach spine first. It was a mystery Jack recognized as one of the blockbuster hits of the year. He looked up at Jack with a quizzical expression, as though Jack presented a bigger puzzle than the book.

"You are Dr. Robert Reese, aren't you?" Jack asked.

The other man scrunched up his brow, contorting his regular features. "I'm sorry. Do I know you?"

Jack stuck out his hand. "Jack DiMarco."

Reese took it, a wary look in his eyes. "Refresh my memory."

"The pitcher with the torn labrum," Jack said. "We spoke a few days ago. You said you were on your way here, that the only people you'd be seeing in the next three weeks were on Tangier."

Reese swung his legs over the side of the hammock and stood up. His book slid off his lap, falling to the porch floor with a loud thunk. Several inches shorter than Jack, he carried himself with the confident air of a successful man. "I remember now. Don't tell me you took that as an invitation?"

Jack wasn't about to admit he realized Reese had been brushing him off. He inhaled the scent of island flowers before answering. "I tried to call ahead to let you know when I was coming, but I couldn't get through to your cell."

"There's no cell phone reception on the island," Reese said, then stopped. "Wait. You never did tell me how you got my number."

Where there's a will, Jack thought, *there's a way.* He'd called in a favor from a former teammate who'd become golf buddies with Reese after the doctor operated on his shoulder.

"Does it matter?" Jack asked.

"I suppose not." Reese bent and picked up his book. "So, tell me. Why exactly are you here?"

"My goal is to play ball again. To achieve it, I need to be operated on by somebody who's tops in the field." Jack omitted the fact that the team doctor of the Owensboro Mud Dogs had advised against surgery, leading to the team releasing Jack. "Lots of people say you're the best."

"Are you trying to flatter me?" Reese asked.

"That depends." Jack cocked his head. "Is it working?"

Reese ran a hand through his white hair. "The reason I vacation on Tangier, that anybody vacations here, is to get away from it all. I should tell you to leave me alone."

"But?" Jack asked, starting to hope.

"But vanity is a weakness of mine," Reese finished. "You understand I can't do the surgery on the island?"

"I just want to get it scheduled. The sooner, the better," Jack said.

Reese walked over to one of two large wicker chairs on the porch and sat down. Jack took the other seat.

"Tell me how the injury happened," he said.

"About a year ago I collided with a base runner and broke my collarbone." Jack stated the barest facts when there was so much more to the story.

"I thought you tore your labrum," Reese said.

"I didn't know the labrum was torn until the collarbone healed. The MRI I had a month ago confirmed it." Jack held up his cardboard folder. "I brought my films, present and past."

"You do understand I need a computer to look at those," Reese said, making no attempt to take the films. "Wait a minute. What do you mean, past?"

"I've had two rotator-cuff surgeries."

"And you want to go through surgery a third time?" The tail end of Reese's question rose.

"If it means I can pitch at a competitive level again, hell, yeah."

"Stand up and show me your range of motion," Reese said.

Jack raised his arms over his head. The right one touched his ear. The left one came close.

"Not bad after a rotator-cuff injury," Reese said, "especially considering you have that tear."

"Tears," Jack corrected. "There is no one big tear, just a number of smaller ones."

Reese stroked his chin. "How old are you, Jack?"

"Thirty-one."

Reese whistled. "Too bad I didn't know about the other surgeries or I could have saved you a trip. A third surgery won't get you where you want to be."

"How can you say that without looking at my films?"

"I don't need to see them," Reese said. "The labrum is collagen based. It can't be strengthened."

"People have surgeries to repair their labrums all the time," Jack argued.

"Yes, they do. But if they're athletes who use an overhead motion, like a pitcher, it's highly unlikely that surgery will yield the desired result," Reese said. "My advice is to go with rehab to strengthen your shoulder muscles and increase flexibility."

"Does rehab ever work?" Jack asked.

"Depends on how aggressive the rehab is," Reese said. "I know of a swimmer with a mild tear who came back to compete in the Olympics. But he was ten years younger than you."

"I'm tough," Jack said. "I've already rebounded from two surgeries. I can rehab with the best of them."

"That may be true, but you've got to understand how far-fetched it is to think you'll improve to the point where you can pitch at a major league level." Reese's pronouncement was distressingly close to what the Owensboro team doctor had said. "Let me give you a piece of advice, Jack. Find something else to do with your life."

Later that afternoon, after an hour-long ferry ride under the unrelenting sun, Jack arrived back at the dock at Onancock. It was larger and more tourist oriented than some of the other small towns and quaint villages that dotted the finger of land that made up the Eastern Shore of Virginia, with a prominent downtown and several hotels and B and Bs. He walked the block into town to find a place to eat. His head hurt from thinking about what the specialist had said.

Find something else to do with your life.

"Like hell," he said aloud.

He'd been working toward pitching in the major leagues since he was a boy. He'd gotten there three times, twice as a September call-up and once as a roster player. Because of the injuries, however, his big-league stat line was meager: three games, four total innings. He refused to believe the dream was over.

He walked past a gift shop and an insurance office before coming to a storefront that looked more like a house than a business. Real estate listings plastered the front window. He slowed, then stopped. The sign above the door said the Realtor dealt in rentals as well as sales, not only in Onancock, but throughout the Eastern Shore.

Jack thought about the Olympic swimmer who'd returned to his previous form. He'd take bets that the swimmer didn't have sisters who popped in on him whenever they felt like it and parents who kept telling him that life didn't end when athletic careers did.

No, the swimmer had probably rehabbed somewhere peaceful and tranquil where he could devote his energy to healing. Somewhere like the Eastern Shore.

Jack pushed through the door of the Realtor's office. The woman at the reception desk looked up, a smile on her face. "Can I help you?"

"You sure can," he said. "I need to get away from it all."

THE SALTY BREEZE BLEW over the rustic outdoor patio of the restaurant, one of the few establishments near Wawpaney with a water view. This view was of a shimmering bay that eventually led to the Atlantic Ocean. The sight didn't have its usual soothing effect on Tara. No surprise. Mary Dee Larson was gazing at her as though Tara had just bitten the head off a seagull.

"You can't be serious!" Mary Dee exclaimed. "That kayaking trip sounded amazing. How could you cancel it?"

Tara popped a coconut shrimp into her mouth and washed it down with some of her happy-hour margarita. Strawberry, her favorite flavor. She intended to enjoy it. Most of the Eastern Shore's hundreds of miles of coastline was bordered by salt marshes, not restaurants. They'd been lucky to snag a table in a prime location. This marked the first Friday after school had been let out for the summer and the place was full, mostly with tourists. Even so, the atmosphere was laid-back. Visitors came to the Eastern Shore for a quiet getaway, usually at a B and B with a semiprivate beach on the bay. The eastern side of the peninsula was largely bordered by marshland and waterways that led to the secluded barrier islands. The hordes of tourists were an hour north in Ocean City, Maryland, and an hour south in Virginia Beach.

"Canceling was surprisingly easy," Tara said. "I got all but fifty dollars back from my deposit, and the airline gave me a flight credit."

Mary Dee set her own margarita glass down on the table with a clink. She thrust out her glossy red lower lip that matched her red blouse. "That's not what I meant and you know it. That trip would have been great for you."

Tara wasn't sure she agreed. Since none of their other friends were kayakers, Mary Dee had persuaded Tara to check out an organization that set up outdoor excursions for singles. The closest kayak trip was on the Snake River in Wyoming. The more Tara thought about it, however, the less attractive the trip seemed.

"I probably would have gotten cold feet, anyway," Tara said. "I mean, why should I go all the way to Wyoming when I can kayak here?"

"For adventure," Mary Dee said.

"And can you imagine the kind of guys who sign up for those sorts of trips?" Tara continued as though she hadn't heard her. "They're probably out for sex."

"So what? Some sex would do you good." She nodded in the direction of four guys they'd known in high school who were across the patio hoisting beers and singing. Tara had dated two of them. "You seem to have already ruled out every man around here."

"The timing is bad, too," Tara said, ignoring her friend's comment. She gazed out into the bay, where the sun was sinking below the horizon in a blaze of red and yellow. "I don't know what I was thinking when I made the reservation, with the anniversary coming up on Tuesday."

Tara had been friends with Mary Dee long enough that she didn't need to explain the significance of the date. The other woman was well aware that was when Tara's father and sister had died.

"You weren't planning to leave until Wednesday," Mary Dee pointed out. "And I thought your mother was going to treat the anniversary like any other day this year."

"I'm not entirely sure she can do it," Tara said. "She might need me to—"

"How about what you need?" Mary Dee interrupted. "They've been gone thirty years, Tara, but you're here and you're alive. When was the last time you did anything for yourself?"

Tara watched the last of the sun disappear before she answered. "I ran five miles last night and had a yogurt smoothie for breakfast this morning."

"Would you stop doing that?"

"Stop doing what?"

"Pretending you don't know what I'm talking about." Mary Dee shook her head. "It used to work but not anymore. I'm on to you, Tara Greer."

Was that really her name? Or was it Hayley Cooper? Tara thrust the ridiculous though from her mind, dismayed that she'd allowed it to surface.

"I'm sorry, M.D.," Tara said. "I know you're only trying to look out for me. But missing the trip isn't a big deal. And it's not like I have a choice."

"You could have chosen to tell your mom no," Mary Dee said. "She didn't have any right to volunteer you like that without asking first."

"I hadn't gotten a chance to tell her about Wyoming yet," Tara said. "Besides, the camp sounds like fun."

Mary Dee thumped the table with a manicured hand. "Doesn't matter. She still shouldn't have volunteered you."

"It's for a good cause," Tara said.

"Yeah, but why are her causes more important than yours?" Mary Dee asked. "She always needs something from you."

"You're exaggerating."

Mary Dee raised her dark eyebrows. "Then why do you live two blocks away from her?"

"You know why," Tara said. "My place was such a great deal, I couldn't pass it up."

"Was that really the reason?" Mary Dee asked. "Or did your mother *need* you to live close by?"

Tara twirled the tiny straw in her margarita glass, not bothering to point out that while she relished her own space she liked being available for her mother. Mary Dee would probably find fault with that, too. "You're being awfully hard on me today."

Mary Dee laid her hand on Tara's arm. "I don't mean to be. I'm only trying to get you to be a little more selfish."

Tara reached across the table, plucked one of Mary Dee's breaded mushrooms from her plate and popped it into her mouth.

"How's that?" she asked.

Mary Dee laughed. "Better. Now, are you going to tell me about that guy I saw you with yesterday?"

Tara blinked, blindsided by the question.

"You didn't really think I'd forgotten about it, did you? So spill."

"He was nobody," Tara said.

"What? A guy that hot—he was definitely somebody."

"A tourist," Tara clarified.

"What did he want?"

It was on the tip of Tara's tongue to repeat the crazy tale Jack DiMarco had spun of the abducted three-year-old and Tara's own uncanny resemblance to the age-progression photo.

"Directions." Tara wasn't sure why she lied, especially because she seldom censored herself in front of Mary Dee. Tara often felt as though her sister's death had created a void in her life that hadn't been filled until Tara had become friends with Mary Dee.

"That's it?" Mary Dee's expression crumbled. "I had such high hopes for you two."

"You're a real pain with that stuff since you got married," Tara complained. "Just because you're in love doesn't mean I have to be."

"Being in love is wonderful." Mary Dee's lips rose in the dreamy smile she got whenever anyone referred to marriage or husbands or love. Then again, she was still a newlywed. "If you'd make room in your life for a relationship, you could feel wonderful, too."

"I've had plenty of relationships," Tara countered.

"Short ones," Mary Dee said. "You find fault with everybody you date."

"That's not true," Tara said. "I'm just not willing to settle for anything less than fireworks, like you have with Bill and my mom had with my dad."

"You should have gone to Wyoming to increase your chances of finding someone, then." Mary Dee gestured to the happy-hour crowd, made up of almost all couples. "Speaking of that, did you at least give that tourist your number?"

"No, Mary Dee," Tara said with exaggerated patience. "I did not give my number to the stranger who stopped to ask for directions."

"What good are you, girl?" Mary Dee asked, shaking her head. "I know you want children some day. You need a man for that."

Tara laid a finger on her cheek. "So now you think the tourist who asked for directions should be the father of my children? I don't even know if he's single."

"You didn't check out his ring finger?" Mary Dee asked.

She had, actually. It was bare. She was uncomfortably aware that she'd found him attractive. No, not merely attractive. Appealing. If he'd been anybody else, she might have found a way to give him her number.

Mary Dee pointed a finger at her. "You did, didn't you? I knew you were attracted to him. Too bad you don't know where he's staying. You could at least have a fling with him while he's visiting."

Tara's heartbeat sped up at the prospect, although she should not have been thinking about Jack DiMarco in those terms. She had ample reason to hope she never saw him again. "I guess I missed my chance, then."

"Too bad." Mary Dee fanned herself. "Now, that's a man who could get a woman thinking about her needs."

Tara's cell phone vibrated and skittered a few inches on the table, as if it were alive. With an apologetic look at Mary Dee, Tara picked it up and checked the display. Her mother. Not that she'd tell her friend that.

"Sorry," Tara said. "I've got to take this."

Mary Dee nodded, watching Tara over the rim of her glass as she sipped her margarita.

"Hey, what's up?" Tara asked, careful not to call her mom by name.

"I think I smell gas in the kitchen!" her mother cried. "I checked and the pilot light's not on. Wouldn't you know the shut-off valve's behind the stove, which is way too heavy for me to move."

Tara turned away from Mary Dee and spoke directly into the phone so her mother could hear and her friend couldn't. "Did you call the gas company?"

"Yes, but what if it takes them an hour to get here like it did the last time?" her mother asked. "I can't stay outside on the porch with Danny for an hour. You know how he gets when his routine is disrupted."

Tara tapped her nails on the table, trying to

come up with the best solution to the problem. "I guess I could be there in about twenty minutes."

"Could you?" her mother asked. "That would be wonderful."

Tara cast a glance at Mary Dee, who was still watching her. Tara wouldn't be leaving her friend high and dry if she cut out early. Mary Dee had mentioned that her husband had rented a movie they were planning to watch tonight.

"I'll leave right now," she told her mom. "In the meantime, open some windows and stay out of the kitchen."

"Already done. Bless you!" Her mother made a few more gratifying noises before Tara disconnected the call.

Taking a deep breath, Tara addressed Mary Dee. "I'm sorry. Something's come up. I've gotta go."

"Of course you do."

Tara finished off the last swallow of her margarita, set enough money on the table to cover their tab and stood up. "I really am sorry, M.D."

"I know you are," Mary Dee said.

Tara turned away from her friend and started for the exit. She hadn't gotten two steps when she heard Mary Dee's voice calling after her.

"Say hey to your mom for me."

TARA GRABBED FOR HER foster brother Danny's soft hand the following afternoon, holding it securely in hers as they crossed the parking lot to the Kroger in Wawpaney. There weren't a lot of choices. The next closest grocery store was twenty miles away.

"You're a good boy to come with me." After picking up Danny from his Saturday swimming lesson at the community center in Cape Charles, where the camp was being held, she'd announced she needed to make a stop. "If I don't buy a few things, my cupboards will be bare. Like Mother Hubbard."

"Your mother's name isn't Hubbard." Danny gazed up at her out of small brown eyes with the distinctive slant characteristic of people with Down syndrome. He was short for his age, another trait common to children like him.

"You're right." Tara sometimes forgot how literal children with Down's were. "It's Carrie. She's your foster mother and my mother."

No matter what the stranger who'd stopped her on the street had suggested.

Tara released Danny's hand to take one of the grocery carts in front of the store, careful to keep him in sight. During the time it had taken Tara to get to her mother's house the night before, Danny had wandered close to the street to follow a butterfly.

"C-Carrie is getting pretty," Danny announced. He had a good vocabulary, although his speech was halting and not quite clear. He also stuttered occasionally. Once school started again, he'd be in speech therapy.

"Right again," Tara said. "Carrie's at the beauty shop. That's why I picked you up from swimming."

Her mother had insisted Danny take the lessons, maintaining that anyone who lived in an area surrounded by water should know how to swim.

Danny scrunched up his face. "Don't like swimming."

That was an understatement. Today had been lesson number two and Danny had yet to agree to get into the water. Afterward the instructor had advised Tara to suspend the lessons until he had a change of heart.

"You can't know you don't like it until you try it," Tara said.

"Know it now," Danny insisted.

"Oh, yeah?" Tara asked. "What if I refused to learn how to drive because I thought I wouldn't like it? Then how would we get to the grocery store?"

Danny looked thoughtful. "Walking."

"Good answer," she said, laughing. It served her right for asking a question with such an easy answer. "Dan the Man strikes again."

Danny giggled at the favorite nickname, and she bent down and gave him a hug. He loved hugs. He'd also been laughing more and more in the three weeks since he'd come to live with her mother. It was a welcome change from the sad little boy who'd kept asking where his real mother was.

She waited for Danny to precede her through the automatic door into the store. "Stay close," she told him.

He moved a step nearer to her.

Tara stopped at a table of navel oranges at the front of the produce section and tore a plastic bag off the roll. "You want me to buy a couple extra for you?"

"Don't like oranges."

"I love them." Tara injected enthusiasm into her voice. She picked out four oranges and dropped the bag into the cart, then pointed to the refrigerated section containing precut bags of vegetables. "How about some baby carrots?"

"No," he said. "No c-carrots."

Her mother was in the process of ensuring that Danny ate healthy foods. Like a lot of Down syndrome children, he was on the chubby side. Diet, however, was only one factor. Many children like Danny weren't active early in life because they had decreased motor skills. Add stunted growth to the mix and weight problems resulted. In Danny's case, they were compounded because he loved to eat with a rare passion.

"I'll give you a hint about what I need next." Tara turned the cart with difficulty, noticing for the first time she'd chosen one with a bum wheel. "Cluck cluck cluck cluck."

"Chicken!" Danny said.

"Right you are." She maneuvered the cart to the top of one of the long aisles and got ready to push it to the refrigerated section in the back of the store.

"Tara!" Mrs. Jorgenson, who'd been her mother's neighbor for as long as Tara could remember, headed toward them with the help of a cane. Otherwise, she was in admirable shape for a woman of eighty-plus, with a trim figure and dark blond hair without a trace of gray. "How nice to see you. You, too, Danny."

"Who are you?" Danny asked.

"You know Mrs. Jorgenson, Danny," Tara said. "She lives in the white house across the street from you."

"Old lady in white house," Danny said. Tara winced.

"That's me," Mrs. Jorgenson said cheerfully. "I'll be eighty-seven on my next birthday."

"I'm ten," Danny said.

"Lucky you," Mrs. Jorgenson said. "Where's your mother, Tara?"

"At the beauty salon," Tara said. "School's out for the summer so I have more time to help her with Danny."

"Such a good heart your mother has," Mrs. Jorgenson said. "I don't know what I would have done without her when Artie was in the hospital. She drove me there every day. Now that he's home, she stops by a few times a week to check on us. Always brings us something home cooked, too."

Tara hadn't known that, but it didn't surprise her—not when frozen dinners filled Mrs. Jorgenson's buggy.

"Artie doesn't feel up to cooking these days," Mrs. Jorgenson said, gesturing to the food she was going to buy. "I was never much good at it."

Danny started down the nearest aisle, darting back and forth as he checked out the items on the shelves. Tara debated whether to call him back and decided against it. The attention span of a ten-year-old, disabled or not, was only so long.

"Nice talking to you, Mrs. Jorgenson," Tara said. "But I've got to go after Danny."

"Certainly dear," the older woman said, shooing Tara away with the motion of her hand.

Tara gave chase, the bad wheel on her buggy causing the entire cart to wobble. "Danny, wait up!"

She needn't have bothered calling out anything. The child had stopped, transfixed by an item on the shelves. Tara groaned even before he reached out and grabbed a jumbo-sized bag of potato chips.

"Look what I found!" Danny thudded toward her on heavy feet. "Chips!"

He put the bag in her cart, his face creased in a

broad smile. Tara did not smile. The salty snack was a terrible choice for a little boy with a weight problem.

She reached inside the cart for the chips and held them out to Danny. "Please put those back, Danny."

"I like chips!" Danny cried.

"I know you do," Tara said. "But they're not good for you."

"They are good!" he protested, his voice rising.

"Not every food that tastes good is good for you." Tara gave up trying to get Danny to reshelve the chips. "I'll buy you a healthy snack."

She headed for the spot where the chips had been with Danny following close behind.

"Want chips!" he yelled at the top of his lungs.

The other people in the aisle, Laura Thompson and her two young daughters, stopped and stared. Tara had taught the older girl, Shelly, in PE last year. She groaned inwardly. Tara was a teacher. She was supposed to be able to handle situations like this.

"Anything I can do to help?" Laura asked.

"Thanks, but no," Tara said. "Please stop yelling, Danny." She kept her voice as calm as possible, the way she did when one of the students at school misbehaved. She placed the potato chips back on the shelf. "Let's go find you something else."

"No-o-o-o-o!" Danny screamed, his face turning red. "Want chips!"

Although her mother had warned her about Danny's tantrums, Tara had never seen one. Her calm voice hadn't worked. Time to try something else.

"Quiet down this instant, Danny!" she said sharply.

"Want chips!" His cry was even more ferocious than the last one. With a defiant look, he snatched the chips from the shelf and took off down the aisle as fast as his short legs would carry him.

"Danny! Come back!" she yelled after him.

He didn't even slow down. With the bag of chips slapping against his hip, he veered right when he reached the end of the aisle.

Tara got behind the cart and followed him. "Sorry about this," she called to Laura and her two daughters as she passed by. She tried to speed up, but the rickety cart slowed her.

"Forget this," she said aloud and abandoned the buggy.

At the end of the aisle she turned in the direction Danny had gone. She stopped in her tracks. The child was nowhere in sight. She couldn't hear him, either.

Her heartbeat sped up and her throat closed. Hayley Cooper sprang to mind. Was this panic what Hayley's mother had experienced when she first realized her little girl was gone?

Tara usually felt safe in Wawpaney, which encompassed a few square miles and had a population of about four hundred. Even during the height of summer, the small inland town didn't get a lot of strangers. Hayley had reportedly been abducted from a small town in Kentucky, proof that bad things can happen anywhere.

Her heart thudded so hard it felt as if it was slamming against her chest. The store had dual exits and one of them was in the general direction Danny had headed. Tara set off again, checking each aisle for any sign of Danny. She spotted people she recognized as she went, but didn't want to linger, asking them if they'd seen Danny. Her panic grew by the second until there was only one more aisle to go.

She was almost afraid to look for fear she wouldn't see him. But, yes! There he was. Not alone, though. A man was crouched down so that he and Danny were at eye level.

Not just any man.

Jack DiMarco.

Her fear over losing Danny subsided, and her heart gave a little leap. If he'd been any other man, she would have attributed the reaction to excitement. But no good reason could exist for Jack to still be in Wawpaney. At the thought, adrenaline of another sort surged through her. She glanced back over her shoulder, battling the urge to flee. Retreat wasn't an option, however, not without Danny.

Gathering her courage, she started forward.

CHAPTER THREE

"HEY, BUDDY, WHERE'RE you going in such a hurry?" Jack crouched so he was eye-to-eye with the boy he'd seen in the parking lot of the grocery store with Tara Greer, the one who'd plowed into him about five seconds ago. The boy didn't seem to be suffering any ill effects from the collision. Jack couldn't say the same for the bag of chips he was clutching to his chest.

"She won't let me have my chips!" the boy cried.

He was different from most other little boys, Jack realized instantly. From his almond-shaped eyes, somewhat flat nose and round face, Jack guessed he had Down syndrome. Like his first cousin's son back in Kentucky.

From the corner of his eye, Jack spotted Tara approaching. Was she the boy's mother? She hadn't been wearing a wedding ring when he'd confronted her the other day, but plenty of women had children outside marriage. She might even be living with the boy's father. Something inside him deflated at the thought.

The boy pointed to Tara. "She's mean!"

It didn't take much brainpower to figure out what was going on.

"She looks pretty nice to me," Jack said. An understatement, he thought.

The boy gazed at him warily and held the chips tighter. He wasn't surrendering them without a fight. Okay. Jack could deal with that.

"You want to see some gross magic?" Jack asked, using two words sure to appeal to any boy.

Just as Jack knew he would, the child nodded.

"I can separate my thumb from the rest of my hand," Jack announced. "Watch."

He placed his left hand palm down with the fingers together and stuck out his thumb. With his right hand, he covered his thumb with a fist and pretended he was trying to detach it. At the exact moment he tucked his left thumb into his palm and jerked his right fist forward, he snapped two of his hidden fingers together.

"Ow!" Jack cried.

"Gross!" the boy yelled, the bag of potato chips falling to the floor.

Just as quickly, Jack brought his hands together and pretended to screw his thumb back on. Then he opened both hands to show that all ten of his fingers were intact.

"Again!" the boy cried, all his attention focused on Jack's hand.

Tara had almost reached them. Jack turned his

head to look at her fully. In a sleeveless yellow shirt, sandals and tight-fitting khaki shorts that extended almost to her knees, she looked even better than she had the first time he'd seen her. Her skin had a healthy glow from her tan and her reddish-brown hair swung loose around her shoulders.

"Let's make sure it's okay with your mom first," Jack said.

"I'm his foster sister," she said shortly. She barely met his eyes, but relief hit him hard at her pronouncement. He checked her ring finger again. Still bare.

Tara stooped in front of the boy. "You shouldn't have run from me, Danny. And you're not supposed to talk to strangers."

So that was how she thought of him. He shouldn't have been surprised after he'd practically accosted her in the street. In retrospect, that probably hadn't been the best way to approach her.

"He took off his thumb!" Danny said. "Do it again!"

"Is it okay with you?" Jack asked.

She didn't answer immediately. Even unsmiling, she was pretty. About the only thing he didn't like about her was the unfriendly gleam in her eyes. There had been nothing frosty about her when she was in the parking lot with her foster brother. She'd been laughing as she leaned over and gave him a warm hug, affection pouring off her. That women, he thought, was the real Tara.

"Use your manners, Danny," she said. "You're supposed to say please."

"Please take off your thumb," he cried.

"Everything okay, Tara?" One of her neighbors, a heavyset man in his sixties, called from the end of the aisle.

"Thanks for checking up on us, Mr. Ganz," Tara called back, geniality radiating from her. "We're fine now."

Jack repeated the trick. It had been one of his younger brother's favorites when they were kids. A wave of sadness hit Jack, as it always did when he thought of Mike. He thrust the melancholy feeling aside, concentrating instead on snapping his fingers to make it sound as though his thumb were breaking off. He winced and grimaced his way through the reattachment sequence until he was supposedly whole again.

Danny clapped his hands.

"Thanks," Jack said. "How 'bout I introduce myself so we're not strangers. I know your name is Danny. Mine's Jack."

"Will you be my friend, Jack?" Danny asked.

"Sure," Jack said. "If that's okay with Tara."

She didn't look as if she wanted to give her permission. "That depends on what you're doing here."

"Grocery shopping." He held up his handbasket. Unfortunately, it was empty. Their aisle smelled of the ground coffee on the shelf behind him. He turned, picked one out at random and dropped it into the basket. Maybe not his smoothest move judging from the way her lips thinned.

"Here in Wawpaney?" she asked.

The skepticism that ran through her question was so heavy she could just as well have accused him of following her. It didn't seem like a good idea to admit he'd decided to come into the store only after seeing her hug Danny in the parking lot.

"Shell Beach doesn't have a grocery store," he said, naming the Chesapeake Bay community about six or seven miles away where he was renting a house. "I'm pretty sure Wawpaney's the closest town."

Her mouth dropped open.

"C-can you take your thumb off again?" Danny interjected.

"Maybe later, buddy," Jack said.

"My name's not buddy," the boy said. "It's Danny."

Jack smiled. "Sorry, Danny. I can't take off my thumb right now. I need to talk to Tara."

"How do you know my name?" she asked sharply.

"You told me," he said. Hadn't she? Suddenly he wasn't so sure.

She shook her head. "I didn't."

That was right. The waitress at the diner had provided Tara's name when she'd spotted the age progression of Hayley Cooper.

"I thought you were passing through town," she said.

"I liked it here, so decided to stay awhile. What better place to hang out than the beach?" When she didn't agree, he looked down at Danny. "You like the beach, right?"

"I like fish," he said.

"Me, too," Jack said. "I was thinking about getting a couple poles so I can fish off one of the piers."

"Danny means he likes the schools of tiny fish you sometimes see in the tidal pools," Tara said. "He gets a bucket and rescues them."

"I'm their hero," Danny said proudly. "Right, Tara?"

"If those fish don't love you, they're crazy," she said, smiling down at him with all the warmth she wasn't showing Jack.

"Crazy fish," Danny echoed. "That's funny."

"Maybe you can show me how you rescue them sometime." Jack nodded to Tara. "You can bring your foster sister with you."

Again a mask seemed to cover the real Tara. "I don't think so."

"But I wanna—" Danny began.

"You've got a busy few weeks coming up, Dan the man," Tara interrupted. "Camp starts Monday."

Although the excuse seemed legitimate, it also sounded like a brush-off. Jack had expected as much, but he also subscribed to the school of thought that you can't get what you want if you don't try for it. He wanted to get to know Tara better and see if he could bring out the softness in her that so intrigued him.

"Jack can come to camp," Danny announced.

"No, Jack can't come," Tara said quickly. "The camp is for kids."

"You're c-coming!" Danny said.

"That's because I'm working there," she said, her voice even. Jack admired her patience. Although Down syndrome children were known for their sweet and cheerful personalities, from first-hand experience Jack knew it wasn't always easy to deal with them. "Now let's say goodbye to Jack so he can get on with his *grocery shopping.*"

She put heavy emphasis on the last words. Yep. She didn't trust him. Jack supposed he couldn't blame her. She didn't know anything about him except that he claimed to be the brother of a private investigator. Never mind that it was the truth.

"Say goodbye to Jack, Danny," Tara said.

"But I don't wanna—"

"Bye, Danny. It was nice taking my thumb off for you," Jack interrupted, loath to cause any trouble between Tara and her brother. He was gratified when the boy giggled. "Bye, Tara."

Her eyes flicked to his. "Goodbye."

She took her brother securely by the hand and led him away, her carriage almost regal. They'd almost reached the end of the aisle when Danny wrenched his hand from hers and ran back to Jack with pounding feet.

"Danny!" Tara called after him.

He ignored his foster sister, not stopping until he reached Jack. His chest heaved up and down.

"Come see me at c-camp," he said somewhat breathlessly. "You can take off your thumb again."

Before Jack could reply, Danny turned and headed back for his foster sister at a slower pace. Over his head, Tara's gaze met Jack's.

He shrugged, trying to convey his apology, not so much over Danny but about the way they'd met. He wished she didn't have reason to be so suspicious of him.

She broke eye contact and in moments she and Danny turned the corner and disappeared from sight.

The big bag of potato chips lay forgotten on the floor.

WAS JACK DiMARCO following her?

The question ate at Tara for the rest of the afternoon and night. She briefly forgot about Jack while helping out at a friend's pub in Cape Charles on Saturday night, but not until she'd visually scoured the vicinity for any sign of him.

Her paranoia was still on full alert Sunday night on the short drive to Cape Charles where she taught spinning classes. The town, founded along the bay as a planned community to serve the railroad and ferry trades, boasted late-Victorian architecture and a sandy beachfront park. It had become home in recent years to a resort retirement community with waterfront homes and championship golf courses, making it feel like a tourist town, albeit a sleepy one.

Tara expected to see Jack's pickup rolling along behind her. It was little consolation that she didn't. If he wanted to find her, he could.

She parked and started up the sidewalk to the fitness club, mentally reviewing the reasons Jack could still be in the Eastern Shore. She supposed it was possible that the beauty of the area had tugged at him, as it had many others. Or maybe he was interested in getting to know Tara better. He certainly acted as though he were attracted to her.

She dismissed the notion, dismayed that it held some appeal. It was far more likely he still thought she might be Hayley Cooper.

"Hey, Tara! Wait up!"

Kiki Sommers, one of the youngest members of her class, rushed to catch up with her. The nineteen-year-old was wearing another of the colorful outfits that were her trademark. This one featured bright pink yoga pants and a sleeveless black-and-white sports top. Kiki's long blond hair was tied back in a high ponytail that swung as she moved.

"Hey, Kiki." Tara opened the door to let the other woman precede her into the brick building that had once housed a YMCA. The fitness club that had taken over the space was prospering, but summers were slow despite the regulars who used the weight room and the diehards in Tara's classes. "Love the outfit."

"Thanks," Kiki said. "I knew it was cute, no matter what JoJo said."

"JoJo?"

"My brother. He moved back home from Virginia Beach a couple weeks ago after he lost his job." Kiki snapped her fingers and turned to regard Tara as she walked through the door. "Hey, I heard you want to get fixed up with him."

"Who does Tara want to get fixed up with?" Dustin Jeffries, an employee not much older than Kiki, asked from behind the front desk. The place was so small, nothing anybody said was sacred. A lounge area consisting of a TV and single sofa was on one side of the desk. Across an aisle on the other side was the all-purpose room where Tara taught her exercise class.

"My brother JoJo," Kiki answered.

"Give me a break," Tara said. "I didn't know your brother existed until a few moments ago. Who told you I wanted to date him?"

"Mary Dee," Kiki said. "She saw JoJo picking me up last week. I thought you did, too."

Tara was going to let Mary Dee have it when she next saw her. Unfortunately that wouldn't be today. Mary Dee was missing class to take her husband out to dinner for his birthday.

"No, I didn't see him." Something occurred to Tara. "How old is he, anyway?"

"Twenty-three," Kiki said.

"Too young for me," Tara said.

"JoJo looks older," Kiki said. Tara thought it was telling that she didn't say anything about her brother's maturity level. So far about the only details she'd provided were that he was unemployed and lived at home.

"Kiki's right," Dustin said. "I've seen her brother. All that facial hair does make him look older. You should go out with him, Tara."

She shook her head. "Is everyone around here trying to fix me up?"

"Yeah," Kiki said. "Pretty much."

"I can find my own man, thank you very much," Tara said, a mental image of Jack DiMarco flashing in her brain.

Kiki clapped. "You've got a man?"

Tara thrust Jack from her mind. "Maybe," she

said, which was the quickest way to get Kiki to stop suggesting a date with her brother.

"Ooooh," Kiki said. "Tell me more."

"Can't," Tara said. "Class is starting in a few minutes. I need to stretch."

She ducked into the all-purpose room, where nine women awaited her, about two-thirds the number that usually showed up. Summer didn't officially start for another week or so but vacation season had begun.

She changed the CD in the sound system to a mix she'd made the night before of songs with fast tempos. She climbed on the bike at the front of the room and started to pedal.

"Okay, class," Tara called above the noise of the gears turning. "Who's ready to work hard?"

"I am!" Kiki, unsurprisingly, was the first to raise her hand.

Forty-five minutes later, Tara was damp with perspiration. She always pedaled with enthusiasm to set a good example for her students. Today, however, she'd put in extra effort, the better to stop thinking about Jack DiMarco and Hayley Cooper—although here at the health club, where she felt so comfortable, she could almost convince herself that Jack's presence in Wawpaney was innocent. He even seemed like a nice guy. He'd helped her out with that situation with Danny and the potato chips, hadn't he? And she hadn't even thanked him.

With the class dismissed, Tara finished off the water in her bottle and bent to remove a towel from her bag. She noticed a flash of bright pink out of the corner of her eye and realized Kiki was approaching.

"Now I understand why you don't want to go out with my brother," Kiki said.

"Excuse me?"

"I mean, JoJo's kind of cute, I guess. But he's got nothing on your guy."

"My guy?" Tara asked.

"About six-two with a body to die for and that gorgeous thick brown hair. Early thirties, I'd say. Really hot. But then, I just love a guy with a widow's peak."

She'd just described Jack DiMarco.

Tara's heart slammed against her chest. "Where did you see him?"

"He was watching the class for a little while," Kiki said. "You had your back to him, so you must not have known he was there."

Tara wiped off her face with her towel to hide her shock. Her hands were shaking. First the grocery store, now the fitness club. This couldn't be a coincidence. Jack must not have believed her rationale when she'd denied she was Hayley Cooper.

"You're a lucky girl," Kiki announced. "I'd pump you for information about him, but I've got to get home. JoJo needs the car."

KiKi gave a wave and hurried off. Tara packed up her things and rushed out of the room. The health club didn't get a lot of traffic in the warm-weather months, but the weight room was never empty. A half dozen men worked out on the machines, but Jack wasn't among them. Neither was his pickup in the parking lot.

Tara left the club and headed toward her car at a jog, thinking about her claim that she'd seen baby photos of herself. She was in front of the pale blue two-story house where she'd grown up before she consciously knew that was where she was headed.

Bright yellow flowers that matched the shutters on the windows spilled out of pots flanking the front door. Not bothering to ring the doorbell, Tara walked in through the unlocked front door, her tennis shoes making soft thudding sounds on the weathered wood floor.

"Mom!" she called. "It's Tara."

Her mother appeared from the back of the house almost instantly, a finger resting against her lips. She was dressed in another of her flowing dresses, this one in pale pink. "Shh. I just this minute got Danny to sleep. He is so excited about camp tomorrow he can hardly stand it."

"Sorry," Tara said, but her attention was only half on what her mother had said. In the hall, pictures were everywhere. Of her sister and father, their heads close together, their smiles almost identical. Of her parents with her sister at a carnival, at a park and in front of a Christmas tree.

There were a few photos of Tara, too, but none of her as an infant or a toddler. In the images, she was either alone or with her mother. Why had Tara never noticed that there were no photos of her with her father or sister?

"Is everything okay, honey?" Her mother's question jarred Tara back to the present. She was gazing at Tara with her forehead furrowed. "You're so darn busy on Sundays, I usually don't get to see your pretty face."

"Everything is fine," Tara said, although suddenly she wasn't at all sure of that. She thought about coming straight out and asking her mother about Hayley Cooper, but rejected the notion. Tara couldn't just blurt out something like that. She searched her brain for an excuse to explain why she'd stopped by. "I'm just making sure we were still carpooling tomorrow."

"Why wouldn't we be?" her mother asked.

"No reason," Tara said and fell silent. What did it mean that she'd never seen a photo of herself with her father or sister? Didn't most parents delight in having their children photographed together?

"Can I make you something to eat?" her mother asked. "Get you something to drink?"

"No, thanks. I need to go home and take a shower." Tara started backing toward the door, then stopped. If she didn't at least ask her mother about the photographs now, she might never screw up the courage. "Mom, can I borrow your photo albums from before we moved to Wawpaney?"

Her mother's hand flew to her throat, a reaction that seemed out of proportion to the request. "Why ever would you want to do that?'

"I guess because I'm curious," Tara said. Her mother continued to gape at her, compelling Tara to come up with a better explanation. "Mary Dee has her kindergartners bring in baby pictures at the start of every year. She brings in one of herself, too. She's always asking to see one of mine."

Her mother's hand was still at her throat. She was so petite, it wasn't much bigger than a child's hand. "The school year just ended."

"Yeah, but I thought I'd have one ready for September. And besides, I'm curious about when we lived in Charlotte. I don't remember ever seeing those pictures." Tara swallowed. "So, can I borrow those albums?"

Her mother's face seemed to lose color, although Tara thought that perhaps her imagination was running rampant. She held her breath as she waited for a response.

"I'm real sorry, Tara," her mother finally said. "I don't have any photo albums from Charlotte."

Tara frowned. Her heart started to thump. "Are you sure? You're always taking photos. You even did that scrapbooking class last year."

"I didn't get into scrapbooking until we moved here." Her mother's voice sounded shaky. "All those pictures I was going to put in albums—I'm afraid they're gone."

"Gone?" Tara repeated, a hitch in her voice.

Her mother averted her eyes—or was that Tara's imagination, too? "A casualty of the move. Such a shame, it was. Some of the boxes had water damage."

Including, apparently, the very box that could have proved Tara was who she'd always believed herself to be.

"I'm sorry," her mother said again.

Tara's throat was so thick she could barely get the words past her lips. "That's okay. I'll see you tomorrow."

She backed out of the house and into the overcast night, automatically placing one foot in front of the other.

I'm sorry, her mother had said.

Tara wondered what exactly she'd apologized for before facing a truth of her own. There was another reason she hadn't been more persistent when questioning her mother. A stronger reason.

If Carrie Greer had abducted her, she didn't want to know.

WHAT WAS HE GOING TO DO for the rest of the day? Jack wondered. It wasn't a great question to be asking himself, considering it was barely past noon.

The beach where he was renting a cottage wasn't wide enough or long enough for running, so he'd jogged along the narrow road through the maritime forest that bordered the salt marsh. He'd also performed the series of shoulder exercises the team doctor had prescribed before the Mud Dogs released him, driven into Wawpaney to buy some toiletries at the drugstore and eaten a sandwich he'd slapped together.

The local newspaper he'd bought at the convenience store lay on the butcher-block kitchen table. He picked it up, struck again by how thin it was. It wouldn't take long to read.

With the newspaper in hand, he headed out to the porch that was just steps from the bay. The low rent on the one-bedroom cottage hadn't made sense until he saw the collection of modest homes on either side of a mile-long street that made up the community. If the houses hadn't been parallel to the water, there'd be nothing special about them. As the Realtor in Onancock had claimed, however, the location couldn't be beaten.

With a narrow expanse of beach just steps from the porch, the warm, salty scent of the Chesapeake Bay in his nostrils and the sound of the lapping waves filling his ears, Jack had to admit she was right. The setting would be even more perfect on a day that wasn't overcast.

He was about to sit down on one of the plastic Adirondack chairs when he noticed two local girls in bikinis about fifteen yards away staring at him. From their gangly figures and coltish legs, he judged them to be about thirteen or fourteen. Their heads were together and their shoulders shook as though they were giggling. The thinner of the two broke away from the other girl and headed straight for him. She stopped just shy of the porch.

"Hey, mister, can I ask you something?" She was still giggling. The sun glinted off something silver and Jack realized she wore braces.

"Sure." He figured the girls had some kind of bet going.

"Are you famous?"

Jack supposed it wasn't outside the realm of possibility that one of the girls had recognized him, although the world he lived in seemed very far away.

"Are you a baseball fan?" he asked.

She seemed surprised by the question. "Sort of. But I know you're not a baseball player."

"How's that?"

"It's baseball season right now," she said. "You'd be playing. You wouldn't be here."

He nodded. Of course she didn't know him from baseball. He'd made three appearances in the major leagues in nine years, none lasting longer than a few innings. Only the most hard-core fan would recognize his name. Even fewer would know his face.

"Sorry to disappoint you, but I'm not famous," he said. "Who did you think I was, anyway?"

"We weren't sure," she said. "But we thought maybe Ryan Reynolds."

"Ryan who?"

"Green Lantern," she said.

"What's that?"

She giggled again. "A movie about a comic-book character. Ryan Reynolds is a movie star."

"Oh." Jack didn't see many movies.

She turned and ran back to her friend, sand kicking up under her feet. Jack sat down, aware his mood had darkened.

He wasn't sure why. For as long as he could remember he'd dreamed of becoming a pro baseball player, not of being famous. When he'd brushed elbows with his superstar teammates during his brief stints in the majors, fame hadn't looked attractive.

The most famous of them, a center fielder who'd won a couple of batting titles, had to switch hotels because of the autograph seekers who mobbed him in the lobby. Somebody had told Jack the player was a virtual recluse in the off-season because it was so difficult for him to go out in public.

No, it wasn't lack of fame that nagged at Jack.

It was the reminder that baseball season was in full swing and he was here at an out-of-the-way beach community on the Eastern Shore instead of on the mound where he belonged.

"What now?" Jack asked himself sarcastically. "You're going to start feeling sorry for yourself?"

That wasn't his style. Neither was talking to himself.

He'd already identified the problem. He had too much time on his hands. Too bad he wasn't one of the sun worshippers who could while away the hours on the beach. Another workout was in his future, but not until at least early evening when his muscles had recovered from his morning exercises. Swimming in the bay was tempting, but he feared his shoulder wasn't yet up to it. He needed to curb his enthusiasm until he could meet with the fitness consultant the guy at the health club had recommended when he'd stopped by the night before.

Jack turned his attention to the newspaper, not exactly sure why he'd picked it up instead of the thicker regional paper. Reading that would have taken longer.

He skimmed a front-page story about a crabber who'd been harvesting the Chesapeake for almost fifty years, scanned a story about beach erosion and skipped a detailed account of the latest Northampton County Board of Supervisors meeting.

He flipped through the rest of the newspaper, finding little to catch his interest. He was about to refold the paper when two words in bold type jumped out at him: Volunteer Opportunities.

Of course. The answer to his boredom. He could volunteer.

He read through the listings, keeping a mental tally of activities that might suit him. Delivering meals to shut-ins. Picking up trash off the beach. Helping kids learn to read.

All the opportunities seemed possible, but none seemed quite right until he reached the last listing.

No experience necessary! Help needed at Camp Daybreak, a summer program in Cape Charles for children with developmental disabilities. You bring the energy. We'll provide the guidance.

The listing included the name and phone number of a contact as well as other particulars about the camp. It went from 9:00 a.m. until 4:00 p.m. daily for the next two weeks and started…today.

This camp was, without a doubt, the one that Tara Greer's brother, Danny, was attending.

Adrenaline surged through Jack for the first time all day. Not only might volunteering at Camp Daybreak bring him back into contact with Tara, he genuinely enjoyed being around children like Danny. Because of his cousin's son, he even had some limited experience.

If volunteering awarded him a chance to change Tara's mind about him, so much the better. He'd seen Tara again last night when he'd stopped by the fitness club. She'd been smiling and laughing, her upbeat personality and a good cheer shining through even as she pedaled faster and faster. He'd been tempted to stick around until her class ended, but was afraid she wouldn't believe it was a chance encounter.

Jack leaped to his feet and went into the rented cottage to find his cell phone. One voice-mail message later, he disconnected the call and made a snap decision. Camp Daybreak didn't end for another three and a half hours. Three and a half hours that would be interminable if Jack spent them here alone.

He had the address of the camp. Why not volunteer his services in person?

CHAPTER FOUR

CARRIE GREER FIGURED now was as good a time as any to get this over with. Actually, considering camp had started a few hours before and the children were settling down to lunch, it was past time.

If nothing else, the confrontation would take her mind off the approaching anniversary of the saddest day of her life and Tara's odd plea to see a baby photo of herself. Carrie always had trouble sleeping in the days leading up to the anniversary. Last night she'd tossed and turned even more than usual, wondering what had prompted Tara's request and worrying that her daughter hadn't bought her explanation.

She shoved the problem to the back of her mind. Now wasn't the time to obsess over things she couldn't change, not when the director of Camp Daybreak was alone in the community center's small office.

"I'll be right back," she told Tara.

"Sure thing." Her daughter glanced up from the long table in the all-purpose room where she was helping one of the ten campers unpack his lunch. The other nine were happily munching on the sandwiches, chips, fruit and assorted goodies they'd brought from home in their packed lunches.

"Bye, C-Carrie!" Danny waved, his face wreathed in the biggest smile he'd worn since coming to live with her. Just as Carrie suspected, this camp was exactly what Danny needed.

She forgave herself for tricking Tara into volunteering by telling her Danny's tuition would be waived. There was a kernel of truth in the claim, since the children of volunteers got the first week free. With both Carrie and Tara helping out at the camp, Carrie had a strong argument for not having to pay for the second week.

If she couldn't sway the director to her way of thinking, Carrie would have to ask Tara for the money. She was loath to do that. Even at half the cost, camps like these were expensive.

The facilities were top-notch. Camp Daybreak had rented space at a privately owned community center that boasted an oversize air-conditioned room. On rainy days, tables could be pushed aside to create an empty space in the center of the room. Campers also had access to a playground and a community pool. The staff was impressive, too. The director was not only the father of one of the campers but a special education teacher, his assistant was a developmental disability nurse and one of the four volunteer camp counselors was a physiotherapist. Another staff member was a speech therapist.

Carrie walked across the all-purpose room, the heels of her sandals making clicking sounds on the linoleum floor, the skirt of her sleeveless cotton dress swishing about her legs. Gustavo Miller was in the cramped office, his head bent over paperwork, one hand poised over a calculator. He didn't look up.

Here goes, Carrie thought.

"Hey there, Gustavo," she said.

His head jerked up, his green eyes fastening on her. The color was quite remarkable, considering his dark hair and swarthy complexion. After a few brief meetings, she'd already noticed he was a man of contradictions. Take his name. Miller was as common as names in the United States came. Gustavo was not.

The intent expression on his face morphed into a smile. "Call me Gus. Most people do."

"I don't believe I will," Carrie said. "Gustavo suits the tall, dark and Latin thing you've got going on."

If he'd been seven or eight years older—in other words, her age—she wouldn't have worded the compliment quite that way. With men as old as she was and older, she was very careful not to flirt.

He laughed, a nice rumbling sound. "My mother's from Argentina, but I'm only half Latin. My father grew up near here in Exeter."

"How interesting. How did your parents meet?" she asked.

"Dad was a month into what was supposed to be a trip around the world when he saw her on a beach in Mar del Plata," he said. "He stayed in Argentina to romance her and six months later they were married. I spent the first ten years of my life in Buenos Aires."

"Now I understand why you have an accent."

"You can hear it, then?" He shook his head, as though he didn't realize how attractive his slightly different pronunciations were. "I learned to speak Spanish first. I've lived in the States so long, though, I keep expecting to lose it. You've got an accent, too. Southern?"

"That's right," she said. "Nothing exotic. I'm just an American girl from Charlotte."

"Nothing wrong with that," Gustavo said. "I quite like Southern girls."

Was he flirting with her? No, that was highly unlikely given their age difference.

She nodded to the empty chair at the table. "Mind if I sit down?"

"Not at all." He folded his hands on top of the papers while she settled into the chair. "Is there something I can help you with, Carrie?"

She shouldn't be flattered that he remembered

her name. She'd been at orientation last week and they were more than halfway through the first day of camp. She'd never heard Carrie pronounced quite that way, though, with the slight rolling of the *r*'s.

Strangely reluctant to bring up the reason she'd sought him out, she asked, "Aren't you going to have lunch?"

"A little later," he said. "But that's not what you came to see me about, is it?"

Still not ready to talk money, Carrie smiled at him. It wasn't difficult. Gustavo had a face that made her want to smile. She got a whiff of something. Not cologne. Something clean and fresh like soap or shampoo. Whatever it was, it made him smell good. "I'm wondering how you got to be director of a camp like this?"

"It's important to me that Susie have the camp experience," he said. "There wasn't a special-needs camp close enough, so I decided to start one. First I had to set up as a nonprofit agency. Then I was lucky enough to get a grant to offset some of the costs. We're starting small this year with the ten campers, but my plan is to keep growing. We might even make next year's camp residential."

"I'm impressed," she said. "You can't have lived here very long or we'd have run into each other."

"About six months," he said. "I've been home-schooling Susie, so haven't met a lot of people yet.

We moved from Baltimore when my grandmother had a heart attack. She was running a bed-and-breakfast. Maybe you know it? The Bay Breeze?"

"That sounds familiar," Carrie said. "It's a two-story house on the water, right? Not far from the Chesapeake Bay Bridge-Tunnel?"

"Right," he said. "My parents moved back to Argentina a few years ago. Dad couldn't get away, so it made the most sense for me to help Grandma run the place until she got better, even though I had to quit my teaching job in Baltimore. Except she never made it out of the hospital."

Carrie's heart twisted and she laid her hand on his. "I'm sorry."

"Me, too. She was a great lady."

"Will you and your wife keep the B and B going?" she asked, realizing she was fishing around for his marital status. His daughter, Susie, was a camper, but thus far he hadn't mentioned a wife.

"I'm divorced," he said. "And no. I've got a special ed job lined up for the fall. I closed the Bay Breeze to guests after my grandma died. I'm putting it on the market once I find another place for Susie and me to live. The place needs too much—how can I put it?—TLC."

"If you're in charge of a camp like this, you must be awfully good at TLC," she pointed out.

He looked down at the table, where her hand still

rested on his, and lifted his green eyes. "Thank you."

She drew her hand back quickly, breaking the contact. Oh, no. Now she'd gone and done it. When she broached the subject of Danny's tuition, he could get the wrong idea.

"I wasn't flirting with you," she blurted out.

"You weren't?" He actually looked disappointed. "You're not married, are you?"

She swallowed the lump in her throat. "Widowed."

"I'm sorry," he said.

"Me, too." She sensed he was about to ask her questions she'd rather not answer and cast around for something else to say. "Besides, you're way too young for the likes of me."

"I doubt that," he said. "I'm forty-seven."

She usually wouldn't reveal her true age unless threatened at gunpoint, but she was trying to make a point. "I'll have you know I'm fifty-four."

"You don't look it." His accented words seemed to glide over her skin. She should be gracious and thank him. Surely she'd blush if she did, though.

"Believe it," she said. "You're the first person I haven't lied to about my age in years."

He threw back his head and laughed, revealing even teeth that looked very white against his tanned skin.

"Is Susie your only child?" she asked, partly because she wanted to know, but mostly to change the subject.

"Yes," he said. "How about you? Do you have other children besides Tara and Danny?"

Carrie didn't pause before answering. "Another daughter. We call her Sunny because she's happy all the time."

"Cute," Gustavo said.

Carrie didn't care to examine why she talked about Sunny as though she were alive. She was about to explain that Danny was her foster child when Susie Miller came running into the office, her face split in a wide smile.

"Daddy!" Susie cried. If she hadn't made sure the entire camp knew she was eleven, Carrie never would have guessed her age. She was short and on the stocky side, with a round, flat face that was always smiling. In her fine, straight brownish-blond hair, she wore a pink bow. "Look what I found!"

Her hands were cradled together. She opened them and a spider with eight spindly legs jumped out on the table. Carrie took an involuntary step backward. It was a daddy longlegs.

"Look how cute it is!" Susie cried.

Gustavo laughed and hoisted his daughter onto his lap. "Only you would call a spider cute. You were careful with him, weren't you, *mi hija dulce?*"

Carrie knew enough Spanish to figure out that translated to "my sweet daughter."

"Yeah. See how fast he moves," Susie said, her attention on the spider. Her speech was quite good, clearer than Danny's. Down syndrome children commonly had significant language delays. She must have had a good speech therapist.

"He's trying to get away." Gustavo blocked a side of the table so the spider didn't scramble to the floor.

"Why?" Susie asked. "We won't hurt him."

"He doesn't know that." Gustavo set his daughter back on the floor and got to his feet. He easily caught the spider in his cupped hands. "Let's take him outside where he belongs."

Susie's face fell. "I didn't mean to make him sad."

"Are you kidding me, sweetheart? If not for you, he might never find his way outside." He slanted a look at Carrie. "You'll have to excuse me. Fatherhood calls."

"Go," Carrie said.

He smiled at Carrie. The bulk of his attention, however, was on his daughter, where it rightly should be. She watched them leave, forming the impression that Gustavo Miller was a very nice man and an even better father.

It wasn't until he was almost out of sight that she realized she never had gotten around to asking him to waive the second half of Danny's tuition.

TARA BLINKED ONCE, then twice. It did no good. Jack DiMarco was still walking toward the community-center pool where in a few minutes she'd be joined by the ten campers and the rest of the staff. She'd volunteered to put up the safety rope between the shallow and deep ends of the pool after the director said it was an ideal time for a water activity. The day was cloudy and a bit gray, perfect pool weather for children who weren't used to spending much time in the sun.

The pool would usually be teeming with kids, but a recent downpour had thinned out the crowd considerably. Half a dozen teenagers swam in the deep end. Otherwise, Tara was alone.

Her heart thudded as Jack got closer. He'd almost certainly lied about his sister being a private investigator. Considering how many times she'd seen him around town, it made far more sense that he was the P.I. in the family.

A P.I. who wasn't satisfied that she wasn't Hayley Cooper.

Her mind raced and her heart beat double time. Where was her mother? Could Tara get rid of Jack before they ran into each other? What could she say to get him to leave her alone?

She'd been about to toss the safety rope with attached floats into the pool. She told herself to act normally, and she threw one end of the blue plastic rope into the water. She bent to fasten the hook to the edge of the pool, drew in a deep breath and got a lungful of chlorine-scented air.

"Let me help you with that," Jack called.

Reluctantly she turned her head to watch him unfastening the lock on the gate and striding to the opposite end of the pool.

She couldn't take her eyes off him. His shorts and T-shirt called attention to his broad shoulders and athletic build. A wave of attraction swept through her. She quickly squashed it, noting the way he exuded confidence. Like a man who was used to getting what he wanted.

He knelt on the concrete, as though he weren't an interloper, as though he belonged.

She needed to accept there was no getting away from him.

"What are you doing here?" she asked.

He lifted his head, revealing the hint of a smile. "Reaching for the rope."

He dipped his right hand into the water, stretched out his arm to forage for the rope and winced. Or at least Tara thought he winced. She didn't have time to wonder about it. She had other things on her mind.

He hooked the safety rope in place, straightened to his full six foot plus and stared at her across the pool. Despite the overcast sky, it was in the mid-eighties. Goose bumps still broke out on her skin.

Her modest one-piece bathing suit was more

suitable for swimming laps than sunbathing, yet she felt naked. She fought the urge to cross her arms over her chest. She would not let him guess how much he unnerved her.

"You know what I meant," she said crisply. "Wherever I go, there you are."

"I can explain that," he began.

She braced herself to hear the reasons he didn't buy her denial that she wasn't Hayley Cooper, wondering if she could counteract them and convince him to go.

Would it be enough to tell him that if she had been Hayley in another life, she didn't want to know?

"Jack! You came!" Danny's excited voice rang out. Moving with unusual speed, Tara's foster brother led a contingent of children and camp counselors to the pool. He was clad in a floral-print bathing suit and so much sunscreen it left streaks of white on his skin.

"Hey, Danny." Jack moved toward the gate and opened it for Danny. "Good to see you again."

He stuck out a hand. Danny ignored it and launched himself into Jack's arms, giving him a huge hug. Jack grinned and hugged him back.

"Will you take off your thumb again?" Danny asked, then added almost as an afterthought, "Please."

"Sure thing." Jack grabbed his thumb and repeated the trick Tara had watched him perform at the grocery store. It really did seem as though he could yank off the digit. This time he made it look as if the detached end of his thumb was wiggling before he brought his hands together and became whole again.

"Yay!" Danny clapped his hands. He turned toward the other campers, who were proceeding more slowly to the pool area. "Come watch Jack take off his thumb!"

Nine-year-old Kim, who was dressed in a pink bathing suit decorated with butterflies, stopped walking and covered her eyes. So did Samantha, the youngest camper at age seven. Neither of the girls had Down syndrome, but their mothers had used the same two words to describe them—*mentally challenged.*

"Yuck," Kim said.

"Yuck," Samantha repeated.

"I wanna see!" A teenager named Brandon who'd suffered a brain injury as a boy spoke for the first time. He used a loping, uneven stride to reach the pool area.

"Me, too!" Susie Miller shouted.

"Again, please!" Danny told Jack. "When I say please, you have to do it."

Jack chuckled. "Please is a good enough incentive for me. But let's wait until everybody who wants to see the magic trick gets here."

A teenager named Brandy, who was volunteering as a counselor to get community service hours, joined the campers gathered around Jack. Tara's mother guided the two youngest girls to the pool area, where they stood back from the group and covered their eyes.

Her mom walked toward Tara, half her attention on Jack and the giggling group of children around him. Tara felt her pulse race.

"How did that man know Danny's name, honey?" Her mother sounded more curious than concerned. "Do you know him?"

Here was another opportunity for Tara to tell her mother about the age-progression photo. If her mom regarded her blankly, Tara could put the matter out of her mind once and for all. But what if her mother looked displeased before answering, the way she had when Tara inquired about the baby photo? What then?

She wouldn't confront her mother, Tara decided. She liked her life precisely the way it was. She wasn't about to do anything to jeopardize that.

"Not exactly." Tara drew out the words to buy herself time while she figured out how to answer. "Remember me telling you about Danny's meltdown at the grocery store? Jack was there. He distracted Danny with a magic trick."

"Oooh," Carrie said, admiration practically oozing from the exclamation. "You've got to like a man who's quick thinking as well as good-looking."

"Can you do any other tricks?" The excited voice belonged not to a camper, but to Brandy.

"I can turn a pencil into rubber." Jack produced a pencil from his pocket with a flourish. "I need one of you to verify that it's a solid lead pencil first. Any volunteers?"

Danny's arm shot into the air. "Me!"

Her foster brother took the pencil. His brows knit together as he carefully examined it for a good fifteen seconds before handing it back to Jack.

"It's solid," Danny said.

"Watch carefully," Jack said.

He held the end of the pencil loosely between his right thumb and pointer finger. With a vertical motion, he moved his hand up and down until the pencil did indeed appear as if it were bending. None of the children seemed to realize it was a clever optical illusion.

"C-cool!" Danny cried.

"He's very good with children, your Jack," her mother said.

Tara had been thinking the same thing. "My Jack?" she exclaimed. "Why do you think he's my Jack?"

"There's gotta be more to the story than you're telling me," her mother said. "Some stranger you met at the grocery wouldn't show up out of the blue at the camp where you're volunteering."

A lump of what felt like panic stuck in Tara's throat. Those were her thoughts exactly.

"It's possible," she said, not believing it.

"Don't worry yourself about it." Her mother wiggled her fingers in the air. "I have my ways of extracting information."

Jack DiMarco, however, dug up information for a living. She didn't truly believe her mother could kidnap a child, but neither could she entirely discount it. A wave of protectiveness swept over Tara, fierce enough that she balled her fists. Whatever her mother might have done, Tara owed Carrie. She needed to make sure Jack didn't go anywhere near her.

She noticed Gus Miller, the camp director, approaching the pool area with Aggie McCorkle, the perpetually cheerful assistant director. Surely he'd notice there was a stranger in their midst? Would he help Tara's cause by asking Jack to leave?

"I'll show you more magic tricks later," Jack told the campers. "Right now, I believe it's time for water aerobics."

How did Jack know what activity was next on the camp agenda?

"Before the children get in the pool, perhaps you'd like to introduce yourself." Tara's mother took a few steps toward Jack. Tara had to call upon all her willpower not to clutch her mother's arm and draw her back. "Some of us haven't had the pleasure."

"Sorry," Jack said. "I should have done that already."

Tara's entire body tensed. It seemed unlikely that Jack would air his suspicions in front of the entire group. Then again, he was a wild card. Who knew what he'd do?

"I'm the one who should make the introductions." Gus edged closer to Jack and laid a hand on his shoulder. "Listen up, everyone. This is Jack, our new volunteer."

Tara's breath caught. How could that be? When camp had started this morning, there were four volunteer counselors in addition to the three-person staff. There had been one more volunteer at orientation last Thursday, but she'd had to drop out because of a family emergency.

Tara gulped, but the ball of panic wouldn't dissolve. Was Jack using an investigative tactic to go undercover as a camp volunteer? Was his objective to gather more information about her?

"Let's make Jack feel welcome," Gus said.

"Hi, Jack!"

"Welcome!"

"Hello!"

While childish voices blended together in greeting, Tara headed straight for Gus. "Can I speak to you for a minute?" she asked in a low voice.

"Certainly," he said, moving with her to a quieter corner of the pool area. "What's on your mind?"

"Why didn't you tell us about him before?" She couldn't make herself say Jack's name. She didn't want to be on a first-name basis with the man set on disrupting her life.

"He just volunteered today," Gus said. "He saw a notice in the newspaper. Lucky for us, because the listing about the camp needing volunteers was supposed to have expired."

Tara didn't believe a newspaper ad had led Jack to volunteer, not when Danny had mentioned the camp to Jack at the grocery store. How hard could it be for a P.I. to find out where on the Eastern Shore a camp for mentally challenged children was being held?

"What about the paperwork? I thought volunteers needed to have a TB test on file and a criminal background check," Tara said. Providing the proper documentation hadn't been a problem for Tara and her mother. Both the school system and the Virginia Department of Social Services had thorough screening processes.

"Another lucky break," Gus said. "Jack works for an indoor sports complex in Kentucky that screens its employees very carefully. They faxed over his paperwork. I gave him an orientation crash course and he was ready to go."

"But...but you don't know anything about him," Tara protested.

"I know enough. I got the owner of the sportsplex on the phone and he gave Jack a glowing recommendation," Gus explained. "Besides, the more volunteers at a camp like this, the better. With Jack, we have the two-to-one camper-to-counselor ratio I was looking for."

Gus tilted his head. "Why are you asking all these questions? Do you have a problem with him?"

Admitting she did would only complicate matters further. "No. No problem."

Another lie. Since Jack had arrived on the scene, she was making a habit of telling them.

WATER SPLASHED UP FROM the pool, the sound loud enough that Jack had to strain to hear Tara. She was leading the water aerobics, which made sense considering she was a PE teacher.

"That's good. Lift your knees. Land on the balls of your feet and push off from your toes," she shouted. "Brandon, we're jogging in place, not running around the pool."

Seven of the ten campers had joined Jack, Tara and the female teen counselor in the shallow end of the pool. The two youngest girls in the camp sat on the edge with their legs dangling in the water. They were both so timid that Jack had felt triumphant when he got them to submerge their feet, especially because the tenth camper steadfastly refused to get near the water.

Danny sat on a chair beside the pool, his arms crossed over his chest. Next to him was a counselor Jack had been told was a developmental disability nurse.

"No!" he'd repeated whenever anyone invited him to join the class. Eventually they'd had no choice but to let him be.

Tara had begun the water-aerobics class by instructing the children to walk in place, which had gone over fairly well. Now that they'd graduated to jogging, however, problems were cropping up.

"I like the way you're chopping your hands through the water, Garrett," Tara called to a twelve-year-old boy who seemed as if he'd rather do anything but exercise. "But you've got to move your feet, too."

"It's hard!" Garrett protested.

"Too hard." A boy named Vince stopped moving altogether.

"Okay, let's all stop jogging," Tara said, as though it were her idea. Very smart, Jack thought. That way, she could keep control of the class. "We'll do something a little more fun. How does that sound?"

Nobody said a word. Many of the children were breathing hard even though they hadn't even been exercising for ten minutes.

"Sounds great," Jack said to help her out. "What's next?"

Tara's eyes briefly touched on him, one of the few times she'd acknowledged his presence since he'd showed up at camp. He hadn't expected a warm welcome, but the chilly reception took him aback.

"I've got an idea," she said. "Be right back."

She waded over to the side of the pool and hopped out, the pool water glistening on her skin. Wrapping a towel around herself and thrusting her feet into flip-flops, she left the pool area and headed for the community center. The children hardly had enough time to splash each other before she was back, carrying a boom box.

"Who's ready for aqua Zumba?" she asked in a loud voice.

She set the boom box down on an umbrella table beside the pool and switched it on. Latin music poured out, the beat catchy enough that Jack felt like tapping his toes. Tara draped her towel over the chair and stood at the foot of the pool.

"Let's dance!" she called, and proceeded to do exactly that. Her hips gyrated, her long legs moved to the rhythm and her slender arms lifted in the air. The motion called attention to her breasts. They were neither too large nor too small. Like the rest of her, they were practically perfect.

"C'mon!" she yelled above the music. "Let's get moving!"

Jack felt properly chastised for being caught staring. Except Tara was talking to the children, not to him. Half of the campers seemed frozen in place.

"You heard Miss Tara," Jack called. "It's time to shake, rattle and roll."

He moved in conjunction with the beat, exaggerating his movements so the campers got the idea. Brandy followed his lead. Susie Miller giggled and copied their dance moves. One by one, the other campers joined in. Except Danny.

The rest of the class passed in a flash, with the children laughing and smiling and creating their own dance moves. As a group, they had a terrific sense of rhythm. Tara abandoned the pool deck for dancing in the water. The assistant director, whose name he couldn't remember, clapping her hands from dry land. Kim and Samantha, the two young wallflowers, even got into the pool and joined in, as did some of the neighborhood kids who'd started to arrive now that the sun was coming out. The only downside was Danny's continued refusal to participate.

"Okay, that's it for today," Tara finally said.

A few of the children groaned. "Already?" Susie called.

"We'll do it again tomorrow," she said. "But now it's time to get out of the pool."

The other volunteers and staff members stood by the pool ladder helping the children out and handing out fluffy white towels. One of them was a petite attractive blonde who could have been anywhere from forty to her early fifties. Jack took a towel from her.

"Thanks," he said while he dried off his upper body. He was lucky that the shorts he wore were fashioned from a lightweight material that would dry quickly. "I'm Jack. We haven't been introduced yet."

"Carrie," she said. "Camp volunteer."

"Which child is yours?"

"Danny." She frowned. "The boy who wouldn't get in the pool. He does the same thing at his swimming classes, darn him."

"Some kids just take a little longer than others to do things," Jack said, although he wasn't sure that was Danny's problem. This wasn't the first activity Danny had refused to attempt. In his peripheral vision he noticed Tara wading through the shallow end of the pool at a fast clip. "If you're Danny's foster mother, you must be Tara's mother."

"And proud of it," Carrie said. "I couldn't ask for a better daughter."

Tara reached the ladder and hoisted herself out of the pool. Water sluiced down her body, causing her skin to glisten.

"Or a prettier one." Jack liked the way Tara looked with her wet hair slicked back from her face. It drew her high cheekbones into prominence and called attention to her bow-shaped mouth. She reached for a dry towel somebody had left draped over the fence and wrapped herself in it.

"I believe I'm going to like you, Jack." Carrie edged nearer to him. "She's completely available, in case you were wondering. No husband. No fiancé. She hasn't even had a boyfriend in a while."

"I was wondering," Jack said in an equally quiet voice. "And I think I'm gonna like you, too, Carrie."

"Speak of the devil." Carrie gestured to her daughter, who was closing the distance between them. "Tara! We were just talking about you."

Tara, who'd been full of smiles during the aqua Zumba, didn't lift her lips. Her eyes seemed to bore into him. "Mom, would you give me a minute alone with Jack?"

"Certainly." Carrie winked hugely at Jack. "I need to take the children inside to change out of their wet clothes, anyway."

Tara waited until her mother was no longer within earshot before she spoke. "I don't appreciate you showing up here and cozying up to my mother."

"Excuse me?" he said.

"If you have something to say, you can say it to me." She spoke in a soft, succinct voice. "There's no reason to—"

"Jack, c-can you do another magic trick?" Danny was behind Jack, tugging at his towel, ignoring the assistant director who was gathering the rest of the children to take into the community center.

"Not right now," Jack said. "Aren't you supposed to be with the other campers, buddy?"

Danny thrust his lower lip forward. "I told you. My name's not Buddy. It's Danny."

"Buddy means the same thing as friend," Jack said. "That's why I call you buddy. I think of you as my friend."

"Buddy," Danny repeated, the pout gone.

"So what do you say, buddy? Ready to go inside?" Jack asked. He raised his eyebrows at Tara in a silent question. It was starting to look as if one of them needed to accompany the child into the community center.

"Go with Jack, Dan the man," Tara told the child in an affectionate voice. To Jack, she said, "Camp's almost done for the day. We can talk when it's over."

CHAPTER FIVE

PARENTS, MOST OF THEM in minivans, started arriving about an hour later to pick up their children at the same time senior citizens were setting up a beginner's line-dancing class. Jack stayed beside the door, alerting the mothers and fathers that their children were inside finishing up an arts and craft project and introducing himself as the new volunteer. After a while, Danny joined him.

"Jack's my buddy," Danny told a woman in a sundress and floppy hat who was the mother of the male camper closest to his own age. "He's not Vince's buddy."

"Only because I don't know Vince very well yet," Jack hastened to reassure his mother. "I didn't get here until after lunch."

"Jack will still like me better tomorrow," Danny said, puffing out his chest.

To her credit, Vince's mother didn't rise to the bait. "You seem like a very likable young man, Danny."

Danny nodded vigorously. "I am."

"There you are, sweet boy." Carrie talked as she

crossed the room toward them. "Are you ready to go? Remember I promised to make you my extra-special pancakes for dinner."

"I'm ready!" Danny said.

"Just let me go tell Tara we're leaving." Carrie started to turn away.

"Did the three of you come together?" Jack asked.

Carrie paused to regard him. "We sure did. Why do you ask?"

"Tara and I still haven't had a chance to talk," Jack said. "I thought maybe I could drive her home."

"Excellent idea!" Carrie said. "Unless it'd take you out of your way. She lives in Wawpaney, just a stone's throw from the elementary school."

"That's no trouble," Jack said. He'd pass through Wawpaney on the way to the remote beach community where he was renting the cottage.

"She's still talking to one of the parents." Carrie gestured to where Tara stood across the room with Vince and his mother. Tara's hand rested on Vince's shoulder and her body was angled toward the boy's mother as though every word she said was important. "Will you do me a favor and tell her Danny and I left?"

"Sure." Jack wasn't about to ask Carrie if she thought her daughter would mind if he drove her home. He knew the answer.

Only a few stragglers remained inside the building. Jack leaned against the wall, waiting until Vince and his mother left. Tara glanced right and left as she walked toward him, the overhead lights making her yellow Camp Daybreak T-shirt seem even brighter. She had lovely legs, with well-shaped calves and good muscle definition. The closer she got to him, the more slowly they moved.

"Have you seen my mother and Danny?" she asked, her demeanor completely different than it had been with Vince and his mother. Again, he wished she'd show him her true self.

"They're gone," he said, raising his voice a little to be heard above the live dance music. "No need to worry, though. I'll drive you home."

Her mouth dropped open and her eyes glinted. "I don't believe this. You got my mother to leave so you could drive me home?"

"She thought it was a good idea," he said.

"Only because she doesn't know you've been following me for the past few days," she retorted.

"What?" He shook his head, finally understanding her cool reception. "I haven't been following you."

"That wasn't you watching my spinning class at the fitness club Sunday night?"

He hadn't realized she'd seen him. No wonder she was so suspicious of him. "Well, yeah, but that was a coincidence."

"How about you turning up here, at the camp, after Danny mentioned it. Was that a coincidence, too?"

"No," he admitted. "When I saw the newspaper ad, I knew it was the same camp."

"I've already told you. I'm not who you think I am," she said. "I don't know what kind of private eye you are, but—"

"I'm not a P.I," he interrupted. "I'm a minor league baseball player."

She shook her head. "Why should I believe you? You told Gus you worked at a sportsplex."

"I do in the off-season," he said.

"Isn't it baseball season now?" she asked. "If you really are a baseball player, why aren't you playing?"

He hesitated, wondering how to phrase it. "I'm recovering from a shoulder injury."

"Why would a baseball player from Kentucky come to the Eastern Shore to rehab?" she asked. "Aren't your doctors and your physical therapist back home?"

The only way to gain her trust was with complete honesty, Jack thought.

"I wanted a second opinion from a specialist who's vacationing on Tangier Island," he said. "I saw him on Friday, the day I talked to you. I didn't intend to stay in Virginia, but the area tugged at me. It seems like a good place to recover."

Her eyes narrowed. Gaining her trust would be harder than he thought.

"Then why volunteer at the camp?" she asked.

"There's only so much rehab you can do in a day," he said. "I'll go crazy if I don't have something else to fill the time."

She seemed to digest his words. "Then you being here at the camp, you're saying it doesn't have anything to do with me?"

Was she always so suspicious? Jack wondered.

"I didn't say that." He kicked up a corner of his mouth. His reaction to the woman he'd glimpsed when she wasn't dealing with him was so strong, he longed for the opportunity to get to know her better. "I was hoping we could be friends."

She resumed shaking her head even before he finished the sentence. "I have enough friends."

He winced. "I deserved that. I don't blame you for not trusting me, but I'm really not such a bad guy." He reached into his pocket, pulled out his wallet and withdrew a business card for the Lexington Sportsplex. He held it out to her. "Call the sportsplex and ask for Kyle Brady, the owner. He's also my brother-in-law. He'll verify everything I've told you."

She kept her hands clasped in front of her. "Why should I do that?"

"Because we'll be working together for the next

few weeks," he said. "It'd be nice not to be adversaries."

She hesitated so long, he thought she still might refuse. Then slowly she unclasped her hands and reached for the card. Their hands brushed for an electric moment. She quickly drew hers back.

"Kyle usually works till nine or ten, so you can call him tonight," Jack said. "He's married to my sister Annalise, but he can confirm that our other sister, Maria, is a P.I. If you want Maria's number, I'll give you that, too."

"No," she insisted. "I don't need her number."

"Okay, then." He opened the door and stepped aside. "Ready to go?"

She regarded him warily, making no move to leave. When she finally went out the door and walked with him to the parking lot, it was in silence. He unlocked the passenger door to his pickup with his remote, then pulled it open.

The rumble of a car engine cut through the quiet. The blue minivan driven by Vince's mother turned into the lot. She pulled up beside Jack's pickup and got out of her van. Vince waved from the passenger seat.

"Vince forgot his lunch box," his mother explained, seeming more serene than annoyed. "Could one of you keep an eye on him while I run inside and get it?"

"It's the lunch box with the sharks, right?" Tara asked in a friendly voice.

"Right. Don't ask me why, but Vince adores sharks."

"I know where he left it," Tara said. "Tell you what, I'll get it for you if you give me a ride home. You did say you lived near Wawpaney, right?"

"Right. It's a deal," Vince's mother said. It didn't seem to occur to her that the passenger door to Jack's pickup was standing open.

"Great," Tara said.

Without looking at Jack, Tara jogged toward the community center. It felt to Jack as if they'd played a game and he'd come out the loser. He didn't like the feeling. He was a man who set goals and expected to achieve them.

For the past few years the goal to pitch in the major leagues had been so all-consuming he'd had no room for another. That had changed.

He intended to get Tara to trust him, no matter what.

THE BEACH WAS DESERTED Tuesday morning except for the lone woman sitting on the sand with her arms wrapped around her knees. She was facing the surf, well beyond the tide line. Waves rolled gently to shore, plovers foraged for food and the scent of the salt water carried on the Chesapeake Bay breeze.

Tara crossed the empty beach toward the woman, her running shoes sinking into the sand, the breeze drying the sweat on her brow from the three-and-a-half miles she'd just run.

With the temperature in the low seventies and the sun starting to rise in the hazy sky, it should have been the start of a beautiful day. Tara didn't even have to worry about Jack DiMarco anymore. She'd called the sportsplex in Kentucky last night as he'd suggested and verified he was indeed a baseball player and not a private investigator.

But the day wasn't beginning well because the woman sitting by herself was her mother.

Tara nearly hadn't come to the beach this morning. She'd almost believed her mother about today being just another day rather than the anniversary of the date she'd lost her husband and older daughter.

Almost, but not quite.

A pelican dived into the bay and emerged on the surface of the water with its breakfast. The unfortunate fish flopped in the pelican's bill before being swallowed whole, its life snatched away in an instant.

The lapping of the waves was gentle, but her mother didn't react to the sound of Tara's approach. Even when Tara sat down beside her on the grainy sand, her mother kept staring out at the bay. A trickle of tears dampened her cheeks. One minute stretched into another, each one more telling than the last.

"I didn't mean to come to the beach today." Her mother finally broke the silence, speaking in a soft, shaky voice that Tara had to strain to hear. "But I woke up before dawn and I happened to see Mrs. Jorgenson getting her newspaper. Before I knew it, I was outside asking her to come and stay with Danny."

Tara heard what her mother didn't say.

"Dad and Sunny were on my mind when I woke up, too," she said. Tara's first waking thought had actually been of her mother. She'd lain in bed in the weak light of dawn, rejecting the notion to go back to sleep until her alarm went off.

As she laced up her running shoes a short time later, she'd been aware that the morning jog she planned to take due west to the nearest beach was for more than exercise.

No matter what her mother claimed, Tara had known she'd find her there. The beach was where her mother had spent the morning of this date for as long as Tara could remember.

"Even after all this time, it hurts like a thorn in my heart to think about them," her mother said. "Looking at the water brings it all rushing back. It doesn't matter that this is the bay and it happened a long way from here at the ocean."

Tara never pressed her mother for the details

of the tragic day. Over the years, however, she'd picked up bits and pieces of information. She knew, for example, that the tragedy had occurred at one of the beaches on North Carolina's Outer Banks. After saving up for months for their first beach vacation, her parents had chosen one of the little towns on the Outer Banks. The location made sense because it was a manageable drive from their home in Charlotte.

"If it hurts so much, why do you do this to yourself, Mom?" Tara asked gently.

"I don't seem to know how to stop." Her mother's gaze was still on the water. "I can picture them clear as day. Sunny was running full tilt for the ocean, laughing and shouting. Scott was coming up right behind her. He swept Sunny into his arms and lifted her into the air, twirling her around."

Tara should stop her mother before she got any further. She parted her lips to speak, but her vocal cords froze. She'd never heard the entire story. So help her, no matter how painful it was, she wanted to hear it.

"I was smiling on my way back to the hotel. I left my beach chair there. Scott didn't want me to go back for it. He said the beach blanket was plenty good enough. He wanted me in the water with him and Sunny. But I wanted that chair."

She took a deep breath, her chest rising and falling raggedly.

"Our hotel was but a couple blocks from the ocean," she said. "Still, it couldn't have taken me more than fifteen minutes to get the chair. I remember humming on the walk back, that song about what a beautiful morning it was."

Her mother swallowed. Again Tara thought about stopping her. Again she let her continue.

"I could tell right off the bat something was dreadfully wrong." Her mother spoke in a monotone. "There were a dozen or so people in a half circle at the shoreline, standing around something. One woman was screaming. Another was crying. I couldn't figure what they were staring at. I thought maybe Scott would know. I looked around for him. Except I couldn't find him. And that's when I knew."

Her mother's pain was so raw that Tara felt it, too. She put her arm around her mother's shoulder, drawing her close.

"A man was trying to do CPR on Scott. He's the one who pulled them out. He said it happened really fast. They were in water about waist-deep when a big wave came. Scott must have lost hold of Sunny, because he started shouting for help. When the man got to him, the water was over Scott's head. He was caught in an undertow." Her mother's lips trembled. "The man maybe could have saved him, but Scott told him to find our little girl. When he did, it was too late for both Scott and Sunny."

Tara squeezed her mother's shoulders tighter, horrified at the scene her mother described. She'd always known her father and sister had drowned, but without the specifics the story didn't have the power to grab her by the heart and squeeze.

"If only I hadn't gone back for that stupid chair," her mother said in a small voice. "Maybe things would have turned out different."

Tara shifted her body so she could look into her mother's face. "It wasn't your fault, Mom. You know that, don't you?"

"That's what my therapist said." Her mother's eyes dropped to the sand. "You didn't know I'd seen one of those, did you now? If I hadn't, we probably wouldn't be living here."

"I don't understand," Tara said.

"Didn't you ever wonder why we live so close to the water when I hate it so?" her mother asked.

"On occasion," Tara admitted. Except for her yearly pilgrimage on the anniversary of the deaths, her mother hadn't spent any time at the beach in years. She'd gone with Tara when she was a child, but only to the parts of the bay where the water was calmest. She'd stayed out of the water herself and had strict rules about how far Tara was allowed to venture into the water. She even stayed out of the pool, although she'd made sure Tara could swim.

"I was still wallowing in grief a year later. My

therapist said what I needed was a fresh start away from Charlotte," her mother said. "A friend of mine invited us to come live with her in Wawpaney."

"I don't remember anyone like that," Tara said.

"I'm not surprised. You were just a little thing when the bank where she worked transferred her—that was about six months after we got here," her mother said. "I had some insurance money from your father. I used it to buy the house from her."

"Did you like it here right away?" Tara asked.

"I didn't like it one bit," her mother said. "But you did. It's a wholesome place to raise a child. And my therapist said I should face my fears if I was ever gonna be happy again."

"You've faced enough for today." Tara stood, extended a hand to her mother and pulled her to her feet. She kept hold of her mother's hand, leading the shorter woman away from the water, feeling more like the parent than the child. She thought of her mother coming to the beach year after year on the anniversary of the deaths, burdened by unnecessary guilt. "She doesn't sound like she was a very good therapist."

"Oh, but she was." Her mother walked with her shoulders stooped and head down. "She gave great advice. I just could never bring myself to take it."

Tara disliked the helpless feeling that swept over her. In an odd way, she understood why her mother relived the day over and over. Before her mother saw the tragedy unfold in her mind's eye, she probably experienced a brief instant when she felt as though she could prevent it from happening. That was ridiculous, of course.

Even if her mother could turn the clock back almost thirty years, she couldn't stop fate from exacting its toll. Neither could Tara, who would have been only two years old at the time.

A chill ran through her despite the rapidly rising temperature. Her mother had said on many occasions that she and her husband had saved up in order to take a family vacation. Yet when she revealed the details of the story, she'd made mention of only three family members.

"Where was I?" Tara asked.

"Pardon me?" Her mother reacted as though the question made no sense.

"When it happened," Tara said. "Where was I?"

A look akin to panic entered her mother's watery eyes. She stammered something unintelligible, then seemed to collect herself. "Why, you were back at the hotel."

Tara's stomach muscles tightened. "Alone? You left a two-year-old alone in a hotel?"

"Of course not." The sun shone down on her mother's pale face, illuminating lines Tara didn't remember noticing. Her mother appeared more ravaged than she had when she was reliving the drownings. "You were…with somebody."

"Who?" Tara asked.

Such a simple question, but it seemed to stump her mother. A long while passed as her mother stared back at her. Tara could almost see her rejecting the answers that occurred to her.

"A friend of mine," her mother finally answered, the words coming out in a rush. Her mother nodded, as though trying to convince herself the answer made sense. "We were on vacation with another couple who had a son around your age. They took you both to the pool."

Tara's mother was breathing too hard. The sun was cruel, showing the tracks of her recent tears on her cheeks. Her brow pinched together, making her expression looked pained.

She was waiting to see if Tara believed her lie. Because it was a lie. Of that, Tara was almost positive.

She was also closer to believing she was that little girl who'd been taken from the Kentucky shopping mall.

She should ask her mother and be done with it. The wind kicked up, blowing sand that stung Tara's ankles. Her mother positioned her body between the blowing sand and Tara. She squeezed Tara's hand, love mixing with the pain.

The question died on Tara's lips. She wouldn't ask her mother about Hayley Cooper, not today on the darkest of anniversaries.

Not ever.

She wouldn't allow Jack DiMarco to question her mother, either, even if he were only the brother of a private eye and not a P.I. himself.

"It was lucky I wasn't on the beach that day." Tara watched the relief pour over her mother's face. "That memory would have stuck with me forever."

Like the recurring nightmare Tara had of the woman who shook her and yelled at her to stop crying.

If Carrie Greer had kidnapped Tara, she very well could have done her a favor. It seemed more and more likely the nightmare woman, and not the one she loved with all her heart, was her biological mother.

THE FITNESS CLUB WAS quiet when Jack arrived late that morning, a departure from Sunday night when music from Tara's spinning class had spilled into the lobby.

The only sound came from a large-screen television, where an ESPN broadcaster was counting down yesterday's top plays. The seating area in front of the TV was empty, and only a few men worked out in the nearby weight room.

The guy working the front desk had directed Jack to an office and advised him to wait there. Jack leaned with his back against the wall across from the TV instead. The personal trainer with whom he'd made the appointment would hardly have trouble finding him in a club this small.

On TV, a teammate of Jack's from when he was a twenty-two-year-old minor league rookie smacked a ball that cleared the center-field wall. That year, the talk had been that Jack and the home run hitter were on the fast track to the major leagues. This was the three hundredth homer of the other player's illustrious career. Jack was reminded again that he'd pitched in only three major league games.

"Are you Jack DiMarco?" The man asking the question strode toward him with a spring in his step. He was well into his sixties with gray islands of hair on either side of his balding head and an impressively fit body.

Jack straightened from the wall and held out a hand. "That's me."

The man grabbed his hand in a firm grip, pumping it vigorously. "Art Goodnight, personal trainer and fitness consultant. And yeah, you heard right. My last name really is Goodnight. You can call me Art."

"I'm just Jack," he said.

"Yeah, yeah. The baseball pitcher." He talked too fast. He shifted his weight from foot to foot, as though it was hard for him to keep still. Judging by his physique, maybe it was. He didn't seem to have an inch of flab on him. His short-sleeved shirt hugged his muscular chest and showed off the definition in his biceps. He was wearing shorts, revealing legs that were as impressive as the rest of him. "What can I do you for?"

"I need some help rehabbing the torn labrum in my pitching shoulder," Jack said.

"Did you have surgery?"

"Two surgeries," Jack said. "Both on the same shoulder, both for my rotator cuff. I would have opted for surgery this time, too, but two doctors advised me rehab is a better option."

"How long ago was this?"

"I broke my collarbone about a year ago in a collision at first base," he said. "The collarbone healed but the soreness wouldn't go away. Nobody realized there was a problem with my labrum until this year at spring training."

"Have you seen a physical therapist?"

"A couple of them." Jack didn't add that neither had let him work out as hard as he wanted to. "I thought it was time to try something else."

"So that shoulder's been through hell." Art's thick gray eyebrows drew together. "I'm not sure I understand. The guy who set up the appointment said your goal is to pitch in the majors again."

"It is," Jack said.

Art whistled. "What do you think I am, son? A miracle worker?"

Jack inhaled. The club had a vaguely metallic

smell combined with air freshener. "I thought you were good at what you did."

"I am good," Art said. "But you're asking for the moon. I'd give the odds at, oh, one in a thousand. And maybe that's too high."

"I'll take 'em," Jack said. "If I can't get my fastball back to where it was, I'll work on my other pitches. So can we start?"

"Not so fast. I've gotta ask you some questions and come up with a fitness plan. That's gonna take a while." Art glanced at the wall clock. "How much time you got?"

"An hour," Jack said. "I'm helping out at a camp and need to get there as soon as I can."

"Follow me." Art took off through the weight room past the treadmills and stationary bikes to the back of the health club. His destination was a small room barely big enough for a desk and two chairs. Jack started to sit down.

"We're not staying." Art grabbed a pen and a lined tablet from the desk. "This office makes me claustrophobic. I think better out there."

He meant the weight room, where he sat down at one of the bench-press machines, perching on the end of the long leather bench. He indicated that Jack should take the machine next to him.

"What kind of camp?" Art asked.

Enough time had passed since Jack had mentioned the camp that he needed to redirect his brain. "A camp for kids with developmental disabilities."

Art pointed at him. "Hey, is that the same camp Tara's working at?"

That was right. Tara worked here. Of course she'd know Art Goodnight.

"It is," Jack said. "Her foster brother Danny's one of the campers."

"I thought the boy's name was Kyle." Art scratched his head. "But maybe Kyle's gone. As soon as one kid moves out, Carrie gets another."

"Tara's mother is working the camp, too," Jack said.

"Aw, hell." Art thumped the tablet against the back of his hand. "If I'd known that, I would have volunteered. I've been trying to get that woman to go out with me for about ten years now."

"Wow," Jack said. "You must have it bad for her."

"I have it bad for a lot of women," Art said with a laugh. "A long time ago, I figured out my best trait was persistence. It works most of the time, but not on Carrie."

"I like that you're stubborn," Jack said. "That's exactly the kind of trainer I need."

"Like I said before, you need a miracle. You know about the anatomy of the shoulder, right?"

Jack nodded. After all his problems, he could probably teach a section about the shoulder in an anatomy class. The labrum was a ring of cartilage surrounding the shoulder socket that helped hold the ball of the humerus in place.

"You having any pain?" Art asked.

"A little," Jack said. "Some in front of the shoulder and some deep inside the joint."

Art bared his teeth and sucked in a breath. "Not great."

Jack was used to reactions like those by now. "The way I understand it, a concentrated workout program will strengthen the muscles outside the joint that help rotate the shoulder."

"Possibly," Art said. "It's more likely you'll work like a dog and still not get the desired result. PT can do wonders for the average person. It can't always make a top athlete as good as new."

Jack felt a scowl coming on. "I'm starting to question how good you are at this."

"Ask Tara," he said. "She can tell you."

Jack sat up straighter. "Tara? Why would I ask her?"

Art tapped his hand rapidly on his thigh. The man had serious trouble keeping still. "Didn't she recommend me?"

"No. I found you on my own," Jack said.

Art pursed his lips, clueing Jack in that he'd said the wrong thing if he expected the man to share additional information about Tara.

"Tara and I are friends, though," Jack said. "I

just haven't gotten around to telling her about my injury. It's kind of tough to talk about."

Art's broad shoulders relaxed, and Jack tried not to feel guilty about his white lie. His sister Maria misled people all the time to get information. Of course, she was a P.I.

"She was an athlete, too. She'd understand." Art paused. "Or maybe she wouldn't."

"What do you mean?" Jack asked.

"Nothing I should have said aloud." Art ran a hand over his face. "It's just that I've never seen anyone as talented as that girl throw it all away like that."

"Talented at what?"

"You name it, she could do it," Art said. "She was one of the best female athletes to ever come out of Northampton High, but volleyball was her best sport. A couple major colleges with top programs even offered her scholarships."

"She didn't accept?" he asked, hardly able to wrap his mind around what he knew the answer would be.

"She said they were too far from home," Art said. "Ended up going to two years of community college, then two years at a small school a few hours from here. Didn't even play organized sports."

"Why was that?" Jack asked.

"I've got my opinions, but it's best I keep them to myself," Art said. "You should ask her."

Jack would love to do exactly that. If, that is, he could figure out how to broach the subject without Tara figuring out he'd been questioning Art Goodnight about her.

Jack nodded, because Art seemed to expect it of him.

"Enough about Tara." Art's pen hovered over the tablet. "Let's talk about you."

"Okay," Jack said, shifting to the all-important task at hand. "Like I said, failure isn't an option. It's not a question of if I'll pitch again. It's a question of when."

He firmly believed that, no matter how many experts cast doubt on his chances of a comeback. He'd defied the odds by even getting to the majors. He'd do it again.

CHAPTER SIX

CARRIE SAT ON A PARK BENCH across the street from the community center, watching the campers and other volunteer counselors gather the rocks they planned to paint later that afternoon, her mind hundreds of miles and almost thirty years away.

"Carrie? Did you hear what I said?"

She looked up to find Gustavo Miller gazing steadily at her with kind eyes. The kindness was nearly her undoing. She blinked to keep the tears at bay. She wasn't as successful at banishing the grief. All day the weight of the past had made it seem to Carrie that she was sinking. She'd gone through the motions at camp, barely any help with the children at all.

"Sorry," she said. "I missed it."

"I asked if you'd mind talking to Susie." He gave a helpless shrug. "She's down about something, but she won't tell me what. I thought somebody else might have better luck getting her to open up."

Susie was sitting by herself on a swing at the playground but not moving. Her head was down and she seemed to be staring at her feet.

"Certainly," Carrie said, rising from the bench. "I'll see what I can do."

She mentally kicked herself for not noticing something was wrong with the girl. Tara had left early after leading the children in a rousing game of freeze tag, checking with Carrie first to see if it was okay.

Saying no wouldn't have been fair to Tara. Her daughter cobbled together a series of jobs in the summer and Mary Dee Larson's father needed her to help out at his ice cream and fudge store.

As she trudged across the playground to the swings, however, Carrie wished Tara were with her.

A sob caught in her throat.

She wanted Sunny with her, too. And Scott. He'd always been so calm and levelheaded. He'd be able to advise her what to do about Tara's sudden interest in the past.

Carrie crossed to the empty swing beside Susie and sat down. The little girl didn't raise her head. Now that Carrie was near, she could tell that Susie's shoulders were shaking.

"Susie, honey, are you crying?" Carrie reached across the chasm between the swings and put a hand on the girl's heaving back. "Whatever is the matter?"

"I'm sad," Susie said through her tears.

Carrie knew about being sad. The emotion

didn't sneak up on you. It festered until the tears spilled over because it was even more painful to suppress them.

Susie must have been down the entire day, yet Carrie had been with her since nine that morning and hadn't picked up on it.

"I'm sorry you're sad." Carrie rubbed the girl's solid back. "You just cry it out and you'll feel better."

Susie sniffed loudly and cried a bit harder. Carrie looked up to see Gustavo regarding them worriedly from where he'd gathered the rest of the campers and volunteers. They appeared ready to go inside. She gestured that he should leave, hoping he'd understand that she and Susie needed privacy. After another few moments, they all headed for the community center.

Finally Susie's sobs subsided. Carrie reached into the pocket of her capris and pulled out a tissue. She got up, bent and mopped the girl's face. Susie's eyes were puffy and red rimmed.

"I try not to cry in front of Daddy," Susie said, her words still broken. "It makes him sad."

Carrie's heart twisted. Surely a father as attentive as Gustavo wouldn't want his daughter to hold back her tears for his sake.

"There's nothing wrong with crying, honey," Carrie said. "Everybody cries."

"Do you?"

"I sure do," Carrie said.

"Doesn't your mommy love you, either?"

Carrie's breath left her lungs. Here it was, the reason for Susie's tears. Her inclination was to assure the girl that her mother did indeed love her. Except she couldn't. She knew nothing of Susie's mother except that the woman and Gustavo were divorced. She could be from the same mold as Danny's mother. The social worker had told Carrie straight up that Danny's mother didn't want him.

"My mama isn't with us anymore," Carrie said.

"My mommy, too," Susie said, misunderstanding. Her lower lip trembled. "She's with a man in a hat."

That made no sense, but it was time to get Susie's mind off her mother. Distraction always worked with Danny.

"Do you like ice cream?" Carrie asked.

Susie stopped sniffling. She nodded.

"I know of a great place that sells the most delicious homemade ice cream and fudge. What do you say we ask your dad if y'all can go for ice cream with Danny and me after camp."

"Yes!" Susie shouted.

It would probably ruin all their dinners, but something about ice cream was comforting. Besides, Carrie needed to fill Gustavo in about what was going on with his daughter.

She stood up and extended a hand to Susie.

"C'mon, let's wash those tears away. I want to see your smile."

Susie bared her teeth in an artificial smile that could have scared a small child.

"Not a fake smile," Carrie said. "A real one."

Susie laughed. Carrie was so relieved to hear the sound that she hugged the child and joined in.

TARA DUG INTO THE VAT OF black raspberry ice cream with her silver scooper and piled the cold treat high on a cake cone. She reached over the counter to hand it to the young girl who'd come into the shop with Tara's mother, Gus Miller, Danny—and Jack DiMarco.

"Here you go, Susie," Tara said.

The girl took the cone, practically jumping up and down with excitement.

Gus stood off to his daughter's side, his arms crossed over his chest, his expression tender. "What do you say, Susie?"

"I say I like ice cream!" Susie answered.

"You're supposed to say thank you," Danny told her in a loud, halting voice.

"Thank you!" Susie shouted.

"Shh," Gus said. "Remember your indoor voice, Susie."

As little as an hour ago, the children could have practiced their manners in front of plenty of customers. The closer it got to dinnertime, however, the emptier the ice cream shop became.

Tara had been expecting some downtime when the contingent from the camp set off the jingling bells above the door. She wasn't sure which one of their group came as a bigger surprise—her grieving mother or Jack DiMarco.

She knew which customer should be less welcome.

Jack might be the baseball player he said he was, but he was also the brother of the P.I. investigating the Hayley Cooper case. Every minute he spent alone with her mother was pregnant with risk.

She needed to avoid him, too. Even if she didn't really want to.

"Put your money away," Jack told Gus, who was reaching for his wallet. "My treat."

"You sure?" Gus asked.

"Positive." Jack stepped up to the counter, rubbing his hands together. The hint of a beard shadowed his lower face, adding an air of ruggedness, making him look even more handsome.

"Everything smells delicious." He drew in a deep breath of the sugar-scented air. "What do you recommend?"

"People drive for miles for the homemade ice cream, but I'm partial to the chocolate butterscotch fudge," she said.

"Then that's what I'll have," he said.

Behind him, Gus and her mother were sharing a table with Danny and Susie. Gus said something and everybody at the table laughed, including her mother.

It was the anniversary, and her mother was laughing.

Tara took a small plastic plate and slid open the glass door of the display case, cutting off a generous piece of fudge from the wedge. She handed the candy to Jack and rang up the sale.

"So," she said, drawing out the syllable, "what are you doing here?"

He extended some bills to her. "I'm about to eat some fudge."

She took his money, putting the bills into a slot and taking out some change. "You know what I mean."

"Danny and Susie asked me to come," he said.

She dumped the change into his hand, careful not to touch him. She already knew she'd get a jolt of awareness if she did.

"The kids said they wanted to spend some time with me because I can't be at camp tomorrow," he said. "I've got to meet with Art Goodnight."

"You know Art?"

"I told you I had a reason for being at the fitness club Sunday night." He had a way of looking at her that made her feel like the only person in the room. "You really should start believing me."

She wet her suddenly dry lips. "I believe you're a baseball player."

"Only because you checked me out," he said. "My sister phoned last night to say you called the sportsplex."

Tara's heart thudded so hard she thought he might hear it. "Your sister, the P.I."

"Nope, the other one. Annalise is married to Kyle. She stays home with their kids and helps him out with the business." His shoulders moved up and down. "Annalise and Maria, they take turns calling me. I think they coordinate who has which days."

"They call you that much?"

"One of them calls every single day," he said. "My mom calls, too, though not quite so often. Why do you think I'm staying on the Eastern Shore?"

She'd thought it was because of her, but then her imagination had been running rampant since he'd arrived in town. She was more than halfway to believing the wild conclusion she'd jumped to. If only she knew more about what had led Jack to her. For the first time, she entertained the disturbing possibility that somebody in town suspected she was Hayley Cooper.

"I thought you were tracking down more leads for your sister," Tara said, steering the conversation in the direction she needed it to go.

"Nope," he said. "She only asked me to track down the one."

"Tell me something," she asked with as much nonchalance as she could muster. Her hands felt as if they were shaking, so she grasped one with the other. "What led you to me, anyway?"

He frowned. "I'm not sure. If you like, I'll ask my sister."

"No, no," Tara said quickly. That could be disastrous. "It doesn't matter. I was just curious."

"It'd be no problem," he said. "She really does call me all the time."

Tara had to clench her jaw so she wouldn't snap at him to forget it. She couldn't afford to protest too much. "Whatever. Like I said, it's not a big deal."

The door burst open, setting off the bells. Mary Dee hurried through, her shirt coming untucked from her shorts and her normally smooth hair looking windblown. She came around the counter.

"Tara, you are a godsend for filling in for me. I had the most awful toothache. The dentist saw me right away, but it turned out I needed a root canal. Then—" She stopped abruptly, turning to Jack with laserlike focus. "I'll be damned. You're the guy who was with Tara last week."

Oh, great, Tara thought, remembering the words Mary Dee had used to describe him. Hot. Sexy. A man who could take care of a woman's needs. What's worse, deep down Tara agreed with those descriptions. She masked her feelings and resigned herself to making the introductions.

"Mary Dee, this is Jack DiMarco. He's renting a place out on Shell Beach," Tara said. "Jack, Mary Dee Larson. She and I work together at Wawpaney Elementary."

"Nice to meet you, Jack." Mary Dee twirled a lock of her black hair around her finger. "What a coincidence that you should run into Tara here."

"Not a coincidence." He gestured behind him to the table where Tara's mother and Danny sat with the Millers. "I came with Gus, Carrie and the kids. I'm volunteering at the camp."

"Really?" Mary Dee pinned Tara with a look. Tara could practically hear the questions running through her friend's brain. But then her gaze swung to the table. "Carrie's eating ice cream and smiling on the anniversary? That's great!"

"What anniversary?" Jack asked.

"Tara hasn't told you?" Mary Dee asked. "It's a really sad story."

"We're trying not to dwell on it," Tara interjected before Mary Dee could continue. "I'd appreciate it, Jack, if you didn't bring up the subject with my mother."

He seemed about to say something, then closed his mouth and nodded. "Sure thing."

"Anything else I can get for you?" Tara asked.

He held up the fudge. "Nope. This'll do it."

"Jack!" Danny yelled from across the store. "Mr. Miller wants to see your thumb disappear."

"Coming," Jack called. To Mary Dee, he said, "It was very nice meeting you." His eyes touched on Tara and held. That damned attraction skittered through her again. "Tara, it's always a pleasure."

He turned and walked to the table. Mary Dee fanned herself with a hand and pretended to swoon. "Now, if that's not a man who could set off fireworks inside you, I don't know who is," she whispered. "We've got to get you some of that."

"No," Tara said, trying to sound as if she wasn't tempted. "We don't."

"Oh, come on. He'd be up for it." She wiggled her brows suggestively. Another time, Tara would have laughed. "I can tell he likes you."

Jack stood at the table, smiling and showing no sign of irritation even though this must have been the fifth or sixth time Danny had asked him to perform the trick. He glanced her way, caught her watching him and smiled.

Tara quickly broke eye contact before she smiled back at him. She needed to keep contact with Jack at an absolute minimum, both for her mother and herself.

The less he knew about their lives, the better. She didn't need Jack—or, worse, the P.I. sister who kept in constant telephone contact with him—speculating about how losing a husband and daughter had affected her mother.

One of them might even entertain the notion that Carrie Greer had replaced the little girl she'd lost with another one.

DANNY SANK TO HIS KNEES on the screened-in porch of the Bay Breeze B and B that Gustavo had inherited from his grandmother, not the slightest bit interested in the stunning Chesapeake Bay view.

Carrie had to admit the objects of Danny's attention were pretty captivating, too.

Three seven-week-old kittens, each one more adorable than the last, played near their mother. The kittens batted at each other with their front paws and meowed.

"They are so c-cute!" Danny shouted.

"Shh," Susie scolded. "You'll scare them."

"I will not!" he protested.

At the ice cream store Susie had mentioned that her great-grandmother's cat recently gave birth to kittens. Danny, of course, had begged to go see them right away.

If these had been routine circumstances, Carrie would have found a way to gently dissuade him. The B and B was a good twenty miles from Wawpaney, not exactly the kind of place to pop in and out. But Carrie was still looking for a chance to tell Gustavo about her conversation with Susie on the swings.

"Can I pick one up?" Danny asked.

"Only. If. You're. Really. Careful," Susie said, enunciating each word clearly.

"I'll be c-careful," Danny promised.

He used excessive care in lifting the smallest kitten onto his lap. Very gently he stroked the kitten's back. It purred. He giggled. Carrie and Gustavo exchanged a smile. Clearly the children would be okay on the screened porch by themselves for a little while.

"Can we go inside?" she asked Gustavo.

"Certainly." He let her precede him through the open French doors. "I don't suppose you're in the market for a cat? They're just about old enough to leave their mother."

"It sure looks to me like Susie wants to keep every last one of them," Carrie said.

"She does, but I've already told her she can only have one," Gustavo said. "I got the mama fixed, too, so we won't have more litters."

Carrie glanced over her shoulder at Danny, who now had two kittens on his lap. "Let me think about it. I just might take one of the kittens off your hands."

"Don't think too much, Carrie," he said, rolling the *r*'s in her name in that way she loved. "People who think about acting usually talk themselves out of it. Remember, do what feels right."

She focused her attention on him. He wore khaki shorts and a cream polo shirt that was flattering with his dark coloring. This close, he smelled great. "It feels right being here with you."

Even to her own ears, she sounded flirtatious. What was the matter with her? At age fifty-four, she should be more in control of herself. Every time she opened her mouth around Gustavo, something came out that he could construe as having a double meaning.

"It's a darn shame you closed the house to guests. It's lovely," she said, to cover her gaffe. She swept a hand to encompass the first floor. A spacious kitchen opened into a den with a brick fireplace, where a paisley-print sofa and love seat were angled for an optimum view of the console television. The opposite side of the room contained a blond wooden table with eight faded upholstered chairs.

"Lovely, but worn around the edges." He indicated the faded wooden floors. "These need to be refinished, the counters in the kitchen should be replaced and all the furniture should be trashed."

"That's all cosmetic." Carrie did a three-sixty, enjoying the late-afternoon light that flooded the house. A view of the Chesapeake was visible through the screen porch. "This old place has good bones."

"Yeah," he said. "But before it can become operational again it needs a good home remodeler and an interior decorator."

"Or an amateur who knows what looks good. The floor should be finished in a warm honey color and the furniture should be moved around to take advantage of that splended view." She walked to an empty spot. "I'd put a brown leather recliner right here. And those faded floral curtains need to go. The only thing behind the house is the bay, so you don't have to worry about people peering in at you."

"If I was keeping this place, I'd take you upstairs to the bedrooms," he said.

She felt her cheeks stain, although she was sure he was referring to touring the bedrooms. Now she was attributing sexual innuendo to the things he said. She needed to make sure there were no misunderstandings.

"If you change your mind, just let me know and I'll *decorate* for free." Carrie emphasized the operative word.

"I'm not changing my mind," he said. "I like teaching too much."

"I've been meaning to ask you about that," she said. "How did you become a special ed teacher?"

"I was already a teacher. But after Susie was born, I went to night school to get certified."

"That must be a great advantage in dealing with Susie," she said.

"The main reason I went into special ed was that I wanted to understand her better."

"Did it work?" she asked.

"Not entirely," he said slowly. "If I understood her better, I have a feeling we wouldn't be having this conversation."

"You figured out I wanted to talk to you about Susie," she said.

"It wasn't difficult," he said. "You wouldn't have suggested ice cream before dinner if you weren't trying to cheer her up."

Carrie's gaze fell on a photo hanging from the wall in the entranceway of the house. Susie appeared to be about a year old. She was sitting on the lap of a smiling woman with delicate features and strawberry-blond hair. Gustavo stood beside them, his arm resting on the woman's shoulder, his expression tender as he gazed down at Susie.

"Is that your ex-wife?" Carrie asked.

"Yeah," he said, his expression unreadable. "That was taken the year before we divorced. It's already been almost nine years. She still lives in Baltimore."

"Susie was crying when you asked me to check up on her," Carrie said softly. "I told her I cried sometimes, too. She asked if that was because my mama didn't love me, either.''

Gustavo swore under his breath. He raked a hand through his dark hair. "Sorry about the language. The whole thing just makes me so angry." He drew in a deep breath and expelled it. "Did Susie say anything else?"

"Something that made no sense," Carrie said. "About her mama being with a man in a hat."

Gustavo's eyebrows furrowed, then smoothed out. He groaned. "Susie must have overheard me talking to her mother on the phone. Victoria was supposed to come down from Baltimore and visit her this weekend. Instead she's going to Manhattan with some guy."

"Oh, no." Carrie laid a hand on his arm, hating to see the pain the situation caused him. "No wonder Susie was upset."

"I could kick myself for letting Susie overhear," Gustavo said. "The thing is, I think Victoria does love her. She just can't deal with Susie not being perfect."

"She's missing out on a wonderful girl," Carrie said.

He gave her a wry smile. "Spoken like the mother of a child with Down syndrome."

"Oh, I'm not Danny's mama. He's my foster child. From what little I know of Danny's real mama, she's sort of like Victoria. Only way worse."

Carrie paused. "She told the agency she couldn't handle a retard."

Gustavo's eyes opened wide. "She used that word?"

"That's what they told me," Carrie said. "She's struggling with her husband not in the picture but she still has custody of Danny's brother."

"Let me guess." Gustavo's lips twisted. "He's not mentally challenged."

"Right you are."

"Have you been a foster mother to other children with special needs?"

"Danny's the first," Carrie said. "Not a lot of foster parents ask to take in special-needs children, so they recruited some of us veterans."

He gave a low whistle. "Carrie Greer, you are my kind of woman."

She felt herself blush at the same time she noticed she was still touching him.

"Don't make me out to be some kind of saint," she insisted. "I need Danny every bit as much as he needs me."

Gustavo tilted his head. "Why's that?"

She hadn't become a foster mother until Tara left home for college. She'd figured out long ago that children who needed her, the way Tara once had, helped fill the hole in her heart. Not completely, but enough so she could function.

The pain of losing both Sunny and Scott at the

same time had been so wrenching it never fully went away.

With a start, she realized this was the first time she'd thought of her lost loved ones since Gustavo had asked her to check on his daughter.

"Carrie?" Gustavo was regarding her curiously. "Are you okay?"

No, she wasn't okay. This was the anniversary of the worst day of her life. "I'm sorry, but Danny and I need to go."

"So soon? I was about to ask you to stay for dinner." He waggled his eyebrows. "I make a mean cheeseburger."

"Thank you," Carrie said firmly, "but no."

"Okay, then what are you doing Friday night? Because—"

"I'm busy Friday night," Carrie interrupted, dismayed that he'd gotten the idea that she might accept a date with him. She headed through the house for the screened-in porch, almost desperate to collect Danny and get away.

No matter what she'd told Tara about treating today like any other day, that was impossible.

Not so impossible when you have Gustavo and Susie Miller to distract you, a voice inside her head whispered.

She shut out the voice, feeling vaguely disloyal.

She didn't want to forget Sunny and Scott. Not today. Not ever.

CHAPTER SEVEN

THE NEXT MORNING JACK turned his pickup from the main thoroughfare that ran through Wawpaney onto Highway 13, the four-lane road that cut a swath through the Eastern Shore.

"I can't thank you enough for driving me and Danny to camp," Carrie Greer said from the passenger seat. She'd pulled her long blond hair back from her face and wore capris and a sleeveless shirt instead of one of her usual flowing dresses. The alterations made her appear younger.

"Thank you, Jack!" Danny called from the backseat.

Carrie craned her head around to look at the boy. "You have lovely manners, Danny." She faced forward again. "Doesn't he, Jack?"

"He does," Jack said. "But you're wrong about not thanking me enough. That makes four or five times since I picked you up."

"We're just so darn grateful you could come get us," Carrie said. "With Tara out on her kayak, I wasn't sure who else to call when the car wouldn't start."

Jack's cell phone had rung after his early morning run, when he was doing some of the shoulder stretches Art Goodnight had prescribed for him. Carrie had told him her problem, explaining that Tara had gotten up at dawn to kayak through the salt marshes at the National Wildlife Reserve and would be a little late to the third day of camp. He'd made a mental note to ask Art about adding kayaking to his rehab when he met with the trainer later that afternoon.

"You did the right thing," Jack said. "Gus suggested the volunteers exchange cell numbers for emergencies just like this one."

"Yes, but it's still a bother," she said. "I know you're not working at the camp today."

"Don't worry about it." One of the infrequent traffic lights that dotted the main road glowed green in the distance. "Shell Beach isn't that far away."

"Shell Beach!" she exclaimed. "Why, I thought you were renting a place in Wawpaney."

"It's near Wawpaney." He sailed through the still-green traffic light. He spotted a car a few hundred feet behind him, but the road in front was empty. "Shell Beach is only six or seven miles away."

"Seven miles of rural road," Carrie said. "I wish you had told me. Surely I could have figured out another way to get to camp."

"What? And deprive me of your company?"

"Scarcely a hardship," she said.

"Okay. Then why deprive yourself of *my* company? I really am delightful," he said, trying to coax a smile out of her. She didn't disappoint him.

"What do you think, Danny?" he called to the boy. "Aren't I delightful?"

When there was no answer, Jack checked the rearview mirror and Carrie swiveled to face the boy. Danny's eyes were closed and his head rested against the seat back. His mouth was open slightly and he was breathing regularly in the rhythm of sleep.

"I'm sure Danny would have backed me up on that if he were awake," Jack said.

"*Toy Story* was on TV last night," she said. "He begged to watch it, so I let him stay up past his bedtime."

"I watched that, too," he said.

"You did not!"

"Yeah, I did," he said. "I love all those *Toy Story* movies. But it would mess with my macho image, so you can't tell anybody, especially your daughter."

"Tara's never gone for the overly macho type, anyway," Carrie said. "Have you asked her out yet?"

"I'm waiting until I grow on her," he said. "She doesn't seem to like me much."

"But you're delightful!"

"I know," he said. "Go figure."

She laughed, a light tinkling sound. "Don't give up on my girl. I met my husband when he crashed into my car in a parking lot and then had the nerve to say it was my fault. I thought he was a real jerk. He asked me out three times before I said yes."

"I take it he wasn't a jerk?"

"The opposite. He was a wonderful husband and a great father," Carrie said. "Sunny adored him."

"Sunny?" Jack asked. "Is that Tara's nickname?"

"Not Tara," Carrie said. "My other daughter. Nobody ever called her anything else."

"I didn't know Tara has a sister," Jack said, not sure why the information that she wasn't an only child surprised him. He was from a family of six.

"Not anymore she doesn't," Carrie said with infinite sadness. "My darling Sunny drowned while we were on vacation at the Outer Banks. Scott did, too. He was trying to save her."

"Did they fall out of a boat?" Jack asked before he could bank his curiosity.

"No," Carrie said. "It was an undertow."

She fell silent, so Jack filled in the blanks himself. The girl venturing too far into the water and getting caught in an undercurrent, her father rushing to the rescue and suffering the same fate. His heart twisted, saddened not only for Carrie but for Tara. He knew what it was like to lose a sibling, too.

"I'm sorry." He thought about what Tara's friend at the ice cream shop had said and concluded that yesterday had been the anniversary of their deaths. He'd been through ten of those sad commemorations himself since his brother died.

"Me, too. I'm sorry every day of my life." Carrie paused. "Do you know that's the first time I've told anyone about what happened to them without crying?"

"Maybe it's time to let go of the grief and focus on the good memories," Jack ventured.

Carrie said nothing. He glanced at her and saw that she was staring straight ahead at the road, her jaw set at a stubborn angle.

Jack started to say something, then thought better of it. Who was he to lecture another person about how to live with loss? Almost eleven years after his family had gotten the terrible news about his brother, Jack was still working on taking his own advice.

LATER THE FOLLOWING afternoon, Tara stood in front of the campers, bouncing on the soles of her feet and holding aloft a beanbag. Because of her PE background, she'd been asked to lead the rainy-day activity. Music with a rhythmic beat played from the boom box in the corner of the room.

"Now that everybody has a beanbag, we're ready to start." She raised her voice to be heard above the music and the steady rain pounding the roof of the community center. "There are a few rules. The first is to keep your eye on the beanbag at all times."

Danny and one of the other campers brought their beanbags up to their faces and held them against their eyes. Tara hid a smile. So did Jack, although Tara had no business noticing what he was doing. It was nuts. Even though it was imperative she keep her distance from him, she kept slanting him secret looks that if intercepted would lead him to believe she wanted to get to know him better. She shifted her gaze back to the campers.

"My bad. I wasn't clear. I mean look at your beanbags like this." She held her beanbag at arm's length and stared at it. "Everybody got it now?"

"I got it!" Brandon called out, mimicking her actions.

Heads nodded from throughout the large space they'd cleared out for the activity by shoving the tables against the walls. Danny dropped his hand with the beanbag to his side.

"Before we start tossing our beanbags, let's go over what high, medium and low mean." She interjected as much enthusiasm into her voice as she could, holding her beanbag at three distinct levels in turn and instructing the campers to do the same. All of them followed suit except Danny. He clutched the beanbag in his hand, a sullen expression on his face.

Oh, no. Tara had seen that look a dozen times since Danny had started living with her mother, most recently during aqua Zumba.

"Now for the challenge." She brightened her voice even more. "We'll toss our beanbags into the air and catch them with both hands. Remember to keep the toss low. Like this."

She threw her beanbag about twelve inches straight up and cradled it with both hands as it came down.

"Now you try it," she said.

Beanbags flew into the air, most reaching far greater heights than the low level she'd demonstrated, many of them thudding to the floor. Danny's beanbag didn't leave his hand.

"That's a good first try," Tara said encouragingly as the children picked up the beanbags that had fallen. "This time we'll concentrate on keeping our tosses low."

She demonstrated again, then instructed the campers to repeat the activity on the count of three. All of them managed to catch the beanbags on the way down except Danny, who hadn't even tried.

"Great!" she said. "Okay, class. Let's see you catch the beanbag three times in a row. Ready, set, go!"

As the other campers did as they were told, she started moving toward Danny. Jack beat her to him.

"Hey, Danny," he said. "Don't you want to give it a try, too?"

"No!" Danny spat out, a scowl on his face. It was a word Tara had heard from him too many times.

"You can do it, buddy." Jack tossed and caught his beanbag a few times. "It's easy."

"No!" Danny all but shouted the word. He plopped down in the middle of the floor, his arms crossed over his chest.

"C'mon, Danny. Don't do that." Jack reached a hand toward the boy. "I'll help you up."

Danny scowled, saying nothing, his eyes fastened on the floor. Jack looked at Tara, a silent plea for help in his eyes. Danny pulled this stunt with regularity and nothing could budge him until he was good and ready to move.

"I'm sorry you decided to miss out on the fun, Danny," Tara said. "Jack, could you help the other campers? I have some new challenges for them."

Jack hesitated, then did as she asked. She went to the front of the group and instructed the campers on a series of variations, including higher tosses and clapping before the catch. The beanbags thudded to the floor so many times the campers were all laughing by the time they finished—except Danny, who hadn't budged.

He eventually joined the other campers, but not until it was time for arts and crafts. For the rest of the afternoon he hardly said a word, even when the developmental disability nurse sat down next to him and tried to coax him out of his bad mood. Jack tried, too. He looked so crestfallen that he couldn't get through to Danny that Tara nearly offered consolation.

Nearly, until she remembered how she was keeping him at arm's length.

As soon as camp ended, she was out the door. She started for the parking lot, then veered past it. She needed to head into town. The rain had stopped and the cloud cover kept the day cooler than it would have been. The short walk to town would do her good.

"Tara, wait!"

It was Jack's voice. She looked over her shoulder. He was jogging to catch up. She considered turning around and ignoring him, but that would be childish. Not to mention, she didn't have a prayer of eluding him. And truth be told, she wasn't averse to spending time with him. She should be. But she wasn't. She slowed down until he was walking abreast of her.

"Where are you headed?" he asked good-naturedly.

"The hardware store." She stepped over a puddle that had pooled on the sidewalk. The grass smelled damp from the recent rain and the air felt heavy, cutting down on the number of people who would usually be walking through town. Signs in storefront windows advertised an upcoming crab and seafood festival and an outdoor concert. "Just know I won't believe you if you suddenly declare that you need to buy some two-by-fours."

"I don't," he said, chuckling. "I do need to talk. About Danny."

She should have figured out right off the bat his reason for pursuing her. He'd clearly been bothered by the boy's refusal to participate in the beanbag activity. Tara supposed she should be grateful he'd come to her about Danny instead of approaching her mother.

"Don't beat yourself up over what happened today," she said. "You've seen how Danny behaves sometimes. He's done the same thing to me and my mother occasionally."

"How long has he been living with your mom?"

"About three or four weeks now," she said. "I don't know much about his background except he and his brother were being raised by a single mother."

"Is his brother in foster care, too?"

"No," she said. "Only Danny. The brother's not developmentally disabled."

Jack swore under his breath. "No wonder Danny's having problems. Any kid would. Imagine if somebody had separated you and your sister."

Tara's heart seemed to skip a beat. "How do you know about Sunny?"

"Your mom told me about her," he said.

She swallowed. Considering her mother never talked about her lost loved ones, that seemed almost impossible to believe. And when had Jack been alone with her mother? He hadn't even been at camp yesterday.

"When was that?" she asked, trying to make her voice as casual as possible.

"I gave your mom and Danny a ride to camp yesterday when her car wouldn't start," Jack said.

Her mother hadn't said anything to Tara about the lift. She kept walking, although she had to consciously tell herself to put one foot in front of the other. What else had her mother revealed?

"I shouldn't have brought it up," he said. "I guess I just wanted to let you know you could talk to me about her."

She swung her head to gaze at him sharply. "Why would I do that?"

"I lost a sibling, too," he said. "A brother."

"I'm sorry," she said, ashamed of herself for snapping at him.

"It's been tough on my family," he said.

"That's the reason your sisters call you all the time," she said with sudden insight.

"It's why I cut them some slack," he said. "I'm the second youngest. Mike was the baby of the family."

"How many years has it been?" she asked.

"Eleven," he said. "He died on 9/11 at the World Trade Center."

"How terrible." She laid a hand on his arm, the horror of the day sweeping through her with new ferocity. But something didn't make sense. If Mike was the baby of the family, he would have been in his teens when the attacks occurred. "What was he doing there? Why wasn't he in Kentucky?"

The questions erupted from her, the words sounding abrupt and almost cruel. She grimaced. "Forget I asked. You don't have to tell me."

"I want to tell you," he said, and she heard him inhale. "He dropped out of high school a few weeks earlier and headed for New York City. He was already eighteen, so there wasn't much anybody in the family could do about it. A friend let him stay in his apartment and got him a job as a busboy at the Windows on the World restaurant."

He recited the horror in a flat monotone, in much the same way Tara's mother had told her the story of the drownings. Whereas Tara could hear her mother's pain underneath the words, his wasn't audible.

"Wasn't the restaurant in the north tower?" she asked.

"The 107th floor," Jack said. "The plane hit below that. Everybody in the restaurant survived the impact, but all the passages below were blocked. None of them got out of the building alive."

"I'm so sorry," she said again even though she was repeating herself.

"Making it worse, we never got to put him to rest," Jack said. "He was one of the many victims whose remains were never identified. There were more than a thousand of those."

"That's terrible," Tara said.

They'd reached the quaint main street of town and walked in silence for a few blocks past a dental practice, an art and frame shop, a coffeehouse and a bait-and-tackle shop.

Tara understood now why Jack had brought up Sunny's death, but thought how different his situation was from her own. He'd grown up with his brother. Tara didn't even have a glimmer of a memory about Sunny.

"Here's the hardware store." She indicated a door with a green awning and assorted tools in the window. "Don't feel like you have to come inside with me."

"You must be joking," he said. "I'm a guy. I love hardware stores."

They entered the shop. The same four elderly men who had been in the store the last time Tara stopped by sat on chairs near the cash register. Mr. Snyder, the youngest of them even though he was probably still at least seventy, got to his feet.

"Hello, Tara." He prided himself on calling his repeat customers by name, as did many of the shop owners on the Eastern Shore. "Who's this young fella with you?"

"This is Jack DiMarco, Mr. Snyder," she said. "He's a tourist, staying out on Shell Beach."

"You're that baseball pitcher, aren't you?" one of the other men called. He stood out from his friends because of his red suspenders and matching baseball cap. All of the men, though, were regarding Jack curiously.

"How did you know that?" Jack asked.

"Recognized the name," the man said. "Art Goodnight's my nephew. He said something about working with a pitcher renting a place out on Shell Beach."

"Aren't you kind of old to be a pitcher?" the oldest man asked. "I thought pitchers nowadays were kids."

"I'm thirty-one," Jack said. "I think I've got some good years left in me."

"Of course you do." Mr. Snyder waved a hand at his friends. "Ignore those guys. They're always gabbing about things they know nothing about."

"Hey!" one of the guys protested.

Mr. Snyder didn't acknowledge him. "What

brings you here today, Tara? Need more of those energy-saving light bulbs for your mother?"

"No. They last a long time, just like you said. Actually, I'm going to refinish a mahogany rolltop desk I got from my mom's house. I'd like to buy stripper and some stain."

"You'll need more than that," Mr. Snyder said. "You ever done that kind of work before, Tara?"

"There's a first time for everything," Tara said. "Just sell me the materials and I can manage."

"I'll help," Jack offered. "I've done a number of pieces for my parents."

"Thanks," Tara said, "but that's not necessary."

"It's tricky refinishing a rolltop, Tara," Mr. Snyder said. "Let your young man help you."

"He's not my young man," Tara began, but she was talking to Mr. Snyder's back. He'd already stepped away to find her supplies. She and Jack followed. The shop owner stopped at shelves stocked with rubber gloves, steel wool, sandpaper, drop cloths and stain.

"Let's see. You're gonna need most of what we've got here," he said. The chimes attached to the front door of the shop sounded. "If you'll excuse me, I need to see to that customer. Your young man can help you pick out the right things, Tara."

"He's not—" Tara began again, but Mr. Snyder was already gone.

Jack jerked a thumb in the general direction of

the front of the store. "According to Mr. Snyder's buddy, I'm your old man."

"You're not my man—young or old—at all." She caught the gleam in his eyes and frowned at him. "You're teasing me."

"Guilty," he said. "But I'm staying until at least July, so I am at your disposal for the next few weeks. You can do what you want with me."

She gave a short laugh. "I'm not going to ask you to have sex with me, if that's what you mean."

"It wasn't," he said, his grin spreading. "I was talking about helping you refinish that piece of furniture."

"Oh." She felt the heat spread across her cheeks. "Sorry."

"No apology necessary." He brushed a strand of hair from her face. "I'm flattered that you look at me and think about sex."

She wondered how this conversation had spiraled out of control so quickly. He was still touching her hair. She wasn't sure why she didn't move away from him. "You weren't listening. I said no sex."

"It's okay with me if we start out slowly," he said. "I'm not the kind of guy who has sex on the first date, anyway."

Now she did step back. "What are you talking about?"

"I'm asking you to have dinner with me this

weekend," he said. "I don't have plans, so you can pick the night."

She had to grit her teeth so she didn't say yes. So what if he was handsome and charming and likable? She should have seen this coming and taken steps to prevent it. It wasn't enough to keep him away from her mother. As she said, she needed to avoid him, too. "Thanks, but no."

"Then I'll pick the night," he said. "How about tomorrow? That way, we can go out again if things go well."

"I meant no, I can't go out with you," Tara said. "Not tomorrow, not Saturday and not Sunday."

He edged closer to her. Her breath caught in her throat. She could smell him, a clean combination of soap, shampoo and his own warm scent. Not for the first time, she wished his sister wasn't working on the Hayley Cooper case.

"Look, I just want to have a few laughs and enjoy your company. Nothing more," he said. "It's not like there could ever be anything serious between us."

"Why not?" she asked, then could have thumped her forehead. If dating him was out of the question, so was forming a meaningful relationship with him.

"As soon as my shoulder's better, I'm signing with whichever pro team offers me a contract," he said. "You'll never leave the Eastern Shore."

She felt her spine stiffen. "How do you know I'll never leave?"

"Hey, I'm telling it like I see it," he said, raising a hand. "I've seen how protective you are of your mother. I can't imagine you moving away from her."

Now he sounded like Mary Dee.

"So how about that date?" he asked. "In case it helps my cause, your mom would approve. She even told me I should ask you out."

He couldn't have said anything more likely to dissuade her from accepting a date with him. He was far too involved with her family already.

"Okay, I hate to be blunt, because you seem like a nice enough guy." She took a deep breath and hoped her lie would sound convincing. "I'm just not interested."

"Ouch." He put a hand over his heart. Despite the overly dramatic gesture, he really did look wounded. "Well, I gave it a shot. No hard feelings, okay? We'll be working together for at least another week, so we can just be friends."

Except they couldn't. Becoming Jack's friend would be almost as dangerous as getting romantically involved with him, maybe more so. She couldn't refuse, though. She couldn't do anything that would make him suspicious of her.

"Sure," she said. "Friends."

"I'll get a handbasket for those materials you

need," Jack said. He was back in a moment, leaning across her to grab sandpaper and stain from the nearest shelf. His arm brushed hers, and warmth spread from her head to her toes. She stepped backward, dismayed by her reaction, hoping he hadn't noticed it.

In minutes, they had all they needed. Jack carried the handbasket to the cash register, then insisted on toting the heavier of the bags back to the community center.

By the time they'd walked a block, more people were out and about, and Tara's nerves were frayed from trying to hide her attraction to him.

"When I picked up your mom and Danny yesterday, she said you were kayaking." He sounded perfectly at ease. "Do you go often?"

She made a concerted effort to focus on the subject, one of her favorites. "As often as I can. There are a lot of beautiful spots you can't reach any other way."

"So you're an expert kayaker," he said.

"A novice," she said. "I took up the sport a few months ago."

He asked her several more questions about kayaking, which she answered at length. Finally something occurred to her. "You're trying to put me at ease, aren't you?"

He shrugged. "If we're going to be friends, I don't want any awkwardness between us."

Here was her chance to set some ground rules and possibly minimize the threat he posed to her family. "Then don't bring up things like my father and sister dying."

"Noted," he said. "I probably wouldn't have mentioned it if the anniversary hadn't been this week. I know those kinds of rememberances can be tough."

"Not as tough as it used to be," Tara said, uncomfortable with the compassion in his eyes. "It did happen almost three decades ago, you know."

"What?" He sounded truly shocked. "I thought it was more recent than that."

Tara bit her lip, dismayed that she'd leaked something he didn't already know. She couldn't backtrack now.

"No, it was a long time ago," she said.

"But your mother said…" He stopped, as though playing over in his mind exactly what she'd told him. "I got the impression Sunny had gone out for a swim. But given what you've said, she couldn't have been very old."

Tara didn't want to tell him her sister's age. With the information he already had, though, he could probably find out the details himself. Or worse, get his P.I. sister to do it.

"She was three." As recently as last week, before her mother had recounted exactly what had happened, Tara wouldn't have been able to provide the details of the story. "She was in my father's arms when a wave swept over them. He lost hold of her."

"You had to have been even younger than that," he said. "You don't remember her, do you?"

Tara's inclination was to claim that she did remember Sunny, except that would be like waving a red flag in his face. Very few people had memories from when they were two years old.

"That's right." Tara needed to add something to throw him off the scent. That is, if he picked one up. "I only know her through pictures and what my mom has told me about her."

"What did she tell you?" Jack asked.

"That they called her Sunny because of her personality." Tara needed to make up the rest. In truth, her mother hardly mentioned her lost daughter. "And that she loved me. She used to hold me on her lap and feed me my bottle even though we were just a year apart."

With a start, Tara realized she'd shared with him the fantasy of only children—having a loving sibling.

He squeezed her shoulder. "The offer still stands," he said. "I'm here if you want to talk."

Except she couldn't talk to him. The more she was around him, the more chance she had of saying something she shouldn't and arousing his suspicions.

She'd been right in the first place. She couldn't be his lover or his friend, no matter how much she wanted to.

CHAPTER EIGHT

THE BEER MUG CRASHED to the floor and bounced, spilling amber liquid onto the wood. Tara grabbed a rag off the bar and hurried to her mother, who stood staring down at the mess.

"Look what I did!" her mother exclaimed. "Oh, I never should have agreed to help out at the pub tonight."

O'Malley's Pub, a bar/restaurant in Cape Charles, was owned by the parents of a guy Tara had dated in high school. She'd worked there as a waitress in the summers when she was a teenager. Her old boyfriend had long since married someone else, but Tara still provided an extra hand at the pub on Friday nights, when the clientele nearly tripled because of the live music.

Her mother was pitching in tonight because one of the regular waitresses had called in sick and the O'Malleys needed an experienced replacement quickly. Her mom qualified, even though it had been many years since she'd been a waitress. Luckily, her neighbor Mrs. Jorgenson had been able to mind Danny.

Tara got down on her hands and knees to wipe up the spill, breathing in the fragrant smell of hops and barley. She looked up at her mother as she mopped. "Everybody drops something sooner or later. Just forget about it and get a refill."

She handed her mother the now-empty plastic beer mug.

"You're right," her mother said. "I used to be a terrific waitress if I do say so myself."

Tara stood up and laid a hand on her mother's arm. Carrie felt fragile, like a porcelain doll. "I know. That's why I recommended you to help out tonight."

"I thought it was because I need the money," her mother said.

"That, too." Of the two of them, it seemed her mother's unemployed status weighed more heavily on Tara. Her mother operated on the assumption that something would come along sooner or later. In today's economy, Tara wasn't so sure about that.

"I'll try to do you proud," Mom said, casting an uncertain glance at Tara before bustling off.

It wasn't the first time her mother had said something like that. Mary Dee's claim about how needy her mother was contained more than a few grains of truth. Lately, it seemed as though her mother craved Tara's approval. Was that because she was seeking forgiveness for snatching a little girl from a shopping mall and raising her as her own?

Stop it, Tara told herself sternly. She didn't know that anything of the sort had happened. What's more, if it had, she didn't want to find out.

Tara crossed behind the bar to rinse out the beer-soaked rag, passing another waitress and George O'Malley along the way. The owner of the bar was a large man with a thick mustache, a shaved head and a soft voice. His green O'Malley's T-shirt stretched over his barrel chest.

"Is your mom gonna be okay?" Mr. O'Malley asked. "She seems overwhelmed."

"She'll be fine once she gets back in the swing of things." Tara winked at him. "She passed down her mad waitress skills to me, didn't she?"

Now, why had she said that? Was she trying to convince Mr. O'Malley she and her mother were related? Or was she trying to convince herself?

He laughed, showing a narrow gap between his front teeth. His son had the same trait, yet Tara couldn't think of a single physical characteristic she and her mother had in common. "My son should have snapped you up when he had the chance," Mr. O'Malley said.

"Don't let Emma hear you say that," Tara said, referring to Mr. O'Malley's daughter-in-law. Earlier in June, Tara had spent all day working beside her at the church flea market.

"I like Emma," Mr. O'Malley said in a voice

that was even softer than usual. He sidled closer to her. "I just like you better."

"If you keep flattering me like that, you'll never get rid of me," Tara said.

He winked at her. His eyes were blue, like his son's. "That's the plan."

"Then it's working." She picked up her order pad, rounded the bar and headed for her section of the main dining area filled with rustic booths and wooden tables. With the live music set to start soon, the dining room was full and more customers were arriving by the minute.

The door to the entrance swung open as she was passing by. She paused, intending to tell the new customer that a few of the bar stools were still empty. The words died on her lips. The customer was Jack.

"Tara!" His sensuous mouth curved into a heart-stopping smile. His jeans and white shirt with the sleeves rolled up would have looked pedestrian on anyone else. On Jack, the clothes called attention to his broad shoulders, hair-sprinkled forearms and long muscular legs. "What a surprise."

It seemed too coincidental that Jack should ask her out for tonight and then show up here at the pub where she worked nearly every Friday. "Is it really?" she asked.

"It sure is," he said. "I figured you for a home-body."

Since that was essentially true, Tara didn't know why it sounded like a criticism.

"I work here whenever there's live music," she said. "That's just about every Friday and some Saturdays during the summer."

"Wow," he said. "You work at a lot of places."

"Only in the summer, a couple hours here and there to help out friends and to make some extra money. I like to keep busy."

Somebody jostled her from behind, causing her to take a step closer to him. Her chest came up against his and her heart sped up. He smelled clean and fresh, like the outdoors. She retreated, breaking the momentary contact.

"You'll want to grab a stool at the bar before they're all gone," she said. "The music should be starting soon."

"Can't wait," he said. "Who would have guessed Gus played flamenco guitar?"

"Gus is providing the live music?" Tara asked. Mr. O'Malley had mentioned he'd scrambled to get a replacement after the originally scheduled act canceled. He hadn't provided any more details, though.

"You didn't know?" Jack asked. "How did you think I found out about this place?"

She thought her mother had told him where Tara worked on the weekends, the same way Carrie had shared a half dozen other confidences with him.

"Hope you enjoy it here. Seems like everybody else does." She gestured at the crowd around them. "I need to wait on my customers so they don't start flagging down the other waitresses."

"Catch up with you later," he said easily before heading to the bar. She watched him go, her gaze slipping from his broad shoulders to his nicely shaped rear end. Just as quickly, she redirected her attention to the restaurant.

She entered the dining room, greeting friends, stopping by booths and tables, taking orders and clearing dishes, trying not to think about Jack DiMarco. She delivered a pitcher of beer and four orders of wings to two middle-aged couples, turned to head back to the kitchen and spotted Gus. Not the Gus who dressed in T-shirts and shorts at Camp Daybreak. In black pants and a black short-sleeved shirt, with the barest hint of gray at the temples of his black hair, this Gus resembled a musician. She intercepted him before he reached the stage.

"Hey, Gus," she said, smiling at him. "I just found out you were the entertainment. I didn't even know you were a musician."

"I didn't know you were a waitress," he said.

"Only sometimes," she said.

"Same for me with the music," he said. "I haven't performed in a while, so it's good to have a friend in the audience."

"You've got more than one friend," Tara said. "Jack's here, too. And my mother."

His dark eyebrows rose. "Carrie's here?"

"The O'Malleys were shorthanded tonight, so I got her to fill in," Tara said.

His face split into a smile that lit up his green eyes. "Then I need to be extra good, the better to impress her."

"You're interested in my mom?" she asked.

"Oh, yeah," he said. "I know she's a widow. I'm trying to take it slow, but patience isn't one of my virtues."

"Did you know my dad and Sunny died in the early eighties?" Tara asked.

His eyes widened and his lips parted. Nope, he hadn't known. Barry Findley, the accountant who did her taxes, motioned for her from one of her tables, where he and his wife, a county librarian, were sitting. No time to elaborate. "I've gotta go, Gus. Good luck tonight. Or should I say, break a leg."

She hustled over to Barry's side, promising she'd bring him a fresh drink pronto. With the pub this crowded, she shouldn't have taken the time to approach Gus.

Poor guy, she thought. Her mom didn't date, not ever, although she'd had her chances. Why, Art Goodnight asked her mother out at least a few times a year. Tara's former volleyball coach had even finagled it tonight so he and his friend were seated at one of her mother's booths.

Tara threaded her way through the tables back to the bar, wondering where her mother was. She didn't have to wonder long. Carrie stood at the end of the bar chatting up the customer occupying the last stool. Tara could see only the back of his head, but knew from his dark hair and the set of his shoulders that it was Jack.

So much for steering clear of him.

She changed direction in midstep, heading straight toward them. Barry would have to wait for his beer. If George O'Malley got wind of her slow service tonight, he might change his mind about wanting her around forever, but it couldn't be helped. Getting her mother away from Jack was more important than any job.

"Hey, Mom. Art needs you at his booth," Tara called as she approached. A white lie, but probably not one her mother would catch her in.

Carrie rolled her eyes. "Is it too late to switch tables? I've got a feeling that darn Art's gonna ask me out again."

"It's too late," Tara confirmed.

"You can handle him, Carrie," Jack said encouragingly.

"Don't you dare use the word *handle* around Art," Carrie told Jack. "That rascal will turn it around and make a joke about how he wants me to handle him."

Jack laughed. Her mother didn't crack a smile, heaving a theatrical sigh before trudging off.

"I like your mom," Jack said.

Tara's mother obviously returned the feeling. Tara wasn't quite sure what to do about that.

"What were you two talking about?" She normally wouldn't ask such a nosy question. These, however, were dire times.

"I offered to take Danny fishing Saturday morning," he said. "Carrie was trying to decide whether to come with us."

Tara's heart felt as if it had been zapped with a defibrillator. "She can't!"

"She can't?" he repeated. "Why not?"

"She has a thing tomorrow." Tara cast about for details, but came up with none. She needed to fake it. "An appointment. She must have forgotten about it."

"Then I guess I'll just pick up Danny when I come by the house," he said.

"No!" Tara blurted out. She didn't want Jack anywhere near her mother's house, not when it was inevitable that Carrie would offer him some Southern hospitality and invite him in. "I'll bring Danny to you."

His brows knit. "Why would you do that?"

Why indeed? Her mind whirred. "Because I want to go fishing with you."

"You do?" He tilted his head, appearing confused. And why wouldn't he be? Just yesterday she'd refused his invitation to spend any part of the weekend with him. The strands of a Latin song filled the bar, loud enough that talking was a challenge.

She ripped a piece off her order pad and handed it to him with a pen. Leaning in close, she said into his ear, "Write down your address and the time we should be there."

She got another whiff of that fresh outdoor scent. The man smelled wonderful, although she didn't detect aftershave or cologne. It was all him.

He turned his head and her lips brushed his cheek. She jerked backward. He smiled at her with his eyes before handing the sheet back to her. "I wrote down my address so you'll have it. Tomorrow, though, you and Danny can meet me at the public pier in Cape Charles. Let's say one o'clock."

He wasn't speaking loudly, but she could read his sensuous lips. She almost groaned aloud that she had attributed the word *sensuous* to them, even though they were. She thought about telling him she didn't need his address, then figured the shorter the conversation, the better. "See you tomorrow."

"Can't wait," he said.

She nodded, pivoted on her heel and returned to work. She wouldn't dare admit she was looking forward to it, too, even though she was.

CARRIE FROZE ON THE WAY to Art Goodnight's table, her attention glued to the stage where Gustavo Miller sat on a stool cradling a flamenco guitar.

No wonder Jack had told her he was at O'Malley's to see Gus. Except Carrie had misconstrued what Jack meant. She'd expected Gustavo to join Jack at the bar to toss back a few while they listened to the music.

She'd never anticipated that Gustavo would be providing the entertainment.

Carrie was so unfamiliar with his style of music that she couldn't have identified it if a customer hadn't mentioned what was on tap for tonight.

Gustavo picked at the guitar, producing a pulsing beat that managed to sound both rhythmic and soulful. The instrument, she realized, was in the hands of a master.

He lifted his head and looked directly at her, as though he'd known she was standing there. A slow smile spread across his face as he strummed the guitar. She felt herself respond with an answering smile.

"Excuse me."

Carrie heard the raised female voice and broke eye contact with Gustavo. A large woman, who was probably a tourist, stood behind her trying to get by, impatience written on her pinched features.

"Sorry about that, hon." Carrie shook herself out of her Gustavo-induced stupor and made room for the woman. She hoped Gustavo hadn't noticed her gaping. Except who was she kidding? Of course he'd noticed. Everybody in the pub had probably seen her acting as if she were in the throes of a crush.

She immediately banished the thought. A woman in her mid-fifties was too old to have a crush. Even if she weren't, she hadn't been in the market for romance for a very long time.

Noticing that Gustavo was an attractive man was a far cry from wanting to press her body against his and feel his mouth moving on hers.

She fanned herself and continued on her original path to the table where Art sat with Fred Marshall, a fisherman who was married to one of Carrie's closest friends in Wawpaney.

She leaned down so the men could hear her over the music. "Did one of you want something?"

"You," Art said with alacrity.

She'd walked right into that one.

"Cut that out. You know I meant something to eat or drink," she clarified.

"Another round would be good," Art said, shoving his beer mug to the edge of the table. Fred did the same.

"Coming right up." Carrie hurried off before Art could make another move. The problem was that she had to keep returning to their table, first to deliver their beers and then to bring the two men another order of breaded shrimp.

She deposited the plastic basket with the shrimp between them. "Here you go. Enjoy."

Her voice boomed into the sudden silence. On stage, the music had stopped. Applause broke out and Gustavo took a small bow.

"Thank you," Gustavo said to the crowd. "I'll take a short break and come back with more live music."

"That's some crazy music. The guitar player's not half-bad, though," Art said, drawing Carrie's attention back to him. "What did you think, Carrie?'

"I usually listen to country, but I enjoyed him very much," Carrie said honestly. "He's quite talented."

"So you like country music," Art said. "What do you say I get tickets to a show in Norfolk and you and me make a night of it?"

What was this? Carrie wondered. Ask Carrie Out week?

"I'll spring for a hotel room if you don't want to drive home afterward," he continued before she could answer.

It wasn't an unreasonable suggestion. To get

to Norfolk, they'd have to cross the twenty-mile Chesapeake Bay Bridge-Tunnel, the only direct link from the Eastern Shore to the more populated Hampton Roads area.

"I don't think—" she began.

"Hell, we can make it a double date. You and Fred's wife, Stella, are friends." Art jerked a thumb at Fred. "I'm sure they'd go with us. Right, Fred?"

"I guess," Fred said, frowning. He didn't seem the type to take in a show.

"What do you say, Carrie?" Art pressed. "Will you go out with me?"

She shook her head. "I can't."

"C'mon, Carrie," he whined. "I've been asking you out for years. What would one little date hurt?"

His eyes were pinched together. Something inside Carrie weakened, although not enough to acquiesce. Art was a nice enough man and she hated to hurt his feelings, but she wouldn't date him no matter how many times he asked. She never dated anyone. She searched for a way to refuse him so he wouldn't ask again.

"She can't go out with you because she's seeing me." Gustavo approached from behind her, encircling her shoulders with his arm. "Isn't that right, Carrie?"

Say no, a voice in her head screamed.

"It sure is," Carrie said.

"Ah, hell," Art said, disappointment lacing his

words. To Gustavo, Art said, "You've got a good woman there."

"I know it." Gustavo gave her shoulders a gentle squeeze. His arm felt good exactly where it was. But when he walked with her away from the table, she sped up so it fell away. No matter what impression they were trying to give Art, they were not a couple.

"Why did you say we were dating?" she hissed.

"Why did you go along with it?" he asked.

"Art's been bugging me for years and I want him to stop."

"This will make him stop."

She ran a hand through her hair. "No, it won't. He'll find out we aren't really dating and ask me out again."

"There's a way to get around that." He brought his head closer to hers. For some reason, she couldn't seem to move away. "Go on a date with me. A real one."

"No." She shook her head vehemently. "I don't date."

"We won't call it a date. We'll be two people getting together so your suitor stops bugging you."

She bit her bottom lip. "That's all?"

"That's all," he said.

Carrie didn't know what she would say until the answer was out of her mouth. "Okay."

"Good." He grinned at her, the same way he had when he'd spotted her gaping at him on the stage.

For a pregnant moment she thought about rescinding her agreement. She even opened her mouth to do so. Then he stroked her cheek and all thought flew out of her mind.

"I'll be in touch," he said.

He left her staring after him, her right hand covering the spot on her cheek where his touch lingered.

THE INSTANT DANNY GOT out of Tara's car, Jack put his fingers into his mouth and whistled. Jack was waiting inside an open-air gazebo on the sand dunes side of the Cape Charles public beach, with only the plastic statue of a dolphin to keep him company.

Danny looked toward the noise, grinned and raised a hand in greeting. Before Tara emerged from the car, the boy was hurrying toward Jack down the sidewalk that ran adjacent to the beach. He wore shorts long enough to cover his knees, a bright red T-shirt and a wide-brimmed beige fishing hat.

Tara followed at a distance, seeming in no hurry to reach him, heightening his anticipation of spending the next few hours with her. She wore a sleeveless white top and blue shorts that showed off her slender, athletic build. He especially liked her long, toned legs. He was grateful his sunglasses hid the fact that he was checking her out. Last night at the pub she'd been friendly and welcoming with her customers, which he'd gathered from watching her at camp was the way she usually acted. He'd put her on the defensive because of how they'd met, but he was determined to draw out the true Tara.

Danny ran straight up to Jack and hugged him, a casual display of affection that Jack thought was kind of nice. Danny drew back. "Do you like my hat, Jack?"

"It's great," Jack said. "Makes you look like a real fisherman."

"That's 'cause it's a real fisherman's hat." Danny fingered the floppy brim with obvious pride. "Mr. J gave it to me."

"Who's Mr. J?" Jack asked.

Tara reached them and stood behind her foster brother. "A neighbor who lives next door to Danny and my mother. He told Danny it was a lucky hat."

Danny tilted his head back to look at Jack from under the brim. "That's why I'm wearing it."

"What are we waiting for? Let's go try it out." Jack gestured at the fishing gear he'd brought along. "I need help with some of this. Danny, can you carry the tackle box?"

Danny nodded, but instead of picking up the tackle box he pointed to a smaller clear container. "What's that?"

"Our bait."

Danny approached the container cautiously and peered at the fat, squirming worms. He made a face. "Why are they pink?"

"They're not regular worms. They're blood-worms. The guy at the bait-and-tackle shop said fish like 'em." Jack gathered the rods and a cooler he'd packed with water and soda. "Can you get the fold-up chair, Tara?"

She picked it up, her mouth twisting quizzically. The sunglasses thing went both ways. He couldn't see her eyes through her oversize pair. "How did you carry all this by yourself from your car?"

"Two trips," he said. "If I like fishing, I might go back to the shop and buy a cart."

"You mean you just bought all this stuff?" she asked, a smile spreading across her face. "Haven't you done this before?"

"Every kid's thrown a pole into the water at some time or other," he said. "How hard can it be?"

"Plenty hard, considering it's the middle of the afternoon. The pier gets a lot more traffic in the morning and after the sun goes down. This isn't exactly prime fishing time."

"Spoken like the voice of experience."

"Hardly," she said. "I've only been fishing once or twice."

Now, that was interesting considering last night she'd jumped at the chance to come with them. "I got the impression you were an avid fishing fan. Did I get it wrong?"

Her mouth opened and closed, as if she were trying to formulate an answer. He'd known something was odd about her request to accompany him and Danny. He still couldn't figure out what.

"Hey! Why aren't you guys c-coming?" Danny demanded. While they were talking, he'd continued down the sidewalk toward the weathered wooden pier that jutted into the Chesapeake Bay. His body was lopsided, the bait bucket weighing down his right side.

"We'll be right there." Tara picked up the tackle box and headed after her foster brother.

Jack gathered the rest of the gear and drew even with her. "You didn't answer my question."

She raised her chin. "Just because I haven't fished much doesn't mean I don't like it."

"Ah, I was hoping you had another reason for coming," he said.

"What other reason could there be?"

"You could have changed your mind about dating me," he said.

She didn't turn her head. Her steps ate up the ground, closing the distance between them and Danny until they were directly behind the boy. "I didn't."

"You sure about that?" he asked. "I've been told I make a great boyfriend."

Danny stopped so abruptly Tara almost ran into him. He turned to face his foster sister. "Is Jack your boyfriend?"

Tara shot Jack what was probably a glare, judging from the tight set of her lips. He tried to indicate with a half shrug that he hadn't realized Danny would overhear.

"No, Danny. Jack isn't my boyfriend," Tara said.

"Who is your boyfriend?" Danny asked.

"I don't have one, silly," Tara answered, affection in her tone.

"Then Jack can be your boyfriend," Danny said.

"No, he can't."

"Don't you like Jack?" Danny asked.

Tara shuffled her sneaker-clad feet. "Of course I do."

"Then why isn't he your boyfriend?" Danny asked.

As much as Jack was enjoying the interplay between the foster siblings, it was time he came to Tara's rescue. "If we don't get out on that pier soon, buddy, somebody else will catch all the fish."

Danny's mouth dropped open. "Let's hurry," he said before he took off.

Jack winced. "My bad," he told Tara. "I forgot he took things so literally."

To Danny, he called, "Slow down, buddy. I didn't mean it. There are plenty of fish in the bay."

The boy ignored Jack, practically running ahead

of them, his body tilting to one side because of the bucket.

"That doesn't look like the same boy who refused to do the shuttle run at camp yesterday," Jack remarked to Tara.

"Yeah, he should have realized your story about someone else catching all the fish sounded—" she paused and a giggle erupted from her lips "—a little too fishy."

Jack laughed, too, enjoying the sound of her laughter, pleased she was starting to lighten up around him. They stepped onto a pier that looked less suited for serious fishermen than for tourists out for a scenic walk. It rose above a rock jetty only a few feet above the water and extended out into the bay before making a sharp ninety-degree turn into deeper water. The slight breeze smelled of salt and the sea.

"Do you have a saltwater fishing license?" Tara asked.

"The guy at the bait shop said we don't need one to fish off the pier," he said. "Something about the city purchasing one. I take it this isn't one of the places you've been fishing?"

"Nope. But I've been here lots of times." Tara indicated a busy stretch of beach that was to the right of the pier. "See the volleyball net over there? A group of us play there after dinner every Monday until it gets too dark to see."

Art Goodnight had claimed Tara was an excellent volleyball player. Jack would love to see her in action.

"And see all the kids on the beach?" she continued. "I used to be one of them."

The bay was so placid that the waves looked more like ripples as the water gently lapped to shore. "Is the water always that calm?"

"Always," Tara said. "Why do you think my mother picked this beach?"

The bay breeze blew Tara's hair across her face. She stopped, set down the tackle box and took a hair tie out of her pocket. While she tied the reddish-brown mass into a ponytail, Jack thought about how the drownings could have affected the dynamics between Tara and her mother. No wonder they were so interdependent. He knew how his own family had banded together after Mike's death.

Ahead of them on the pier, Danny was looking over the railing into the water. Jack and Tara resumed walking, passing an elderly fisherman with graying hair and a leathery, tanned face. He looked up from the hook he was baiting.

"Any luck?" Jack asked.

"None so far," the fisherman replied. "The fish, they ain't biting today."

"Hate to hear it," Jack said and waited until the man was out of earshot before remarking to

Tara, "Let's see what difference Danny's lucky hat makes."

It didn't take long for the results to come in. An hour later, Danny reeled in his third catch of the day, a small saltwater fish called a spot.

"You were wrong, Jack!" Danny cried. "The other people didn't c-catch all the fish. I am."

"Yes, you are." Jack took the hook out of the fish's mouth and held the fish out to Danny. It wriggled in his hand, making it hard to hold. "You want to throw this one back, or should I?"

"Tara can do it!" Danny said.

She shook her head. "Oh, no. I'm not touching that slimy thing."

Jack laughed and tossed the fish gently into the water. Relief hit him when it swam off, alive and well.

"Can I go watch that boat?" Danny pointed to a sailboat with a multihued mast off in the distance.

"Sure thing, little brother," Tara said.

Danny laughed and practically threw himself into Tara's arms for a spontaneous hug. "I like when you call me that."

Both Jack and Tara smiled as they watched him dash off to the end of the pier, which wasn't far from them.

"He's a great kid, isn't he? I'm glad fishing kept his attention."

"Good thing we caught a few," Jack said. "That lucky hat sure came in handy."

Her smile grew. "Should we throw in another line?"

"Maybe not today," he said. "I'd be bummed if we caught a really big fish. I forgot to buy an ice bucket, so we couldn't keep it."

"Danny won't eat fish, anyway," Tara said. "All he wants is mac and cheese and cheeseburgers."

"I think I was the same at that age."

He stood beside her with his elbows on the rail, gazing into the sparkling water. A sense of contentment washed over him. He doubted he'd enjoy fishing nearly as much if Tara wasn't with him. She was definitely starting to treat him with less suspicion and more warmth.

"Speaking of my mother and food, Danny and I shouldn't stay much longer, anyway," Tara said. "I'm not working at the pub tonight, so Mom invited me over for an early dinner."

"Six o'clock, right?" Jack asked.

She turned her head sharply. "How do you know what time my mother's serving dinner?"

"She invited me, too."

"When was this?"

"Last night at the pub," he said. "She said in case we didn't catch anything, she'd make chicken."

"But…" Tara seemed at a loss for words. "Don't you have something else to do tonight?"

"Nope," he said. "The woman I asked out said no."

She didn't even smile at that. Considering they'd been getting along well up to this point, Jack couldn't make heads or tails of it. He'd even been about to ask her out again. "I hate to say anything against my mother, but she's not a very good cook."

"Then I'll look forward to the company."

"Let me put that another way," Tara said. "She's a *bad* cook."

"Her cooking can't be as bad as my mom's," he said. "Once my mom tried to cook frozen ravioli in the oven. Another time she didn't use enough flour and her cookies started to boil. The worst, though, was probably when the Thanksgiving turkey caught fire."

"It did not!" she exclaimed, her eyes bright.

"Technically, it was a grease fire that started when she was trying to take the bird out of the oven," he said.

"Nobody got hurt, did they?"

"Just the turkey," he answered.

She covered her mouth with her hand, but a laugh erupted from between her fingers. Their eyes met and he joined in, looking forward to the evening ahead, her mother's bad cooking and all.

CHAPTER NINE

JACK FINISHED HIS LAST spoonful of Cajun chicken pasta and followed it with a bite of French bread, savoring the flavors that melded in his mouth.

"That was delicious, Carrie," he said. "Best meal I've had in weeks."

"Why, thank you." Carrie bowed her head slightly in acknowledgment. "If there's one thing I know how to do well, it's cook."

Jack tried to catch Tara's eye from across the table in a dining room that, like the rest of the house, was more cozy than formal. Tara's attention was riveted on her food, understandable considering how wonderful it tasted. He suspected, however, that Tara was deliberately ignoring him.

Earlier today on the pier, he could have sworn they'd made a connection.

Then why had she lied about her mother being a terrible cook? The only reason Jack could fathom was that she hadn't wanted him at dinner.

Danny rose from the table, shoving his chair backward so that it made a scratching sound on the hardwood floor.

"What are you doing, Dan the man?" Carrie asked.

"I need to go to Billy," Danny said. "He misses me."

Billy was Danny's new kitten. Danny had been so eager to show it off that he'd been waiting on the front porch with the kitten when Jack arrived.

"You can't check up on Billy until you're excused from the table," Carrie said.

Danny screwed up his face. "How do I get excused?"

"You know how," Carrie said, no hint of impatience in her voice. "You ask."

"C-can I be excused?" Danny asked.

"Yes, you most certainly may," Carrie said.

The boy stomped off toward the sunroom where Carrie had insisted he keep the cat while they ate. His footsteps sounded like miniature bursts of thunder.

Tara finally looked up from her food. "Tell me again how you got this cat, Mom."

In a pale orange v-necked shirt and comfortable-looking white shorts, Tara wasn't dressed much more formally than she'd been at the pier. Yet with her hair wavy and loose about her shoulders, she exuded a casual chic. He liked the way her nose sloped and the bow shape of her mouth. He'd like that mouth more if it smiled at him. Or, better yet, molded to his.

"A friend was giving them away," Carrie said. "It seemed to me that having a pet would be good for Danny."

"Isn't Billy one of Gus's kittens?" Jack asked. A few days ago at camp, Susie had announced that her great-grandmother's cat was a mom.

Carrie pursed her lips and shifted in her chair. "Yes."

Tara rested her forearms on the table and leaned forward. "Why didn't you say Gus was the friend in the first place?"

Carrie waved a hand. "No particular reason." She stood up. "Who's ready for dessert? I made key lime pie."

"I am," Jack said. "As good as that dinner was, no way am I passing up anything you made."

Tara half rose. "I'll help you serve, Mom."

"No, no," Carrie said. "You just sit back down and enjoy Jack's company."

The instant her mother was gone, Tara's eyes met Jack's. "Did you see what she did?"

Jack lifted a corner of his mouth. "Offered you a very wise suggestion?"

"Not that," Tara said. "She totally didn't want us to know Gus gave Danny the kitten."

He'd picked up on that, too. "Why wouldn't she want us to know?"

"Maybe because there's something going on

between them," Tara whispered. "Gus told me at O'Malley's pub that he had a thing for her."

"Sounds like a good thing."

"You don't understand. My mother hasn't shown any interest in a man since my father died." Tara bit her lip. Footsteps sounded from the kitchen. "You've got to help me find out if something's going on between them," she finished in a rush.

Carrie reentered the dining room carrying two plates of key lime pie topped with generous dollops of whipped cream. She placed the desserts in front of Tara and Jack and rejoined them at the table.

"Looks delicious," Jack said. "Aren't you having any, Carrie?"

She tossed her blond hair and patted her stomach, which looked flat even under her billowy print dress. "I'm watching my weight."

"Since when?" Tara asked.

"You know what they say—a woman can never be too rich or too thin." Carrie shrugged. "I'm never gonna be rich, so I might as well be thin."

"You look great to me." Jack's eyes touched on Tara. "You both do. You're built alike, even though Tara's a lot taller."

"I take after my father," Tara said. "He was tall."

Jack had already noticed that. Family photos plastered the walls, including a few of her late father and sister. Sunny had been fair, like Carrie, but Mr. Greer had dark hair and eyebrows. Tara didn't share his high forehead and the long shape of his face but, as she said, she'd inherited his height.

"You all have one thing in common," Jack said. "Good looks."

"Such a charmer you are," Carrie said.

He grinned at her and dug in to the pie, moaning softly while he chewed and swallowed. "You should reconsider having a piece, Carrie. This is some seriously good pie."

"Thank you," Carrie said. "Is your mom a good cook?"

Jack smiled. "My dad is. My mother swears that's the reason she never perfected the art."

Carrie laughed. "What do your parents do?"

"They own a real-estate business together," he replied. "I already told you about my brother. I've also got two sisters, Annalise and Maria."

"What do they do?"

"Annalise is a wife and mother. She stays home and raises my two nephews, exactly what she's always wanted to do. Now, Maria, she's the opposite." He took a breath, about to tell Carrie what his sister did for a living.

"She's single," Tara cut in, sending him a sidelong glance that looked as if she was trying to communicate something to him. "Jack's sister Maria doesn't have plans to get married any time soon."

"Is she dating anyone?" Carrie asked.

Jack gazed across the table at Tara and raised his eyebrows, curious as to what she'd say next. Even though it was true that Maria wasn't in the market for a husband, he hadn't told Tara that.

"Nobody in particular," Tara said. "She's like Jack. She plays the field."

"Is that so?" Carrie frowned before directing her attention to Jack. "I hadn't figured you for a player, Jack."

"I'm not." Jack shook his head, looking directly at Tara. She'd explain later what was going on. For now, he was willing to play along. "Especially not compared to my sister, I hear."

"Maria's a little older than Jack, so the whole family's hoping she'll settle down," Tara said. "Isn't that right, Jack?"

"That's right," Jack agreed.

"I should certainly hope so," Carrie said.

It was time, Jack thought, to change the subject.

"By the way, Carrie, I've been meaning to ask if you need me to watch Danny for you Wednesday night," he said. "I know that's one of the nights Tara has spinning class."

"Would you?" Carrie clasped her hands in front of her. "You are a terrific guy."

"Just tell me when to be here," Jack said.

"Why do you need a babysitter, Mom?" Tara asked. "Where are you going Wednesday night?"

Carrie hesitated. "Out to dinner with a friend."

Tara considered her. "The same friend who gave you the cat?"

After a long moment, Carrie said, "The same one."

"So you're going on a date with Gus?" Tara asked.

"Not a date," Carrie protested, shaking her head so quickly her hair rustled. "We're just two people having dinner together."

That must have been the wording Gus had used when he convinced Carrie to go out with him. Jack wondered if that tactic would work on Tara. After he finagled it so he could walk her home tonight, he might find out.

TARA STIFLED ANOTHER of the yawns that had been occurring with increasing frequency as the evening wore on. Though it was only a few minutes past nine, at any other time she would excuse herself and go home.

Not tonight. No way would she leave Jack alone with her mother. After she and Jack pitched in to help Carrie with the postdinner cleanup, Danny had corralled the three of them into admiring Billy the kitten. Now Danny had gone to sleep and they were sitting on her mother's spacious front porch, the best part of the house.

"Tara, honey, you seem all tuckered out," her mother said. "You should go home and go to sleep."

Tara blinked a few times to clear the fatigue from her eyes and injected brightness into her voice. "I'm fine."

"You sure about that?" Carrie asked. "We had a late night yesterday at O'Malley's. And didn't you get up early this morning to kayak before you went fishing?"

"Yes, but I'm not..." Another yawn interrupted what Tara had been about to say. "Okay. I admit it. I'm tired."

"If you're too tired to walk home, maybe Jack can drive you," Carrie suggested.

"Be happy to," Jack said.

"I can walk. It's only a few blocks." Tara immediately realized her mistake. She'd stayed this long only because she was afraid to leave Jack alone with her mother. And now she'd passed up a chance to get him out of the house. "But if Jack is ready to leave, perhaps he can walk with me."

She read surprise on his face. No wonder. She'd been sending hot and cold signals at him since they met.

"Sounds good to me," Jack said. "I've got a fear of being the thing that wouldn't leave, so I was just about to say my goodbyes."

"You don't have to be afraid of anything like that," Carrie said. "Remember how delightful you are."

Jack slapped his forehead. "How could I forget?"

They both laughed at what was obviously an inside joke. Great. Her mother was becoming buddies with the man who threatened life as she and Tara knew it.

Tara stood up. "Thanks for dinner, Mom. Ready to go, Jack?"

"Yes." He rose, crossed to where her mother sat on a wicker chair and smiled down at her. "Thanks for inviting me, Carrie. As fantastic as dinner was, the company was even better."

"You're welcome any time, Jack," her mother said. "I'd love to have you over again."

"Don't think I won't hold you to that," he said.

Tara's temples throbbed. Could the situation get any worse? This time she made herself yawn, even adding a sound effect.

"I better get your daughter home before she passes out on her feet," Jack told her mother. He crossed to Tara's side and put a hand at her elbow. Warmth spread underneath his hand, unwelcome but not surprising.

She moved from him so his hand fell away, then she hurried down the porch steps. "Bye, Mom," she called.

Jack caught up to her on the sidewalk when she was almost even with the next house.

"When you decide to leave," he said, "you really get up and go."

"It is getting late," Tara said, although that

wasn't exactly true. "And it's not like you needed more time to flatter my mother."

The instant the words left her mouth, Tara knew she'd said the wrong thing. What's more, she'd sounded petty and mean-spirited. Her stomach turned.

"I'm sorry," she said. "I shouldn't have said that."

"Your mom deserved the praise," Jack said. "She's a nice person and an excellent cook. Gourmet quality, even."

The canopy of trees they were passing under obscured the full moon—perfect timing. It afforded Tara a few moments to get her thoughts in order. The trouble was they were as jumbled as the ingredients in her mother's chicken pasta.

"Why did you tell me she was a terrible cook?" he asked.

They stepped into the moonlight and her respite was over. He was gazing down at her as he walked in that effortless, loose-limbed way that was so attractive. She'd dated a fair bit over the years but seldom had a man ever been so focused on her. It was as though he was watching every nuance of her expression. If she told him anything other than the truth, or at least a sanitized version, he'd know she was lying.

"I didn't want you to come to dinner," she said.

"I figured that," he said. "But why? And while

I'm wondering about things, what was the deal with what you said about Maria?"

Tara felt her heart drumming against her chest. He was already suspicious of her motives. It wouldn't take much of a leap for him to resurrect the suspicion that she might be Hayley Cooper, especially now that he'd seen the photos in her mother's house. Tara might be tall like her father, but she didn't resemble anyone in her family. How she handled his questions was vitally important.

"I was trying to get off the topic of what Maria did for a living," Tara said. "I don't want my mother to know she's a private investigator."

"Why not?"

"Mom always has a tough time getting through the anniversary week of my father's and sister's deaths," Tara said. The statement had the benefit of being true. Even now, she was reluctant to lie to him. "I couldn't let you say anything to upset her."

"I wouldn't do that," Jack said.

"Not intentionally," Tara said. "But I'm the only family she has left. How do you think she'd feel if she knew you came to Wawpaney because you suspected she'd abducted me?"

"Whoa," Jack said. "I never suspected that."

"Not now that you know her, no. Now you see how ridiculous that is." Tara was gaining momentum as she talked. Even to her own ears, she sounded convincing. "The reason you and I met was because I happen to resemble this missing girl. Do you really think my mother needs that extra stress in her life this week?"

"When you put it that way," Jack said, "I guess not."

Tara felt almost light-headed with relief, but she wasn't through yet. "Then promise me you won't mention it to her."

Jack waited a few beats before answering. She held her breath the entire time.

"I promise, except maybe you're not giving her enough credit," Jack said. "I realize losing your father and sister devastated her. But as you pointed out before, it happened a long time ago. She might be ready to move on."

"I'll believe that when I see it," Tara said.

"We're already seeing it," Jack said. "She's going out with Gus Wednesday night, isn't she?"

Tara sent him a sharp look. The moon was bright enough that it cast a soft glow over him, illuminating his classic features and highlighting that attractive widow's peak. "How did you know about that, anyway?"

"Gus told me," he said.

"Gus actually used the word *date?*" She put emphasis on the last word.

"Gus said he asked your mom to dinner," Jack said. "I'm not sure if he used the word date or not."

"So it's possible he didn't specify that it was a date? Did he say where he intended to take her?"

Jack laughed. "I didn't ask follow-up questions."

"Why not?" she demanded, but she was smiling when she said it.

"I'm a guy," he said. "That's not what we do."

"You ask me a lot of questions," she pointed out.

"I'm trying to get to know you better," Jack said. "I've got a couple questions in mind right now."

The toe of her sandal caught in a crack on the sidewalk. She stumbled. His hand shot out to right her.

"Thanks," she said.

"That's me," he said, "the knight in shining armor coming to the rescue."

"Ha! I wouldn't go that far."

"You can't blame a guy for trying," he said.

They walked in silence for a few paces past the modest houses with the well-kept yards that were a staple of the neighborhood. The streets were quiet, as they usually were at this time of night, whether it was a weekend or weekday.

The turmoil was inside Tara. She felt her stomach tightening in anticipation of what he might ask. After another few paces, she noticed he was still holding her arm. "You can let go now."

"Do I have to?" There was a chuckle in his voice.

"Yes." She didn't feel any less tense when he was no longer touching her, not with the uncertainty of what he'd ask hanging over her. "What did you want to ask me?"

"How good a volleyball player are you?"

She relaxed, but only slightly. "I'm decent. Why?"

"I heard you were a star in high school and that you passed up scholarship offers."

Tara doubted her mother had revealed that information. Her mom had gently dissuaded her from taking one of the scholarships, pointing out how far the colleges offering them were from home.

"Art's been talking about me, hasn't he?" she asked.

"How did you know it was Art?"

"Logic. He's the one most likely to phrase it like that." She nodded across the empty street to indicate they should cross. It was so quiet she could hear the click of her sandals on the pavement. But then serenity was abundant year-round in Wawpaney. Her mother always said that was the quality she liked best about the town. "I don't think I passed up much of anything."

"A full ride to a Division one college sounds like something pretty great to me."

"It's a gamble is what it is," she said when they reached the other side of the street. "You're involved in sports. You know athletic scholarships don't come with four-year guarantees. Get injured and you can kiss your scholarship goodbye."

"Athletes recover from injuries all the time." Jack sounded slightly defensive. "Sometimes they come back stronger than before."

"Yeah, well. I wasn't willing to take that chance. Volleyball wasn't that important to me. It's not like I could make a career of it."

"Misty May-Treanor and Kerri Walsh did." He named the two most celebrated female beach volleyball players in the United States. The two-time Olympic gold medallists had both been college stars before transitioning to the two-player beach game.

"They beat astronomical odds," Tara said. "They're the exception, not the rule."

"What's to say you wouldn't have been an exception?" Jack asked.

"Lots of things. My talent level, for one."

"Art said you're oozing talent."

"Art exaggerates." She slowed down and indicated her house. She hadn't left the porch light on, but the moon illuminated everything she loved about the place. The flowers she'd planted along the perimeter of the house. The uneven roof line that lent the home character. The coat of pale yellow paint on the stucco walls. "There's my place."

"Nice," he said. "How long have you lived there?"

"About eight years," she said. "The location's

perfect, close enough to Mom if she needs anything, far enough away for privacy."

"It's kind of dark," he said. "I'll walk you to
the door."

He took her gently by the arm, something he
seemed to like to do. She expected to tense at his
touch. Her body relaxed instead. Had he been any
other man, she wouldn't fight the attraction.

"What if I come watch your volleyball game
Monday night and judge for myself whether Art
is right?" he asked.

The ball of anxiety she thought had dissipated
rose to her throat. "I'd rather you didn't."

"Then here's another question for you," he said.
"What can I do to convince you I'm a good guy?"

The melancholy note in his voice tugged at her.
How could she claim to have a negative impression
of him after watching him interact with Danny and
the other kids at the camp? If she'd been dating
him, she'd heartily approve of the way he treated
her mother.

"I already know you're a good guy," she said.

He cocked his head. "Then why have you been
trying so hard to keep me at arm's length?"

Her skin tingled where he still touched her.
What excuse could she give that would both be believable and convince him to stay away from her?

"I don't quite know how to explain it," Tara said.

"I guess it's because you make me…uncomfortable."

He looked her straight in the eye. "You mean because I'm attracted to you?"

She'd meant because he was a danger to her. The sexual pull between them, though, complicated matters even further.

"Yes," she said.

He let go of her arm and touched her cheek. "It doesn't make me uncomfortable that you're attracted to me."

She rolled her eyes. "That's because you're a man."

He laughed. "Good point. For a minute there, I thought you'd deny there was something between us."

"Would it do any good if I did?"

Two of his fingers slid to the pulse point at the side of her neck. "Not when I can feel your heart racing."

"Damn heart," she said.

He laughed again. "What are we gonna do about it?"

"Nothing," she said. "I'm not in the habit of making out with the tourists."

"Very glad to hear it," he said. "But you know what they say? There's an exception to every rule."

"Why would I make you the exception?"

"Because this feeling, this chemistry that's between us, it doesn't happen very often."

Tara swallowed. "All the more reason to resist it. When something burns this bright, this fast, it will fizzle just as quickly."

"Let's find out." He traced her lips with his fingertips. "If it fizzles like you say, our problems will be solved."

Something was off with his logic. The trouble was, something was equally wrong with Tara's brain. She couldn't think, could barely form a coherent thought. He was standing so close she imagined she could feel the heat of his body. Or maybe the heat was coming off her.

Her back was against the front door. He placed one hand on either side of her. Most of the men she'd dated had been roughly her height. Jack was at least four inches taller. He put a finger under her chin and tipped it upward, then he dipped his head.

Their mouths met in a slow, sweet exploration. The contact was featherlight, yet Tara couldn't deny—from the jolt that traveled through her—that she wanted more from this man. She reached up and twined her arms around his neck, pulling his mouth down more securely on hers.

He tasted delicious, better than her favorite ice cream. His tongue traced her lips, then parted her mouth and delved inside. She circled it with her own tongue, dimly aware there should be some reason to resist him but unable to bring to mind what it was.

As his tongue thrust inside her mouth, she matched his motions. Their bodies plastered against each other, pressed so closely together she could feel the muscles in his chest, the flat plane of his abdomen, the unmistakable rigidness of his erection.

With her back against the door, there was nowhere to go. That didn't matter. She no longer thought about getting away from him. She only wanted to be closer.

His hand traveled up her rib cage and cupped her breast. She moaned, leaning into his hand. Liquid heat pooled in her center. She rubbed against him. This time he was the one who moaned.

She deepened the kiss. Sensations flooded her until nothing was more important than this moment and this man. The kiss went on and on and on. Then suddenly there was air where his mouth had been. Her fingers were still tangled in his hair. She tried to pull his head back down to hers and met resistance.

"Why did you stop?" Her voice sounded breathless.

He cleared his throat. "I'm trying to prove I'm a good guy."

She blinked up at him, not understanding.

"I'm gonna hate myself for this," he said. "But

if you're not inviting me inside, we need to stop right now."

He was asking if she intended to invite him not only into her bed but into her life. Temptation gripped her. A little voice inside her head whispered for her to take a chance.

Yes, he was a tourist who would soon leave the Eastern Shore. He was also the first man who had excited her in a very long time. A man she'd met only because his sister suspected she might be the missing Hayley Cooper. A cold chill ran through her. That was a possibility Tara hadn't been able to rule out.

She wet her well-kissed, swollen lips and cleared her throat. "I'm not inviting you in."

He winced, stepped back from her and covered his heart with his hand. "I was right. I do hate myself."

She couldn't help but smile. "You are a good guy, Jack DiMarco."

She unlocked the door and backed inside, her eyes still on his. With the moonlight glowing down on him, he looked open and honest.

"Are you at least okay with me coming to your volleyball game?" he asked.

She shouldn't be, for the same reason she hadn't invited him inside.

"C'mon." He cocked his head. "We good guys, we're hard to find."

She bit her lip, intending to say no. No words came out of her mouth, but her head nodded. She shut the door on his smile, aware that their experiment had failed.

The kiss hadn't extinguished the sizzle. It was still burning brightly.

CHAPTER TEN

TARA SAT BOLT UPRIGHT in bed on Monday morning, her heart pounding and tears running down her face. She imagined that she could feel the woman's fingers digging into her shoulders even though that was impossible.

It had only been a dream.

Or a memory.

The sequence was always the same. A dark room, Tara's own choking sobs and then the woman grabbing her shoulders and shaking her so that her head snapped back and forth.

"Stop that damn crying, you little brat!" the woman would yell. Her face was usually in shadows, but not always. A light shone somewhere in the room.

Tara could never figure out why she was crying or exactly where they were. The only thing of which she was absolutely certain was that Carrie Greer was not the woman shaking her.

The images had come to her over the years dozens of times, dating back to early childhood. They intruded on her when she was both awake and asleep, although it was impossible to pinpoint the first time it had happened.

As Tara got older, the woman rarely encroached on her thoughts during the day. At night, the dream came less and less frequently until years passed without Tara being wrenched out of a deep sleep.

If Tara had thought about the woman at all in the past few years, it was to convince herself she was the stuff of nightmares.

Jack's appearance in Wawpaney had cast that theory into serious doubt. The specter of the woman had nagged at her all day Sunday, through morning services at church to the local talent show she'd volunteered to judge in the evening.

If Tara was Hayley Cooper, it made sense that the woman was a real person from her past. Maybe the woman was even her biological mother, the very woman who had hired Jack's sister to find her little girl.

Tara kneaded her forehead, feeling the beginnings of a headache coming on. No matter what Carrie Greer had done, Tara intended to protect her. The uncertainty, however, was slowly driving her crazy.

She switched on her bedside lamp, blinking against the sudden influx of light. The darkness of the night peeked through a crack between the windowsill and the bottom of her mini blind.

It didn't matter that dawn was still hours away.

She'd never be able to go back to sleep, especially when there was a computer in her living room.

A short time later she was sitting at the rolltop desk she intended to refinish, tapping her fingers on the faded surface as she waited for the desktop computer to boot up. It was at least six or seven years old, a computer-age dinosaur.

Now that she'd made the decision to try to find out more about Hayley Cooper, she could hardly contain her impatience.

The first time they'd talked, Jack had told her his sister had put Hayley Cooper's age-progression photo on a missing-persons website.

The icons on her desktop slowly appeared. She moved her mouse to the icon for the internet and clicked, waiting for long minutes to get online. She typed "missing persons cold cases" into a search engine. Dozens of results popped up. She clicked on the first one.

A website materialized with a photo of the missing person of the week, a young Chicago woman who'd disappeared six years ago after a night of drinking. Had Hayley Cooper's photo appeared in that very spot on this exact website?

She found the search function on the page and typed in Hayley Cooper's name. Her fingers shook so much it took her three tries. Side-by-side photos appeared. One was the age progression of the woman who looked so much like her. The other was of a very young girl, her lips creased in a closemouthed smile that didn't quite reach her eyes. Honey-brown bangs fell into her eyes. Was it significant that Tara couldn't remember having bangs?

Hayley's vital statistics at the time of the abduction were beneath the photo: three years old, thirty inches tall, twenty-eight pounds, golden-brown hair, brown eyes. Her date of birth was more than a year after Tara's own, a reassuring sign. Also noted was the date of her disappearance and the fact that it was a nonfamily abduction. The date was April 14, 1984. That was twenty-eight years ago.

Tara scrolled down the page to the two short paragraphs that provided the details of the disappearance.

Hayley was last seen in the women's department of a Macy's Department Store at the Green Acres Mall in Oak Hill, Kentucky. She liked to hide in the circular racks of clothes whenever she went shopping with her mother. This time, when her mother tried to get her to come out she was gone.

Police found no witnesses. Hayley has not been seen again, but her family believes she is alive and may not know she was abducted.

That was it. Tara had no memory of ever disappearing inside a clothes rack. However, she could easily envision a little girl hiding from a mother who was cruel to her. Maybe the girl hadn't been snatched from the women's department. Maybe she'd been trying to get away from her mother. Maybe whoever came across her had found her crying and unhappy. Maybe it hadn't been so much a crime, but an opportunity to help a child in need.

Tara closed her eyes and ran a hand over her face. She didn't know that had happened and she certainly hadn't discovered anything on the website that would lead her to believe she was Hayley Cooper.

Before she realized her intentions, she was on a popular internet auction site, searching for a home paternity kit and making sure it could also verify maternity. Or not. She bought one from an official-sounding lab with DNA in the name, paying more for shipping so it would arrive more quickly. Her stomach churned and rolled as she finalized the payment.

That done, she leaped up from the computer, her head feeling as though it might explode.

She crossed the room to the window, drawing aside a blind. The weak light of dawn cast a hazy glow over her yard and the street in front of her house. She had plenty of time to go for a run and not be late to carpool to camp. It wasn't quite bright enough unless she wore the reflective vest her mother had bought her for Christmas, the one she'd stuffed into the back of a drawer.

A half hour and about four miles later, sweat dripped down her face and from between her breasts. She'd run faster than she ever had before, hoping to clear her mind. It hadn't worked. She couldn't stop going over the details of the case or thinking about the woman in her dream.

She slowed to a walk, her mind still racing. Yes, she looked eerily like the grown-up version of Hayley Cooper. And, yes, she could come up with a scenario that explained the woman in her dreams. But there were other facts that pointed to Tara being exactly who she'd always thought she was.

Tara was more than a year older than Hayley Cooper. She wasn't sure exactly when she and her mother had moved to the Eastern Shore, but it was highly possible it had been before the Hayley Cooper kidnapping.

She did some mental calculations. She was thirty-two. She and her mother had moved to Wawpaney sometime after the drownings, when Tara was three years old. That was twenty-nine years ago. In 1983.

Hayley Cooper had been abducted in 1984.

The dates didn't add up!

Her elation faded as quickly as it had appeared.

The dates didn't add up as long as her mother had told the truth about when they'd moved to Wawpaney.

But how could Tara ever determine that?

It wasn't yet six-thirty. The neighborhood was just waking up, with lights shining from the occasional window and the distant sound of a car motor starting.

She was almost surprised to find herself on her mother's street, although it probably wasn't a coincidence, considering what was on her mind.

A movement caught her eye—a woman, walking down her sidewalk with the aid of a cane to where a newspaper lay in her driveway. She recognized Mrs. Jorgenson, her mother's longtime next-door neighbor. She remembered Mrs. Jorgenson once telling her she'd resided in the same house for fifty years.

Mrs. Jorgenson would have been living next door when Tara and her mother moved in.

"Mrs. Jorgenson!" Tara called, raising her voice to be heard and waving.

Mrs. Jorgenson stopped and pivoted, waiting while Tara jogged to catch up to her.

"You beat me out of bed this morning, Tara," Mrs. Jorgenson said. "I'm usually the early bird in the neighborhood and I haven't even had my coffee yet."

"Coffee," Tara said. "Do you think I could have a cup?"

Mrs. Jorgenson looked surprised. However, she was much too polite to point out it was rude to invite yourself into a neighbor's house before seven in the morning.

"Why, certainly," she said. "Come on in."

The kitchen felt too warm after the cool air of the morning. Mrs. Jorgenson led her to the kitchen, which was small and cramped but somehow inviting.

"Artie's not awake yet, so we need to be quiet," she whispered. "How do you like your coffee, dear?"

"Extra cream and extra sugar, please." Tara hoped that by diluting the strong taste she might be able to tolerate it.

A pot of coffee was already brewing. In no time, Mrs. Jorgenson set a full coffee mug in front of Tara.

"Thanks." Tara took a sip and tried not to grimace. She was too impatient not to get right to the point. "You've always been such a wonderful neighbor. How long has it been?"

Subtle, Tara thought. Really subtle.

"How long has what been, dear?"

"How long have you and my mother been neighbors?"

"Oh, heavens. A long time."

This wasn't going well. "Do you remember me as a little girl?"

"Of course I do," Mrs. Jorgenson said. "I remember the day you moved in. You were, let me see, three or four years old, if I'm not mistaken. Such a quiet thing. But that was understandable, considering what you and your mother had been through."

"So you knew about the drownings right away?"

"Oh, heavens, yes. Dawn told me before you even moved in."

"Dawn?"

"Your mother's best friend from high school. She and your mother had lost touch, but when your mother called and told her what had happened Dawn invited both of you to come live with her."

"I don't remember Dawn," Tara said.

"Such a nice lady she was," Mrs. Jorgenson said. "Never raised her voice to anyone. She moved away about six months after you got here."

"Because of a job transfer?" Tara provided the reason her mother had given.

"That's right," Mrs. Jorgenson said. "She moved here because of a man. I think she met him on vacation. Dawn was so smitten she bought this house. Wouldn't you know, she caught him cheating. She was a bank teller, so it wasn't hard for her to get a transfer."

That synced nicely with what Tara's mother had told her. "And I was three, you say."

"Yes," she said. "Three when you moved in."

"So that was 1983," she said.

"That sounds right," Ms. Jorgenson said.

For the first time since Jack had shown Tara the age-progression photo, she didn't feel as if a weight was pressing on her heart. If she'd been here at the Eastern Shore in 1983, she couldn't possibly have been abducted from a shopping mall in Kentucky in 1984.

Had she known that last night, Tara very well might have invited Jack into her bed. She almost snorted. Who was she kidding? She would have dragged him there.

IF JACK HADN'T HAD AN agenda, the throbbing in his shoulder would have driven him back to his bay-front house after camp and rehab on Monday afternoon. The ibuprofen tablets he kept there didn't help much, but sitting still usually did.

Though, if he'd taken it easy today he might not be suffering. Operating on the principle that more is better, he'd gone against Art Goodnight's advice to work out the shoulder only once a day to speed up the excruciatingly slow healing process.

The throb in his shoulder told him he shouldn't have.

He heard the thwacking sound of hands hitting

balls and voices celebrating a point being scored before he saw the group playing volleyball on the strip of beach adjacent to the public pier in Cape Charles where he and Tara had fished with Danny.

The net was set up beyond the surf line, with six players on each side, only a few of whom were women.

Jack hung back on the wooden walkway, his attention snagged by one of them. Tara was taller than some of the men and nearly as tall as the others, but that wasn't what set her apart. Neither were the long, toned limbs left bare by her sleeveless red top and navy shorts. Something else was at play, a characteristic shared by every top athlete Jack had ever known.

Confidence radiated from her, and not only because of the way she carried herself. Her weight was balanced on the balls of her feet and her head mimicked the motion of the volleyball. Anyone watching could tell she wanted the ball to come to her.

She was in her team's front row in the outside hitter position. A guy on the opposing team served a bullet that one of Tara's teammates bumped to the setter, a short woman in the center of the front line. The woman got under the ball and sent it looping in a high arc over to Tara.

Tara leaped, elevating herself over the sand with impressive loft. While airborne, she cocked her right elbow and spiked the volleyball. It shot over the net, finding an empty space on the court and kicking up sand.

"Damn, Tara!" exclaimed a big, barrel-chested guy who looked as if he could lift the combined weight of his teammates. "Do you have to keep doing that to us?"

"Yes, she does," retorted the short woman who had set Tara up for the spike. It was Mary Dee, her friend from the ice cream shop. "It's only fair. You had her on your team last week."

"I tried to get her this week, too," the big guy said. "But she wouldn't take a bribe."

"You only offered me five bucks, Butch," Tara said.

"Hey, I'm not a rich man," Butch said.

"And that's why Tara's gonna make you pay," Mary Dee retorted.

Smiling to himself at the good-natured banter, Jack resumed his walk to the beach, the sand getting in his sandals. He'd never get tired of breathing in the salty air. A few players noticed his approach, including Mary Dee.

"Jack!" she called, waving wildly. "Are you here to play?"

He imagined lifting his arm to serve a volleyball and the shoulder gave another throb.

"To watch," he called back, his eyes glued to

Tara. She nodded in greeting, her teeth flashing in the rapidly fading daylight.

A smile was a good start. She'd given him a few of them today at camp, too. He interpreted the smiles to mean she didn't regret their kiss Saturday night. He was increasingly certain he'd been right to ask if she wanted to stop.

When they made love, he wanted her to be sure.

"Is that your husband, Mary Dee?" asked a skinny teammate who would be the next server.

"No, sir," Mary Dee said. "Jack's here for Tara, not me."

"I heard that, Tara. He'll make you nervous," Butch called from the other side of the net in a teasing singsong voice.

"You wish!" Mary Dee hollered.

Jack retraced his steps, sitting down at the bottom of the wooden stairs so he wasn't directly in Tara's line of vision. Nerves could do funny things to an athlete. He'd seen baseball players who should have been stars crumble when the going got tough.

The game resumed, with Tara spiking the ball with precision whenever it was within reach. The only snag her teammates ran into was getting the ball to her. When she touched it, whether from the back line or the front, her team usually got the point. Eventually they won the game.

Tara's teammates gathered around her when it

was over, exchanging high fives. "MVP! MVP!" Mary Dee chanted.

Tara slung an arm around her friend. "Only because you set me up."

"Many can be set up," Mary Dee said. "Only a few can dominate a game."

"I hardly dominated," Tara said.

Jack got to his feet and approached the two women, not only impressed with the way Tara had played. Proud, too. Mary Dee gestured to him.

"Settle this for us, Jack," Mary Dee said. "Did Tara dominate or didn't she?"

"Tara dominated," he answered.

"Told you so." Mary Dee smiled at Jack, displaying a charming gap between her front teeth. "You should take Tara out for a drink at O'Malley's."

"Don't pay attention to my friend," Tara told Jack. "She thinks it's her duty to arrange my social life."

"Who can't use a little help from their friends?" Mary Dee shot back. "You are going to take her out, right, Jack?"

"I was about to ask before you beat me to it." A corner of Jack's mouth rose. "But I don't want to step on anyone's toes. Doesn't the whole group go out?"

"We used to, back when most of us were single," Mary Dee said. "Now it's hit or miss. Tonight's a miss. Listen, I've gotta run."

Mary Dee hugged Tara, hanging on to her for an extra few seconds. "Do yourself a favor and go out with the man, Tara," she whispered into her friend's ear, loudly enough that Jack heard. To Jack, she said, "Hope I'll be seeing a lot more of you, Jack."

"You, too," Jack said.

Mary Dee picked up her flip-flops and took off through the sand, hurrying to catch up to one of her teammates. The rest of the crowd had also dispersed, leaving Jack and Tara alone on the beach.

"Well, that sure was embarrassing," Tara said, brushing back some stray hairs that had come loose from her ponytail. "Please don't feel obligated to take me out."

"Okay." Jack rubbed his chin. "Then how do you feel about coming back to my place to see my etchings?"

Amusement played about her lips. "You have etchings?"

"I might," he said slowly. "Except I'm not really sure what etchings are."

"Maybe another time," Tara said, laughing. Even in the dim light he could see the sparkle that came into her eyes. "On second thought, I believe I will take you up on that drink."

He felt his face split into a wide smile. "Chalk one up for the good guys."

"Don't get ahead of yourself, pal. It's only a drink."

"I'm looking forward to it." He reached out and touched her cheek, mostly because he couldn't stop himself. "But when I was smiling, I was thinking about the 'maybe another time.' I really like the sound of that maybe."

She let him keep his hand exactly where it was and smiled, too. "It doesn't take much to make you happy, does it?"

He elevated his eyebrows. "Come to my place one day and you'll find out."

"C'mon, let's go to O'Malley's." She started for the wooden walkway, probably thinking she'd put an end to the subject. She didn't know him very well yet. Once she did, she'd discover he finished what he started, even if it was only a conversation.

He fell into step beside her. "I was serious about the invitation."

"Good." Her voice was matter-of-fact. "Because I was serious about the maybe."

This time Jack kept the smile to himself. Something had shifted in their relationship since Saturday. Whatever had caused the shift wasn't important.

The important thing was that he was finally making progress with Tara.

TARA SAT ACROSS FROM Jack a short time later in a booth at O'Malley's, trying not to stare at him. Even though the dinner hour was over, the pub was doing a fair bit of business. Jack, however, was by far the most interesting customer.

Of course, he'd also held that distinction Friday night when the place was packed.

What a difference a few days made. Now that she knew for certain that she wasn't Hayley Cooper, she could finally stop viewing him as a threat and get to know him as a man.

A man who was intensely appealing.

Goose bumps broke out on her arms even though she'd thrown a light athletic jacket over her sleeveless top. Thinking about how appealing Jack was reminded Tara that Mary Dee had urged her once to describe what she was looking for in a man.

Integrity. Kindness. A sense of humor. A way with kids. An active lifestyle.

Jack had all those traits and more wrapped up in a sexy six-foot-two package. She liked the way he looked, too, from his square chin to his chocolate-brown eyes to the thick hair that sprang back from his widow's peak.

She also liked that he didn't wear his clothes tight to show off his lean, muscular build and his broad shoulders. She narrowed her eyes. Was one of his shoulders drooping?

"Did you have the surgery on your right shoulder?" she asked.

"Surgeries," he corrected. "Two of them. Both on the right shoulder. Why?"

"You're holding the shoulder funny," she said. "Like it hurts."

"You know what they say." Both corners of his mouth rose, then fell. "No pain, no gain."

"That saying doesn't refer to shoulder surgeries. It's about working out," Tara said. "What exactly happened, if you don't mind my asking?"

"It's a long story," he said.

She indicated their full mugs of beer. They'd ordered a couple of drafts at the bar, where she greeted some people she knew, and carried them to the booth in the dining room. "I drink slowly, so I've got time."

"Where do you want me to start?" he said.

"How about the first shoulder surgery?"

"That would have been my third year of pro ball," he said. "I didn't get drafted until I finished college. Third round by the Cincinnati Kings. I was progressing through the minor league ranks pretty well, even got a call-up to the bigs one September and an invitation the next season to spring training. That's when the doctor ordered an MRI of my sore shoulder and we found out I had a torn rotator cuff. So I had my first surgery."

"What went wrong?" she asked.

"At first, nothing. I worked myself into shape and two years later I was back at spring training with a real chance to make the team. They decided they wanted to take a longer look at me and sent me back to the minors. That's when I reinjured the shoulder and had to go under the knife again." He stared down at the beer before gazing back up at her. He looked as if he was trying to smile, but he didn't manage it. "The Kings cut me loose."

"How long ago was this?"

"Almost five years ago," he said. "But I didn't give up. I took a lot longer rehabbing the shoulder this time, then played for an unaffiliated team before getting signed by the Carolina Stars."

"I've heard of the Stars," Tara said. "Weren't they an expansion team in the major leagues a few years back?"

He nodded. "That's probably why they took a chance on me. The snag was that I'd be strictly a relief pitcher."

"Did it work out?"

"Surprisingly well," he said. "I moved from A ball to AA to AAA, then was called up in September. And last year I made it to the show. On opening day, I was on the Carolina Stars roster."

She leaned forward, eager to hear the rest of the story. The couple in the booth closest to them got up to leave, giving them some privacy. "Did you get into any games?"

"One," he said. "In that game, I tried to tag a runner out at first base and broke my collarbone in the collision."

"Your collarbone? I thought the problem was with your shoulder."

"It is," he said. "The collarbone healed, but the soreness remained. I didn't do well in spring training this season and got sent back to AA ball. The problem wouldn't go away. This time the team doctor figured out I had a torn labrum."

Tara winced. Volleyball players used the same overhead motion as pitchers to spike and serve. One of the players on her high school team had suffered a similar injury to the one Jack described, then had given up the sport entirely.

"A torn labrum doesn't regenerate, does it?" she asked.

"I've come back from injury before. I can do it again," he said with a stubborn tilt to his chin. She noticed that he didn't answer the question.

"Will you have a third surgery?"

"No. There's a school of thought that physical therapy is better than surgery for torn labrums. That's why I hired Art Goodnight. I'm working on strengthening the other muscles in my shoulder."

Something about the story seemed off. "And the Carolina Stars' doctor—he thinks you can come back from this and pitch again?"

"That's what *I* think," Jack said. "The Stars cut me, too."

Tara had formed the impression that he had a job in baseball waiting for him once his rehabilitation was over. She couldn't have been more wrong. "It sounds like a long shot."

"I've beaten the odds before," he said. "I'll do it again."

"You sound pretty sure of yourself," she said.

"I have to be," he said. "Baseball's my life."

"Oh, come on," she said. "There's more going on in your life than that. I know you work at the Lexington Sportsplex."

He shifted in his seat. "I fill time at the sportsplex between baseball seasons."

"Fill time doing what?" she asked. "It's an indoor sports facility, right?"

"Yeah." He shrugged. "It's not a bad job. I do anything that needs doing, but mostly I help supervise the running of the indoor leagues."

"That sounds like fun," she said. "I wouldn't mind doing that."

"Wouldn't you rather be playing volleyball?" he asked.

"Are we back to that again?" She shrugged. "I've already told you. There's more to life than playing sports."

"Tara!" Mark Ames, a guy she'd dated before he moved out of the area, appeared as if out of nowhere. He approached them with a giant grin on his face. "I knew stopping by the pub tonight was a good idea. You look more beautiful than ever."

Mark had always been effusive with his compliments, which was probably one of the reasons Tara had dated him. His good looks hadn't hurt. He bore a vague resemblance to a young Brad Pitt.

"Mark! What a surprise!" Tara said. "Are you visiting your parents?"

"Haven't you heard?" he asked. "I'm back for good. Dad's getting up there in years, so I'm going into business with him."

Mark's father owned a wholesale seafood business. Before Mark had moved to New York City to work for a friend's sightseeing company, Mark had vowed never to work in the seafood business. Now wasn't the time to bring that up, though. The two men were sizing each other up, like boxers before a fight.

"Mark, this is Jack DiMarco," Tara said. "Jack, Mark Ames."

Jack stuck out a hand first. "Nice to meet you."

Mark hesitated only slightly before taking it. "Likewise. I guess I shouldn't be surprised Tara is seeing somebody."

Tara waited for Jack to correct him. The pause lengthened until it became obvious he didn't intend to.

"What do you do, Jack?" Mark asked.

"I'm a pro baseball player," Jack said.

Mark screwed up his forehead. "I didn't know the Eastern Shore had a pro team."

"It doesn't," Tara cut in. "Jack last played for the Carolina Stars. He's here rehabbing his pitching shoulder."

"So you're a tourist." Mark sounded pleased by his conclusion. "How long will you be here, Jack?"

"I haven't decided yet," Jack said.

"Not long, then," Mark said, nodding slowly. "Good to know."

Mark's comments were getting weirder by the second. Although they'd had some good times, things had never been serious between Tara and Mark. When he moved away, she'd been only mildly disappointed.

"How about you, Mark?" Tara asked. "Is this a temporary move? Or will you settle down here?"

"I'm staying. I'll give you a call sometime. We can get together so I can tell you all about it." He gestured in the direction of the bar. "I'm here with a friend, so I should go. Catch up with you later."

Mark nodded at Jack, who returned the gesture. Jack watched the other man leave before bringing his attention back to her.

"Old boyfriend?" he asked.

"I wouldn't call him a boyfriend exactly but we did go out a few times before he moved to New York City," she said. "A friend of his owns a boat tour company and asked Mark to be one of his boat captains. He must have gotten tired of it."

Jack twisted his beer mug left and right and watched the amber liquid slosh before raising his eyes. "Should I be worried about him?"

She could pretend not to know what he was talking about. Now that she'd verified she wasn't Hayley Cooper, however, there wasn't any need.

She kept her eyes trained on his and shook her head. "No."

"You want to get out of here?" he asked.

She didn't think about it. She just nodded.

He took a swallow of his beer, removed his wallet from his back pocket and slapped some money on the table.

A few people window-shopped along the street outside the pub and a noisy group of tourists was leaving a nearby restaurant, typical activity for a Monday night in summer. Since Jack had left his truck at the fitness club, she'd driven them from the beach to the Cape Charles business district. Her car was parked between two others under a street light.

Jack didn't touch her as they crossed the road, yet she'd never been more aware of him. The tourists were laughing and talking in loud voices, yet she could hear Jack's every breath and sensed the power of his lean, athletic body as he moved.

Her breaths were coming too fast and her palms

growing damp. What exactly had she committed herself to inside the pub by admitting she preferred Jack to Mark Ames? Was Jack expecting her to come to his place or to invite him to hers?

Each step she took closer to the car, it grew harder to breathe. Last night after verifying she wasn't Hayley, she'd all but decided to have a fling with Jack. Now she wasn't sure she could go through with it. She'd always been conservative where sex was concerned. She liked to take her time getting to know a man before going to bed with him. She and Jack hadn't even been on an official date.

"Everything okay?" His voice broke into her toughts. "You seem nervous."

It seemed pointless to deny it. "I am."

"You don't need to be," he said. They reached the driver's side of her car. She turned to face him, and he cupped her cheek. The moonlight softened his features. Her gaze went to his lips, and she remembered what they'd tasted like. Maybe she could throw caution to the wind and indulge herself, after all.

She waited patiently for him to give her one of the standard lines used by guys who were trying to get laid.

I'll be gentle with you.

You won't have to do anything you don't want to do.

You can trust me.

"I can wait until you're ready, no matter how long it takes," he said.

Had she heard him right?

"Excuse me?" she asked.

"Like I told you before, I won't pressure you," he said. "Until you're sure, nothing's going to happen between us."

She frowned. "Nothing at all?"

He laughed and dipped his head, capturing her lips with a swiftness that made her head spin. Her lips clung to his as his mouth moved over hers. She wound her arms around his neck, bringing him closer, opening her mouth in invitation. The kiss went from G-rated to scorching hot in mere seconds.

Suddenly it occurred to her that they were in full view of the noisy tourists and any car that passed by.

She pulled back at the same moment he did, bringing an abrupt end to what had been an amazing kiss.

"Wow," he said.

She wet her lips and cleared her throat. "Are you still okay with taking it slowly?"

"Yeah." He didn't even pause to think about it. "It's enough right now to know I'm the only man in your life."

"Really?" She wasn't sure why she kept pressing him. *Yes, you are,* a little voice inside her head whispered. *You want him to persuade you.*

"Really." He gave her a swift kiss on the lips and pulled back almost before it had begun. "Be careful driving home. I'll see you tomorrow afternoon at camp."

With a smile that looked wistful, he turned and walked in the direction of the fitness club where his car was parked. She stood watching him for long moments, not sure how she managed to resist the overwhelming urge to call him back.

Once she was inside the car, she sat behind the wheel, her head falling back against the cushioned headrest. Her heart was still beating too fast.

Had she really by her silence just said no to a man who'd made it a point not to capitalize on her weakness for him? A man like that came around very seldom, if at all.

She jolted herself out of her stupor and fished in her handbag for her keys. A noise startled her. The ring tone of a cell phone, she realized, but not her phone.

On the passenger seat beside her, the display of a dark-colored phone lit up. Probably Jack's. He'd ridden with her from the beach to the pub. The phone must have fallen out of his pocket.

She picked it up and looked at the name on the display. Maria, it read. Jack's sister, the private investigator who was looking into the Hayley Cooper case.

The phone stopped ringing, no doubt because the caller had been directed to voice mail. Jack's sister would have to wait until tomorrow when Tara returned his cell for Jack to call back.

Tara tossed the phone onto the passenger seat and inserted the keys in the ignition. Before she started the car, Jack's cell phone flashed the message that he had three new voice mails. Were they all from Maria? Maybe there was a family emergency and Jack's sister needed to talk to him right away. The cell phone would be the only means she had of reaching him.

Tara pulled out of the parking spot and turned down the street where the fitness club was located, hoping to see Jack's white pickup. It wasn't there.

She pulled over to the curb, leaving her engine idling while she thought. If Jack's sister had urgent news, it possibly couldn't wait for tomorrow. Then again, hadn't Jack said his sisters called all the time?

Tara dug through her purse until she found the piece of paper where Jack had written down his address. Now she had the option of driving to his beach house tonight and giving him the cell phone.

Of course, if there was no family emergency, maybe she and Jack would do something about their attraction for each other.

Tara put the car in gear and drove, not only unsure of what to do, but of her motivation. She was still trying to decide as she approached the fork in the road that led to Shell Beach.

CHAPTER ELEVEN

JACK LEANED BACK ON THE recliner in the living room of his beach house, letting the ice do its magic on his shoulder.

His first move when he got back to the house had been to strip off his shirt en route to the freezer. He kept special inserts there that fit under his cold therapy wrap. Compression straps kept the wrap in place, enabling him to remain mobile.

Tonight he needed ice for more than his injury. The drive from Cape Charles had taken a good twenty minutes or so and his body still hadn't cooled down from that kiss.

Before he started second-guessing himself for passing up yet another chance to make love to Tara, he picked up the TV remote and switched on a television sports channel.

The Cincinnati Kings were playing the Carolina Stars, the two organizations that had given up on him.

The camera panned in for a close-up of the Stars pitcher, a baby-faced kid Jack didn't recognize. The pitcher appeared to be in his early twenties. If things had gone differently for Jack, he would have made it to the majors at about that age and stuck.

The young pitcher stared down the batter, nodded at the catcher's signal, reared back and let the ball fly.

In time with the pitcher's release, Jack's shoulder gave a sharp twinge. It hurt a little more, though, to watch the batter swing and miss.

Not so long ago, Jack was throwing pitches like that.

He clicked a button on the remote and the television screen went dark. He picked up an issue of *Sports Illustrated* from the side table. The cover story was about the strides the Carolina Stars had made since joining the league as an expansion team.

About ten paragraphs into the story, a quote from the general manager jumped out at him. "Thanks to our excellent scouting system, we identified players we've been able to develop into solid major leaguers."

Jack had been one of those players before he got hurt.

A rapping sounded on the front door. Glad for the interruption, he set down the magazine and got out of the recliner. He didn't have a clue who it could be. In the short time since he'd rented the beach house, this was his first visitor.

He pulled open the door.

Tara stared at him, her eyes huge in her pale face, her lips parted as though asking to be kissed. She'd shed the jacket she wore in the pub and was dressed as she'd been when she played volleyball, in short shorts and a sleeveless top that hugged her breasts. As in the pub, her hair was loose around her shoulders. His body reheated despite the cool from the ice wrap.

"I sure am glad you're exercising your prerogative to change your mind," he said.

He put out his left hand, inviting her to take it so he could pull her inside. She placed something small and hard in his palm. His cell phone.

"You left this in my car," she said. "I thought you might need it. Your sister's called twice since I noticed it."

He felt as if she'd thrown a bucket of ice water in his face. "Annalise?" he asked.

"Maria," she said. "Her name came up on your screen."

"Come on in." He stepped back to make room for her as he checked the phone, noticing how she hesitated before crossing the threshold and pushing the door shut behind her. He dragged his gaze from her and focused on the phone.

"There are some texts, too." Jack clicked through to his messages and read the ones from Maria. He sighed aloud. "She wants to know if I'm okay."

"That's it?" Tara asked like a rational person

who understood too much checking up bordered on paranoia. Too bad his sisters didn't share that mind-set.

"That's it. When I didn't answer her text, she called a few times. When I didn't answer the calls, she texted again." He held up a finger. "Please excuse me a moment."

With his right arm hampered by the wrap, he used his left hand to both hold the phone and type in the text. Im foine? Tslk tomorrow, it read. Maria would have to deal with the typos. He hit the send button.

"That should satisfy her for tonight." Jack was pretty sure Maria would understand that he'd call her in the morning. At least he'd spelled tomorrow right.

"You weren't exaggerating when you said your sisters call all the time, were you?" Tara asked.

"Nope. Not at all."

"Then I'm glad they can't see you now," she said. "That thing on your shoulder looks kind of worrisome."

"It's nothing," he said. "Just a way to promote healing. I was getting ready to take it off when you knocked on the door."

He pulled apart the Velcro compression straps, resulting in a distinctive ripping noise. He shrugged out of the wrap, noticing that Tara's brown eyes had gone wide. She was gaping at his bare chest.

"I take off my shirt when I put on the wrap," he explained. "I can feel the ice working better against my bare skin."

"You don't have any scars." She took a step toward him and he picked out a light, floral scent. Even after playing volleyball, she smelled great. "Just a couple faded marks."

"From the small incisions the doctor made for the arthroscopic surgeries," he said.

"Did the surgeries hurt?"

"Surprisingly, they weren't too bad," he said. "Rehab hurts like a bitch, though."

She reached forward with her right hand and lightly trailed her fingers over the barely visible wounds. He sucked in a breath, afraid to act on her signals in case he was misinterpreting them.

"I have a confession to make," she said in a soft, breathy voice. "I was pretty sure your sister didn't need to talk to you tonight."

Her lips replaced her fingertips on his shoulder, planting soft kisses at the site of his surgeries. She raised her eyes to his. "The phone was an excuse for me to do what you said when I got here."

"What did I say?" He barely got the question past the thickness in his throat. His short-term memory seemed to be malfunctioning.

"That I was exercising my prerogative to change my mind." She traced his lips with her fingertips. "I'm sure now, Jack."

Good things come to those who wait, he thought. He didn't dare say it aloud. He didn't dare say anything for fear she might change her mind again.

That, he didn't think he'd survive.

Her lips grazed his. "Aren't you going to show me where the bedroom is?" she asked, her breath warm and sweet against his mouth.

He almost laughed. The beach house consisted of a combination kitchen/living room, bathroom and single bedroom.

"It's behind door number one." He reached for her and led her there, pushing open the partially cracked door with his foot, telling himself not to rush things. With Tara, he wanted to stretch out his time. "The view from the bedroom is the reason I picked this place."

Through the open blinds the moon reflected off the sand and the gently rippling water of the bay.

On most nights, Jack kept the lights in the bedroom off in order to see the water of the bay through the open blinds. He let go of Tara's hand, crossed the room and pulled the blinds shut, plunging the room into darkness.

"Why did you do that?" she asked.

He switched on his bedside lamp and rejoined her at the foot of the bed. "I'd rather look at you than the view."

Her lips parted and she shook her head. "There you go again."

"I don't know what you mean."

"Why do you think I'm here?" she asked.

He shook his head, still not understanding.

"When you say things like that," she said, "I can't resist you."

"Let's find out if I can do some other things you won't be able to resist." He grinned and pulled her against him. Even her height was a turn-on. Her mouth was just inches below his, waiting for his kiss.

He claimed her soft, willing lips. He'd already figured out she liked long, drugging kisses. She opened her mouth in invitation and his tongue tangled with hers, teasing and tasting. Jack had never been addicted to anything in his life, except perhaps baseball. It occurred to him that he could get hooked on Tara.

He threaded one of his hands in her hair and slid the other slowly up her rib cage until he caressed her full breasts through the material of her shirt. She gasped against his mouth. His body grew hard in response, even harder than when he'd seen her at the door.

She lifted her arms and he pulled her sleeveless shirt and then her sports bra over her head. His fingers were shaking slightly, something that had never happened to him before. For a moment he didn't touch her. He just stared. Her breasts were high and firm, the nipples already taut. Naked from the waist up, she looked like a goddess.

"I've been imagining you like this since I first saw you," he said.

"Really?" Her voice was low pitched and throaty. "In front of the elementary school when you thought I was that missing girl?"

"Maybe not then," he said. "But for sure at the grocery store. I had some naughty thoughts in the produce section."

With her eyes dancing, she moved her hands to her waist and slowly shimmied out of first her shorts and then her panties.

Her legs were long, her stomach flat and her hips slightly rounded, all things that were evident when she was clothed. But her high firm breasts were large for a woman as thin as she was.

"You're gorgeous," Jack said. "Absolutely gorgeous."

"No fair," she said. "I'm the only one who's naked."

He fixed that in record time, wincing in pain when he accidentally jerked his shoulder.

"Does your shoulder hurt?" she asked.

He ignored the throbbing. "It's nothing."

Tara closed the slim gap between them, lightly tracing the shape of his sore shoulder. He groaned and cupped her buttocks, bringing her securely against him, letting her feel how much he wanted her. He couldn't remember ever desiring a woman more.

She lifted her mouth and he covered it with his in a hungry kiss, his tongue advancing and retreating, his hands roaming over her lovely naked skin.

The bed was nearby. He wasn't sure how they got there, but suddenly they were tumbling together to the mattress. The thought ran through his mind that he was falling for her.

He rained kisses from her neck to the slope of her breasts. His tongue circled her nipple, which was already a hard peak. Soft sounds of pleasure escaped her lips. Pressing herself against him, she moved her hips in invitation.

"Ah, Tara," he said.

"Don't you dare ask me if I'm sure," she said.

Jack laughed, amazed that she could both turn him on and amuse him at the same time. "Wouldn't dream of it."

He intended to ease slowly inside her, but then she moved her lower body upward in blatant invitation. He entered her, unable to hold himself back any longer. He didn't have to, because she met him thrust for thrust.

His last coherent thought before he lost himself in her was the same one he'd had when they tumbled together to the bed.

He was falling for her.

TARA CAME SLOWLY AWAKE on Tuesday morning and stretched her limbs, feeling as content as a cat. No, scratch that. As content as a woman who'd been made love to by the most delicious man not once, but twice in—she checked the bedside clock—nine hours.

She sat bolt upright in bed, the sheets falling away from her naked breasts. It was already seven o'clock, and she needed to be at camp by nine.

The view of the bay was once again on display through the bedroom window. Jack must have opened the blinds when he awoke so she could enjoy the view. She smiled at his thoughtfulness. But where was he? She ran her hand over the side of the bed on which he'd slept and found it cold to the touch.

A murmur of voices drifted through the open door of the bedroom from the main part of the house. Did Jack have company? She listened more closely and could make out only Jack's voice. He must be on the telephone.

She pulled her shirt over her head, tugged on her panties and got out of bed. She peeked around the side of the door. Jack sat on one of the kitchen chairs with a cell phone to his ear, his long, hair-sprinkled legs extended in front of him. His dark hair was tousled, he could have used a shave and he wore gym shorts and a T-shirt. Under the shirt his abdomen was flat and firm. She'd run her hands over the play of muscles just last night. Warmth spread through Tara as she remembered the other things they'd done to each other in bed and the way Jack had made very sure her needs were satisfied before meeting his own.

"I'm not becoming a recluse, Maria," he said into the phone with what sounded like exaggerated patience. "I'm rehabbing my shoulder in a place where I can get some peace and quiet. There's a difference."

He fell silent as he listened to what was being said on the other end of the line. Suddenly his brows rose and his lips curved into a smile that crinkled the skin at the corners of his eyes and mouth. He'd spotted her.

He pointed at the cell phone, silently mouthing the words *"My sister."*

She nodded and gestured toward the bedroom, hoping to convey she was going to use the bathroom and get dressed. Luckily she had a change of clothes in her gym bag, which Jack had fetched from the car the night before.

A short time later, she walked into the main living area of the house. Jack was still on the phone. He'd moved from the table to the refrigerator. He was bent at the waist, peering inside. He removed a carton of orange juice.

"Uh-huh." He seemed to be only half paying attention. "Yep. Sure thing. Don't worry, okay?"

He poured some orange juice into a glass, nodding once more. "Love you, too."

He clicked off the phone, picked up the orange juice and turned back toward the table. This time when he saw her he didn't smile. "You're dressed. I was hoping you'd stay naked."

She laughed. "Can I have some of that juice?"

"You can have mine." He set the full glass on the table. Before she could pick it up, Jack reached for her.

He captured her mouth in a slow, thorough kiss. She wrapped her arms around his neck, savoring the now-familiar sensations he could elicit so easily from her. Too soon, he lifted his mouth. He kept his arms locked loosely around her waist.

"Good morning," he said.

"Yes," she said, feeling happiness rise in her. "It's a very good morning."

"Sorry about the phone call," he said. "I wanted to call Maria before she rung me and woke you. She's an early riser."

"You shouldn't have let me sleep so long," she said.

His eyes sparkled so they appeared a lighter shade of brown. "It was the least I could do after I tired you out."

She lifted her lips and bestowed a swift kiss on his mouth. "You could also feed me. Got any yogurt?"

"Nope," he said. "How about some bacon and eggs?"

She wrinkled her nose. "I'm not a big breakfast eater. A granola bar will do, if you have it."

"I think I do." He let her go and opened the door to a skinny closet in the kitchen, removing a bar from a package. She sat down at the table beside the orange juice, taking the apple-cinnamon granola bar he handed her. She could smell the bay through the screens on the house's open windows.

"Did you convince Maria not to worry about you?" she asked.

"I'm not sure that's possible," he said, then pointed at her. "Hey, by the way, I asked who tipped her off about you looking like Hayley Cooper."

Tara's breath caught before she remembered that she couldn't be Hayley. She relaxed. Jack's sister's investigation into the old case no longer posed a threat to Tara or her mother.

"What did your sister say?" Tara asked.

"It was somebody from a conference you attended earlier this year," he said.

She'd been to only one conference in recent months. "The conference in Virginia Beach? The one for elementary school physical education teachers?"

"Yeah. That's the conference Maria mentioned," he said. "The tipster was a teacher, too. After she got home, she saw the age progression of Hayley on one of the missing-persons websites and thought it looked like you."

"Why would somebody from the conference be looking at missing-persons websites?" Tara asked.

"I know the answer to that one," Jack said. "A student from her school was missing."

"I wonder if that was the case in Williamsburg," Tara mused. "It got a lot of press. Turned out the little boy's father took him. I think he's back with his mother now."

"My sister says most missing kids are snatched by people they know, usually parents," Jack said. "Stranger abduction is actually pretty rare."

That wasn't any consolation for Hayley Cooper's parents, Tara thought.

"Why did the teacher go to your sister and not to me?" Tara asked.

"I don't think she knows you except in passing," he said. "She didn't even give us your name. And you've got to admit you do look a lot like that photo. As soon as I saw you walking to Wawpaney Elementary, I realized you were the woman I was coming to see."

"I guess the resemblance is why I'm curious about Hayley." Tara didn't see any harm in admitting that. Not now. "I read about her on that website, too."

"Then you know as much as I do," Jack said.

"Not quite," Tara said, tearing open the wrapper

and biting into the granola bar. "Did your sister tell you why Hayley's parents hired her now after so many years had passed?"

"As a matter of fact, she did," he said. "Hayley's father wants to sell their house and move to Arizona, where their grandchildren are."

"Hayley has siblings?" Tara asked.

"At least one," Jack said. "Hayley's mother wants to spend more time with her grandchildren, too. But she's afraid moving would be like giving up hope that Hayley will ever come home."

"That doesn't make sense," Tara said. "Hayley was only three when she was abducted. She wouldn't remember where they lived."

"Maria didn't say the mother's reason was rational," Jack said. "I guess what it boils down to is that she needs closure."

"I can understand that." Tara took another bite of granola and chewed slowly while she thought. "If she knew for certain that Hayley was dead, she could grieve and put her to rest. Not knowing what happened to her daughter must eat at her."

Jack nodded. "Unfortunately Maria says it looks like the case will never be solved. Too many years have passed."

Tara popped the last bite of the granola bar into her mouth and washed it down with the rest of her orange juice. She stood up, trying to put Hayley out of her mind. She felt for the little girl's family, but there was a lot of sadness in the world. She couldn't obsess over their loss simply because she and Hayley shared a resemblance, not when there was nothing she could do to help them.

"I've gotta go," Tara said.

"Go?" Jack reached for her hand and drew circles on the inside of her palm with his thumb. Shivers ran down the length of her body. "Camp doesn't start until nine."

Even though Jack touched only her hand, Tara felt as if her knees were about to buckle. It was ridiculous the effect the man had on her. Ridiculous and thrilling.

"I carpool with my mom and Danny. I need to pick them up at eight-thirty."

His eyes grew heavy lidded. "I need you."

She smiled at him. "I thought I gave you enough of what you needed last night."

"Not even close." With a quick tug, he pulled her down onto his lap. She fit against him perfectly, she noticed. "It's not even seven-fifteen yet. Are you sure you can't stay longer?"

She ran a hand over his square jaw, needing to touch him. "Don't you have to run on the beach or rehab your shoulder or something?" she asked, her voice breathless.

"Later. Right now I'm exactly where I want to be." His breath caressed her lips as he talked. She could feel his erection against her thigh.

"This isn't fair," she said.

"Sure, it is," he said.

She wasn't surprised at his response. After hearing the saga of his shoulder injuries, she understood him better. He was a professional athlete. He'd do whatever it took to come out on top.

He nuzzled her neck. Delicious goose bumps rose on her flesh.

"What do you say?" he asked. "Especially if I promise to make it quick."

Unable to resist the sensations spiraling through her a moment longer, she wrapped her arms around his neck.

"Don't you dare make it too quick," she whispered against his mouth.

JUST AFTER NINE ON WEDNESDAY, Tara fished the key to her mother's house from the pocket of her shorts, unlocked the front door and hurried inside the empty house. Danny and her mom had already left for camp. Tara would get there later. She was spending the morning as an emergency fill-in volunteer at the Barrier Island Center, where she was due in a half hour.

It felt as if all she'd done for the past two mornings was rush. Of course, the fact that she and Jack had indulged in some morning delight for the second consecutive day contributed to that. She didn't regret telling him to take his time, though.

Their lovemaking had been worth every frantic second since.

She was a little sore, but in all the right places and only because she'd spent two nights in a row with Jack after not having sex in more than a year. Her drought was definitely over. What's more, she had absolutely no regrets.

A warm feeling swept through her at the thought. She identified it as contentment.

The only downside was she barely had time to catch her breath.

"It's your own fault," Tara said aloud as she ran lightly up the stairs to the closet in the guest bedroom her mother used for storage.

While listening to Gus Miller perform flamenco guitar the other night, she'd remembered a box of maracas she'd used while teaching her physical education students aerobic dance. She'd forgotten to have a look for them until this morning.

And once she got something in her head, it stayed put. Today, she'd decided to bring the maracas to camp for a musical activity.

Tara glanced at her watch and slowed her breathing. If she left her mother's house in the next ten minutes, she'd be at the center on time.

She yanked open the closet door and groaned. Boxes were stacked from floor to ceiling. She'd have to wait until later in the week to bring the maracas to camp, after all. No way did she have time to search these boxes for them.

Tara was about to shut the closet door when she glimpsed writing on one of the lower boxes. Could it be? She got down on her knees. Yes! She'd written "Maracas" in black magic marker on the outside of the box.

Getting to her feet, Tara unstacked boxes until she reached the one she wanted. She slid the box free and heard the sound of cardboard ripping from the top of the box below it. She inspected the damage. The box was so old and brittle that part of its top had come loose.

The cover of what appeared to be a photo album peeked through the opening. Tara frowned. Hadn't her mother said all her albums sustained water damage in the move? She chewed on her lower lip. No, her mother had said she didn't have photo albums from when Tara and Sunny were babies. Maybe this album and whatever else was in the box were from a different time. One thing was for certain. She didn't have time to figure it out now.

She got up, intending to restack the boxes. She hesitated, then pulled out the box with the photo album. It would be fun to look through it when she had time. Maybe it contained photos from before her parents had children. She doubted her mother would mind.

A short time later, Tara put the box of maracas

on the passenger seat of her car and then deposited the other box in the trunk. She slammed the trunk shut.

"Tara!" Mrs. Jorgenson waved at her from her porch across the street.

"Hey, Mrs. Jorgenson." Tara waved back, then moved toward the driver's side of her car, hoping the woman got the message that she was in a rush. She enjoyed talking to the older woman, but not today.

"Wait a minute." Mrs. Jorgenson shuffled down the few porch stairs, holding tight to the railing with one hand, gripping her cane in the other. She wore a summer housedress and slippers. At the bottom of the steps she leaned on the cane and walked toward Tara, talking as she moved. "I was just thinking about you. I heard a trunk slam, looked out the window and there you were."

Resigning herself to a few moments of conversation, Tara crossed the street and met her mother's neighbor on the sidewalk. The scent of the pine trees in Mrs. Jorgenson's front yard filled the air. Again Tara noticed the slippers. Whatever her mother's neighbor had to say must be important.

"I hear you have a new man in your life," Mrs. Jorgenson announced. "I met him the other day. Such a charming one, he is."

"He is charming," Tara agreed, feeling her lips curl into a smile. There wasn't any reason to hide the way she felt about him. "Kind, too. Not to mention considerate."

"And handsome," Mrs. Jorgenson chimed in.

"Yes." Tara stopped herself from going further. She was starting to sound like the president of Jack's fan club. "I'd love to stay and talk, Mrs. Jorgenson, but I can't. I have somewhere I need to be soon."

"This won't take but a minute," Mrs. Jorgenson said. "I got something wrong the other day and I wanted to make sure to correct it."

Tara's entire body went still. Like a portent of doom, a chill ran through her even though the temperature was in the low eighties. She had a crazy urge to cover her ears and start humming.

"It's about when you and your mother moved here to Wawpaney," Mrs. Jorgenson said. "I told you it was 1983."

Tara nodded, remembering the elation that had coursed through her when the elderly woman verified that fact, which proved Tara couldn't be Hayley Cooper.

"Well, that's what I got wrong." Mrs. Jorgenson smiled as she talked, as though she weren't about to turn Tara's world upside down. "It was 1984."

The year Hayley had been kidnapped.

The meager breakfast Tara had eaten rose in her stomach as though she was going to be physically ill. She swallowed, telling herself she was overreacting. Mrs. Jorgenson didn't seem really sure of her dates. The elderly woman could just as likely be wrong about this date as the other.

"It was a long time ago," Tara said. "I don't see how you can be sure."

"Oh, I'm positive," she said, still beaming. "My daughter graduated from high school in 1984. We had a big party and you and your mother were there."

"That doesn't mean we didn't move to Wawpaney in 1983," Tara said, which was a perfectly logical statement.

"You didn't move to Wawpaney in 1983." Mrs. Jorgenson clasped her hands together, looking proud of herself. "You and your mother moved in the week of the party."

Don't panic, Tara told herself. *Not yet.* "You remembered all that between yesterday and today?"

"*I* didn't remember," Mrs. Jorgenson said. "My daughter did. She was visiting yesterday afternoon and asked about you. She didn't always like you, but she said she's developed a soft spot for you over the years."

Tara was almost afraid to ask the obvious question. "Why didn't she like me?"

Mrs. Jorgenson laughed. "Because of something that happened at her party. I'll tell you this. Lizzie wasn't too happy with me for inviting you and your mother, especially because you were like strangers to her."

Tara wasn't sure whether she was frustrated or glad that Mrs. Jorgenson had a rambling way of getting to the point. It flashed through her mind that she'd be better off without hearing what the other woman had to say.

"Don't you want to know what happened at the party?" Mrs. Jorgenson didn't wait for her to respond. "It wasn't funny then, but it certainly is now. I don't know how I could have forgotten it. Lizzie certainly never did. You stuck your hand in her graduation cake!"

CHAPTER TWELVE

LATER THAT WEDNESDAY, Carrie edged her chair closer to a table covered in brown paper, within reach of a mallet, a knife and a roll of paper towels. Good thing she'd looked out the window and glimpsed Gustavo coming to pick her up dressed in jeans and a casual shirt. The little black dress she'd changed out of was not the best choice for a meal eaten with fingers.

"I hope it's okay that I brought you to a crab house," Gustavo said. Painted on the wall behind him was a cartoon image of a crab. Carrie didn't have a clue how the man managed to look so handsome with that image as a backdrop. "I love these places."

Carrie usually did, too. She couldn't say for sure why she'd had a vague sense of disappointment when she'd discovered where they were going.

"I can see why." Carrie eyed the plate of blue crabs in the middle of the table that Gustavo had ordered for them to share. "What could be better than crabs when you're on the Eastern Shore?"

Champagne. Caviar. Duck à l'orange. The answers popped into her head one after the other.

"Now you're talking." Gustavo grinned and plucked a crab from the plate. He twisted off the claws and legs, then flipped the crab to reveal its underside. In seconds he'd removed the shell and the gills and snapped the crab body in half. He pulled out some meat with his fingers, put it into his mouth and chewed. "Mmm. Heavenly."

His enjoyment made up for their casual surroundings and a clientele that included families and one very noisy group that was celebrating a birthday. Carrie knew that because the guest of honor, who was probably in his sixties, was wearing a paper party hat. Oh, well. She shouldn't have expected candlelight and a table with a view of the water, anyway.

"Didn't you say you were from Baltimore?" Carrie reached for her own crab. "The way you're acting, I'd swear you hadn't had crab in forever."

He paused in the act of extracting more crabmeat. "Not crab I've cracked myself. Usually when I go out, Susie's with me. Crab houses frustrate her."

Carrie nodded, understanding without explanation that most children with Down syndrome had poor manual dexterity. Danny certainly did. He'd never have the patience to extract his own crab meat.

"Not much frustrates that girl," Carrie said. "She's always the first one to give me a holler when it's time to try something new."

This afternoon, the new experience had been the maracas Tara had used in a musical activity. Susie was the first to grab one. She shook hers with gusto, giggling in delight. Before long, all the children had followed suit. Even Danny.

"I'm impressed, too. I love her so much." He grinned at her. "But I'm glad we didn't have to bring her along tonight. I owe Jack."

Gustavo's babysitter had canceled at the last minute. When Jack found out, he'd offered to watch Susie, too, if Gustavo brought her over to Carrie's house.

"Jack's a fine young man," Carrie said.

"It took me a while before I figured out where I'd heard his name before," Gustavo said. "Turns out I was at the game where he broke his collarbone. It was last year, when the Stars were playing in Baltimore."

"That sure is a coincidence," Carrie said, shaking her head. "But what's this about Jack breaking a collarbone? I thought his problems were with his shoulder."

"He has injury problems is how I understand it," Gustavo said. "It's too bad."

"Jack sure seems motivated to pitch again." She dug some crab out of a shell with her fingers. "Let me ask you something, Gustavo. Did you notice anything going on between Jack and Tara today?"

He didn't answer until he'd finished chewing a mouthful of crab. "Like what?'

"Oh, I don't know," Carrie hedged. "I thought Tara had been more cordial to him until today."

"Sounds like you want them to get together," Gustavo said.

"I sure do." Carrie sighed. "Sometimes I think it's my fault Tara's thirty-two and still single."

He stopped picking the crab and directed all his attention her way. Even in the crowded room, he made her feel as if she was the only one present. "How could it be your fault?"

"Tara's always been so particular," she said. "That's a real problem when you live on the road less traveled like we do. There aren't very many eligible men here who are the right age to begin with."

"I don't see how it's your fault that she's picky."

"I worry she won't settle for anything less than what I had with Scott," Carrie said. "Once I met him, that was it for me."

"How old were you?"

"Seventeen. He was, too." She shook her head. "It seemed like we'd have forever together. It turned out we only had seven years."

"Must have been seven good years," Gustavo said.

"Not all of them." Carrie pursed her lips. "Wow,

I can't believe I just admitted that. But it's plain true. We broke up and got back together a half dozen times, both before and after we got married."

"My marriage was the opposite. Sometimes I think Victoria and I got married because it was expected of us," he said. "We never argued, not even after we had Susie. By then, I knew what kind of person Victoria was. It wasn't as though anything I said would change her."

"Scott and I went at it all the time," Carrie said. "I used to wish we didn't argue so much. But as low as our lows were, our highs were pretty darn high."

"Is that why you don't think you'll fall in love again?"

"I won't," she said. "I've accepted I'll only ever love one man."

"Even though he died almost thirty years ago?"

Carrie pursed her lips. "Who told you how long ago it was?"

"Tara. She told me Sunny was gone, too." He didn't look upset that she'd led him to believe Sunny was alive, only puzzled. "Why didn't you want me to know?"

It was easier to pretend he was only asking her about Scott. "I don't like to have to explain why I don't date."

"You mean because most men would think it

was time to move on after thirty years?" Gustavo asked.

"Exactly," Carrie said. "It's darn near impossible for them to understand I don't need another man in my life."

"Fair enough." Gustavo regarded her for long moments. "I can accept that as long as you don't set your feet in stone. One of these days you might feel differently."

"I won't," she said quickly.

"I don't know about that," he said. "Life is full of surprises. Look at Jack and Tara. They'd never have met if his sister wasn't a private investigator."

"Jack's sister is a private eye?" Carrie asked. Why hadn't she known that?

"Yeah," Gus said. "He mentioned it in passing the other day. He wouldn't have stopped in Wawpaney if he hadn't been checking out a lead for her."

Carrie felt the blood rush to her head and heard the pulsing sound of her heartbeat in her ears. She forced herself to calm down. This was paranoia at work. Years had passed with no hint of anyone suspecting what she'd done.

"What kind of lead?" She was amazed that her voice was steady.

"I'm not sure," Gus said. "I just know it didn't pan out."

Carrie schooled her features. Her heartbeat returned to normal. She'd overreacted, just as she suspected. There was no reason to believe anyone would come after her, not after all this time. Besides, Gustavo said the lead had gone nowhere. Carrie had absolutely nothing to worry about.

Gustavo went back to eating his crab, taking time out between bites to charm her with stories about life with Susie and the cats he'd inherited from his grandmother along with the B and B.

She wondered what Gustavo would think of her if he knew her secret, then she shoved that out of her mind, too.

Nobody would ever know.

SWEAT DAMPENED TARA's brow and dripped down the vee of her Dri-Fit shirt on Wednesday night. Her heart beat too fast even now, after the cool-down and stretching portion of the spinning class. For the moment, her mind was mercifully empty. She clapped. "Great class today," she said. "You ladies worked really hard."

Kiki, her most die-hard pupil, slumped over her bike, her chest heaving, the hair around her face dampened with sweat so it appeared a darker shade of blond. "I don't think I can stand up."

"Me, either."

"My legs don't just feel like jelly. They've turned into jelly!"

Some of the other women chimed in with their

thoughts. Since there had been only eight women present tonight, Tara was starting to think she might have gone overboard.

She took a step and almost collapsed. Yeah, she'd definitely overdone it. The upshot was that exercising had only temporarily helped her mental state. Now that the class was over, she was once again consumed with the possibility she might be Hayley Cooper. She locked her knees, waiting for her legs to regain their strength.

The women stretched, then started gathering their things. Kiki walked up to Tara without the usual bounce in her step. "What was with you tonight, Tar? I thought I was gonna die."

Tara had to pause and process what Kiki had said. She needed to do a better job of focusing on the here and now rather than what might have happened in the past. "I doubt that. You're nineteen years old and in the best shape of anybody in the class."

"And you're avoiding the question. What's going on with you?" Kiki narrowed her eyes, then snapped her fingers and pointed at Tara. "You're having guy trouble, aren't you?"

Tara wasn't sure how to answer. If Jack had never set foot in Wawpaney, she'd never have known about Hayley Cooper. Did hiding her suspicion from him that she was the abducted girl constitute guy trouble?

"You are!" Kiki cried. "I'm an expert at recognizing the signs, and you've got 'em, girl. Dark circles under your eyes. Frown lines on your forehead."

"Maybe I have dark circles because I stayed up most of the night having sex," Tara said, hoping to shock the younger woman. She should have known better.

"Then what's with the frown lines and the exercising to exhaustion?" Kiki asked. "Hello? A lot of sex is a good thing."

Tara cracked a smile for the first time since discovering she'd been the most memorable guest at Mrs. Jorgenson's daughter's graduation party. In 1984, not 1983. "You make it sound so simple."

"It is simple," Kiki said. "Give yourself permission to enjoy yourself. No reason for things to get heavy. It's not like you have to marry the guy."

"Tara's getting married?" Art Goodnight appeared behind them. Tara hadn't even noticed him enter the room where they held the spinning classes. "To who?"

"I'm not marrying anybody." Tara figured she might as well explain so she wouldn't have to field more questions. "Kiki was just saying you don't have to marry someone just because you're dating them."

"Absolutely right." Kiki picked up her empty

water bottle and gave a fluttering wave. "See you next class, Tara."

"I wish your mom thought like that. I've been trying to get her to go out with me for years," he said. "Every time I ask, she tells me she doesn't date."

So that was the reason Art had sought her out. He was fishing for information about her mother, the woman who may have taken Tara from a shopping mall when she was three years old. Tara's stomach pitched and rolled.

"Any chance you know if that's still true?" Art asked.

Tara brought her mind back to the conversation. She supposed there was no reason not to tell him what he wanted to know. "My mother's out with Gus Miller tonight."

Art swore under his breath. "Then they are dating. I half thought she and that flamenco guy were pulling my leg."

"Doesn't seem that way."

"Let me know if they break up," Art said. "It's the least you can do for your old volleyball coach."

Tara reached down and grabbed her gym bag, almost desperate to get away from him in order to have some time alone to think. Except it was also crucial that she act normally and not let anyone know what was going on inside her head.

"You mean the guy who's been telling Jack

DiMarco stories about me?" she asked, making her voice light. "That coach?"

"Hey, Jack asked about you," Art said, the words sending a chill up Tara's spine. She reminded herself that Jack didn't suspect anything. "If you want, I'll tell you stories about Jack."

On another day, Tara would have laughed at his response. Despite his faults, which included having a really big mouth, Art wasn't a bad guy.

"I already know Jack is rehabbing his shoulder so he can pitch in the majors again," Tara said.

"He told you that?" Art shook his head. "Guess he must still believe it."

Tara stopped thinking about herself. "What do you mean?"

"Jack will never pitch in the big leagues again," Art said. "He's got too much damage to his pitching shoulder."

A few minutes later Tara walked to her car as though in a trance, her mind ping-ponging between her own predicament and Jack's. If she hadn't been distracted, she would have picked up the impossibility of Jack's situation before now. She'd witnessed the pain his shoulder was causing him and heard about how the doctors had said another surgery wouldn't help. Why, then, did he persist in believing he could again reach the very best level of baseball?

She settled into the driver's seat, jumping at a

noise that shattered the quiet. She groaned when she realized it was only the text tone on her cell phone. She picked up the phone. The message was from Jack. Her heart gave a happy leap. She clicked through and opened it.

Help! Your mom and Gus went to bingo after dinner. Kids wearing me out.

She sat in the darkening twilight staring at the text, wishing she could control how she felt about him. At camp this afternoon she'd made a half-hearted attempt to put distance between them. He'd wrecked her already weak resolve when he'd taken her aside and whispered he could keep what was between them a secret as long as she liked.

She wanted to confide in him then and there, but she couldn't risk it, not with his sister investigating the Hayley Cooper case. Besides, discovering she and her mother had moved to the Eastern Shore in 1984 wasn't definitive proof of anything.

Tara put the key in the ignition and started her car, her destination clear. She would have headed over to her mother's tonight even if Jack hadn't sent the text, if only to distract him from noticing there were no photos of herself as a young child in the house.

Jack had given her no reason to believe he suspected she was anyone other than Tara Greer, which was probably who she was. Even now she'd put her chances at better than even that Carrie hadn't abducted her. But what if she had? And what if the woman in Tara's nightmares was real?

She took a deep breath. She couldn't avoid Jack, not when she saw him every day. Two days of camp remained, including Friday's field trip to Chincoteague Island that they were both chaperoning.

It went without saying that she needed to maintain a working relationship with Jack. The wild card was whether she could continue to be as close to him as she craved to be.

Before she pulled out of the parking space, she opened a message prompt on her cell phone and typed, On my way.

Although she had no clue what she'd do or say when she got there.

YELLOW LIGHTS FLASHED low to the ground in Carrie Greer's backyard, giving away the ever-changing location of the fireflies that had emerged at dusk.

"I got one!" Susie Miller yelled. She ran up to Jack, her hands cradled in front of her.

Very slowly, almost reverently, Susie opened her hands. The firefly she'd captured flashed its light, then flew away into the darkening night.

Susie let out a cry of delight. "I knew I could catch one!"

She'd been attempting it for at least fifteen minutes, ever since she'd spotted the blinking lights in the backyard and asked Jack if they could go outside to try their luck. Danny had been sitting on the bottom step of the back porch with his arms folded across his chest for about as long.

"Hey, buddy," Jack called to him. "You ready to give it a try?"

"No!" Danny provided the same answer he had the past three times Jack had asked. It was the identical response he'd repeated when Jack offered him the Wii remote so he could play a game of video bowling with Susie.

"You really like that word no, don't you, pal?" Jack asked.

Danny thrust his lips out in a pout. "No!"

Jack scratched the back of his neck. Why had he believed he'd be any good at babysitting? And where was Tara? He'd sent her the text nearly forty-five minutes ago, strategically timing the missive for after her spinning class.

"I'm tired," Susie announced and plopped down in the middle of the yard. Her abrupt change of mood didn't surprise Jack. He'd noticed at camp that most of the children had quick mood changes, switching from happy to sad and back again in a flash.

"Firefly chasing will do that to you," Jack said.

"They're called lightning bugs," Susie corrected.

"Okay. Lightning bugs."

Now neither child was smiling. A firefly flew near Jack and he snagged it out of the air, pretty sure neither Susie nor Danny had noticed.

"Hey, who wants to see a magic trick?" he asked.

"Me!" Susie got to her feet and came toward him, her good humor already restored.

"How about you, Danny?" Jack asked.

Danny's scowl started to waver. "What kind of magic trick?"

"I can pull a lightning bug out of your ear," he said.

Danny uncrossed his arms and rose from the porch step. "C-cannot."

"Watch me." Jack surreptitiously maneuvered the firefly in his hand until he held it firmly but gingerly between his thumb and forefingers, hidden from view.

One of Jack's uncles had taught him the other magic tricks he knew. He was making this one up on the fly. He decided the trick needed all the help it could get. Perhaps a magic word? He searched his mind for one.

"Shazam!" he called out.

Jack touched Danny behind the ear, then extended his arm in front of him with a showman's flourish. He opened his fingers. Almost as though the firefly were cooperating with the trick, it flashed its light as it flew away.

"Cool!" Danny yelled, his smile back.

Susie jumped up and down.

"Shazam?" Tara asked. He turned toward the voice. She was standing not six feet behind them wearing jeans, sandals and a pretty yellow top, her hair damp. She must have gone home and taken a shower and changed before coming over.

She'd been more distant at camp this afternoon than he would have liked, but he wasn't discouraged. She was here, wasn't she? Jack felt himself grinning. Just looking at her did that to him. "The trick doesn't work unless you say the magic word."

Danny ran up to Tara and hugged her. "Jack pulled a lightning bug from my ear!"

"I saw," Tara said, hugging him back. Although she was as affectionate with the boy as always, Jack noticed lines of strain around her mouth. He vowed to take her mind off whatever was troubling her.

"For my next trick, I will pull a quarter out of Susie's ear." Jack needed to talk fast before one of the children suggested he perform the firefly trick again. He couldn't catch another of the insects without somebody noticing. "I will also make juice appear."

"How?" Danny asked.

"I'm going to take the juice carton out of the refrigerator," he said.

"That's not magic!" Susie exclaimed.

"That's tricky is what it is," Tara said with a small chuckle.

Jack grinned at Tara and placed a hand on the shoulder of each child. "Magicians are supposed to be tricky."

A couple glasses of juice and three magic tricks later, the four of them retreated to the family room. Danny asked if he could turn on the Nickelodeon channel, which was playing a popular cartoon. Within minutes, both children were asleep.

"Cartoon reruns will do that to a kid," Jack cracked in a hushed voice from next to Tara on the love seat. She held herself stiffly, cementing his suspicion that something was off. After the nights they'd spent together, she should be curled up against him.

"What was with the SOS?" she asked in an equally quiet voice before he could attempt to get to the bottom of what was wrong. She flipped her hair back over her shoulder and he got a whiff of a pleasing floral scent, the same one from when they'd made love. "It didn't seem like you needed help when I got here."

"Only because I'd resorted to cheap magic tricks," he said. "I thought for sure I'd accidentally crush that firefly before I pulled it from behind Danny's ear."

"Danny liked the tricks," she said, looking down at her hands instead of at him. "He likes you."

"Didn't seem that way before you arrived," Jack said. "I couldn't get him to do anything."

"He acts that way sometimes." Tara glanced at him, then just as quickly glanced away. "You've seen how stubborn Danny can be at camp. It doesn't matter what you do or say. He just refuses to try."

"I wish I knew why," Jack said, rubbing the back of his neck. "I think I'll mention it to Carrie. She's bound to have more insight than I do."

"She's trying her best," Tara said, an edge to her voice. "She's a great mother."

"I know that." He narrowed his eyes. Something was definitely different between them than it had been the previous two nights. "Is something bothering you?"

She chewed on her lower lip, then nodded. She turned to him, still not quite meeting his eyes. He tipped up her chin so she had to look at him.

"Before you start," he said, "I want to state for the record that I thought the last few nights were pretty terrific."

"They were." She took a measured breath and exhaled just as slowly. "But is it really wise for us to get involved, Jack? You're just passing through. Soon you'll be gone."

He tucked a strand of still-damp hair behind her ear and ran his fingers over her jawline. She had such smooth, pretty skin. "We're already involved."

"We can cut it off right now. Before either one of us gets in too deep." She sounded hesitant, as though that wasn't what she really wanted.

Jack could almost hear the sizzle of attraction between them. He felt a corner of his mouth rise. "Why don't we go with the flow instead?"

"That might not be wise," she said, but she was nodding. He wondered if she realized she was giving off mixed signals.

"Breaking things off makes even less sense. I see you at camp every day, Tara. What will stop me from falling more deeply for you?"

"Not having sex with me," she said in a soft whisper.

He shook his head. "That won't do it."

"Really?" She seemed doubtful.

"Really." He moved closer to her on the love seat, took her hand and brought it to his lips. Very slowly he turned it over and kissed her soft palm. He spoke equally quietly, although there was no chance the two sleeping children could hear them. "Don't get me wrong. I love having sex with you. But I think you're pretty great out of bed, too."

A faint red stain traveled from Tara's neck to her face, charming him. Not many women in his acquaintance blushed.

"And you're very charming," Tara wet her lips,

bringing his attention to her mouth. But kissing her would be a bad idea with the kids only a few feet away.

"I won't pressure you, Tara," he murmured close to her ear. "I'd like to spend the night with you, but that's entirely up to you."

While he talked, he ran a hand up the length of her arm and felt her shiver. The air felt charged, the sexual tension between them like a living thing.

"No fair," she said in a breathy voice. "How can I think clearly when you're touching me?"

He grinned. "Then why try?"

"Because I have to," she answered, suddenly serious. "I've never been the kind of woman who leaps before she looks. I need to figure out some things on my own. Do you understand?"

He withdrew his hand so that he was no longer touching her and forced himself to smile. "I'm nothing if not understanding."

But he didn't understand. Not really.

CHAPTER THIRTEEN

VERY EARLY THE NEXT morning, Tara flicked on her porch light and padded out to the darkened curb in front of her house where she'd parked her car. The pavement felt cool under the soles of her bare feet and the neighborhood was quiet except for the hum of cicadas.

Not much went on in Wawpaney before dawn broke. Tara should know. This was the second time this week she'd been awake before the sun. She stood peering down at the trunk of the car, hugging herself despite the moderate temperature. The sky was clear, portending beautiful weather for the next-to-last day of camp. That was later. Right now Tara had to drum up the courage to deal with the murky nature of her past.

"Okay, Tara," she whispered aloud. "You can do this."

She uncrossed her arms and unlocked the trunk, lifting out the box she'd taken from her mother's house a few days before. A couple moments later she set the box on the kitchen table. The light over the table hurt her eyes after the darkness outside.

What was she waiting for?

Since her discovery that she and her mother had moved to the Eastern Shore in the same year Hayley Cooper had been abducted and Tara had withdrawn from Jack, she'd been miserable.

She couldn't continue this way. She was sleeping in fits and starts, missing having Jack beside her. The nightmare images of the woman shaking her were occurring with increasing regularity. This Thursday morning, as Tara had lain awake in her bed, she'd finally accepted the inevitable.

She needed to figure out once and for all if she was Hayley.

The simplest course of action would be to ask her mother. Tara rejected the idea, as she'd already done a few times previously. She couldn't do that to Carrie, not without proof. Her mother had endured enough heartache in her life. It could shatter her to know her own daughter suspected her of this unspeakable crime.

If Tara was her daughter.

Tara blew out a shaky breath.

Carrie truly had done her a favor if she'd taken her away from the woman of her nightmares. Except something had nagged at Tara since Jack had relayed more details about the case earlier in the week. If Tara had been born Hayley Cooper to the cruel woman, she had left behind others. A father.

At least one sister and perhaps even more siblings. And now nieces and nephews.

The reasons that Tara needed to know who she was were stacking up.

The box of photo albums could provide the answer.

If one of the albums contained a photo of Tara with her father or with Sunny, she'd know for certain that she'd been born a Greer.

If not...

Taking a deep breath, Tara unfolded the worn flaps of the cardboard box and pulled out the top album. The cover was shiny and looked almost new. She flipped it open to page after empty page. Except that didn't mean the other albums were devoid of photos.

She peered into the box at the rest of the contents. Whereas the top item was an unused photo album, the others weren't. Her high school yearbooks were arranged side by side with their spines showing.

Relief hit her with the impact of a freight train.

She sank into one of the kitchen chairs, her stomach fluttering until she felt almost giddy with relief. Maybe her mother had been telling the truth about her photo albums being damaged in the move.

Maybe? Tara shook her head. Most likely. As in, most likely her mother hadn't kidnapped her.

Carrie was an advocate for children in need. She was a foster mother, for goodness' sake. She solved problems for children. She didn't cause them.

On the heels of that thought came another: the empty photo albums and the box full of old yearbooks didn't prove a thing.

"This is ridiculous!" Tara shouted.

She rose to her feet and yanked open the drawer in the sideboard beside the kitchen table. Inside was the DNA testing kit that had arrived from eBay yesterday.

The kit suggested getting a tissue sample from the parties in question by swabbing the inside of the cheek. However, there were other ways to establish paternity. Or, in Tara's case, maternity.

She crossed to her coat closet and took her purse off the large hook where she'd hung it. Rummaging inside the handbag, she pulled out the item she'd impulsively removed from her mother's bathroom last night. It was a brush complete with dozens of strands of long blond hair. In the back of her mind, Tara must have known it would come to this.

Tara sat back down at the kitchen table and dug into the DNA testing kit until she found the sheet of paper with the detailed directions. She learned that if she paid significantly extra, she could get the results within a day of when the lab received the kit.

The extra cost would be worth it, she decided.

So would the next-day service she'd spring for when she got to the post office when it opened that morning.

Most likely the results would be exactly what she wanted to hear. Until then, she was going to try her best not to worry about it.

DANNY BOUNCED UP AND down in his seat on the tour boat on Friday and pointed to something brown near the shore of the nearby island.

"I see a pony!" he cried.

Without much hope, Jack looked toward where Danny was pointing. He'd learned that the wild ponies living on Assateague Island could be viewed only from the water, but they didn't always cooperate with the tourism industry. The boat captain who ran Assateague Nature Cruises had already taken a few detours through the salt marshes on the outer reaches of the island searching for them, to no avail. The dolphins hadn't made an appearance, either. So far the highlight of the trip had been a bald eagle too far away to see clearly.

"Oh, my gosh!" Tara said. "You're right, Danny. That's a pony."

Dark sunglasses covered a good portion of her face, causing her flashing teeth to seem very white. Her hair was in a ponytail, the wind whipping tendrils loose that danced around her forehead. She was wearing an orange life jacket like the rest of them. Hers didn't detract from her tanned and toned arms. He thought she looked beautiful.

She also looked untroubled.

They hadn't traveled in the same car during the ninety-minute drive from the community center in Cape Charles. When they'd arrived at the floating dock at the waterfront park in Chincoteague, however, he'd noticed the tension that had surrounded her in recent days seemed to have lessened.

A single boat was too small to accommodate all of them, necessitating a split into two groups. Jack had suggested he and Tara help chaperone the five children who had already boarded the first boat, along with Aggie, the assistant director, and Brandy, the teenage volunteer. Tara had agreed without an argument.

He was starting to be optimistic she'd given up on the ridiculous notion that they should end things.

"Let's take a look," the boat captain yelled above the sound of the motor. He rotated the wheel and cut his speed, maneuvering the boat into a salt marsh. From their perches on white poles that marked publicly leased oyster grounds, a dozen or so double-crested cormorants soared away until they were black specks against the blue, cloudless sky.

"Is it Misty?" Susie Miller asked. Somehow

she'd ended up in their boat instead of with her father and Carrie.

"Good question, but it's *Misty of Chincoteague*," Brandy said, naming the book that had helped make the ponies famous. "Not Misty of *Assateague*."

"It's not Misty," the captain said above the hum of the outboard motor. "They're sometimes called the Chincoteague ponies, but they all live on Assateague."

He'd already told them that about 150 wild ponies lived on the barrier island, a 14,000-acre wildlife refuge free of human residents that bordered the Atlantic Ocean on one side and a string of bays on the other.

"I see two ponies!" Susie yelled.

Their view of the second pony had been blocked by the stout, wide body of the first one. The second pony had a similar short-legged build but showier coloring, with black markings on its white coat.

The captain cut the engine and let the boat drift not fifteen yards from where the ponies grazed on salt marsh grasses. The animals didn't seem to notice or care that they had an audience.

"I told you I saw a pony!" Danny said, his chest swelling with pride.

Jack patted him on the back. "Good eye, buddy. Without you, we might not have seen any."

"Look!" Danny got to his knees on the padded

bench seat that lined one side of the boat, shielding his eyes from the sun despite his sunglasses. "Another one."

A tan pony with a white mane emerged from the brush and joined the first two. Jack caught Tara's eye and grinned at her, enjoying this unbridled side of her foster brother.

"Can I stand up to get a picture?" Tara asked.

"As long as you're careful," the captain said.

She pulled a digital camera out of her bag and rose, almost immediately stumbling over a backpack. Jack shot out of his seat and righted her before she could lose her balance.

"I've got you," he said, keeping his hands on her shoulders and her body in front of him. He immediately thought about how much he missed being this close to her. He'd never been a patient man, but wasn't sure how to convince her they should be together. She snapped a few photos, including one with the five children in the foreground.

"It's wild to see ponies living on the coastline," Jack said, hiding his disappointment when Tara broke away from him and sat back down. "How did they get here?"

"Nobody's real sure," the boat captain said. "We like to think they swam ashore in the 1700s from a shipwrecked Spanish galleon."

"What's a galleon?" Danny asked.

Jack hadn't realized Danny was paying attention to their conversation, as intent as he was on the ponies. He sat down beside the boy and ruffled his hair. "Just a boat, buddy."

"Can the ponies swim?" Danny asked.

"Absolutely," the captain said. "Every July we round 'em up and drive 'em across the channel. We've got vets on hand to give them their annual checkups. After that, the town holds an auction."

"What's an auction?" Susie asked.

"It means people can buy some of the ponies," Aggie explained. The camp's second in command had been much quieter than usual, confessing earlier that the boat ride was making her feel queasy.

"Can we buy a pony?" Danny asked Tara.

Tara laughed. "A pony wouldn't be too happy in my mother's backyard. There's not enough room."

"Then can we watch them swim?"

Jack started to tell Danny he'd bring him back to Assateague for the event in July, then stopped himself. If things went according to Jack's plans, he would be picked up by a minor league team by then. The prospect usually cheered him. Not today, though. Today he realized success in his career would take him away from Tara and her family.

Once the children had their fill of looking at the ponies, the captain headed back through the salt marshes to the open water of the bay. They passed under the Chincoteague bridge and in no time were once again at the floating dock.

Jack disembarked first, helping the children step off the boat onto the dock and making sure Aggie was okay until she got her land legs back. Tara was last. He extended a hand to her, reluctant to let go of her when she was safely on shore.

"Jack's your boyfriend now," Danny said, grinning at them. "Boyfriends and girlfriends hold hands."

"He's got you there, Tara," Jack said, holding tight. "That's the truth."

Tara made a face at him and slipped her hand from his, but she was laughing. Yes, things were definitely looking up.

"Looks like the other boat isn't back yet," Jack said.

"Let's hope things went smoothly, for my mother's sake," Tara said. "Considering how she feels about the water, I'm shocked she agreed to get on the boat."

"Your mother's stronger than you give her credit for," Jack said, a thought he'd had more than once. "Maybe she's finally ready to let go of the past."

"I hope so," Tara said.

Aggie nodded toward the swings and monkey bars on the other end of the park. Her color was already coming back. "Let's wait for the rest of our group at the playground. How does that sound, kids?"

"I want to go to the playground!" Susie yelled. "Let's race!"

Four of the children took off, some with stumbling gaits, all of them laughing.

"Wait up," Brandy called, dashing after them and looking more like a kid than a counselor. Aggie followed at a slower pace. Danny walked a few steps, then sat down, right in the middle of the sidewalk.

"Oh, no," Tara said as an aside to Jack. "Not again. He seemed like he was doing so much better today."

"I've been thinking about Danny's situation," Jack said so only Tara could hear. "You know, with his mom giving him up but keeping his brother."

Tara nodded. "It had to affect him, but I can't begin to figure out what's going on in his head. My mother can't, either. She's making him an appointment with a psychologist."

Except Danny must be leaving them clues. Jack thought back to Wednesday night, when Danny had refused to bowl on the wii or try to catch the fireflies. Was there a pattern to the things he refused to do? The boy usually cooperated at camp, discounting the times he wouldn't take part in the physical activities.

Eureka! Jack thought.

"That's great about the psychologist, but right

now would you let me handle Danny, Tara?" he asked, his eyes on Danny's sad slouch.

"Sure," she said, touching him briefly on the arm. "Give it your best shot. I'll be at the playground."

Jack waited until Tara was gone before he sauntered up to Danny and stopped. "Hey, buddy. What are you doing down there?"

Danny thrust out his lower lip and crossed his arms over his chest. *If you can't beat 'em,* Jack figured. He plopped down on the sidewalk next to the boy.

Danny's chin came up. "You're not 'sposed to sit on the sidewalk."

"You're doing it," Jack pointed out.

"You're 'sposed to tell me not to," Danny said.

"Nah," Jack said. "I don't feel like it. Kind of like you didn't feel like racing the other kids."

Danny said nothing. The wind whipped through the park, creating a whistling noise. In the distance, Jack could hear the other campers laughing and shouting on the playground. A group of people waiting to board another tour boat talked among themselves, their voices carrying on the breeze.

"My little brother would never race me when we were growing up," Jack said. "I was older than Mike and he hated to lose."

"My little brother always wins," Danny said.

"That's how it happens sometimes," Jack said.

"But just because you come in second doesn't mean you should stop trying."

Danny shook his head. "No. Trying doesn't work. I c-can't do it."

Jack sensed the boy was trying to tell him something important, but he was having a hard time following his train of thought. "What can't you do?"

Danny was silent for a long time before he muttered, "Anything right."

"What?" Jack said. "Who said that?"

Danny's lower lip trembled. Whoever had implanted that idea in his head had dug deep.

"Well, whoever it was, they were wrong," Jack said. "You can do lots of things."

Danny blinked back tears. "No, I c-can't."

"Hey, you're the one who spotted the pony today. And remember all those fish you caught?"

Danny shook his head as though Jack hadn't spoken. "Something wrong with me."

"No way, bud," Jack said with feeling.

"Something wrong with me," Danny repeated. "That's why she didn't want me."

Jack digested the information and swallowed a groan. Now they were getting to the crux of the matter. "Are you talking about your mother?"

He nodded, tears running down his face.

Ah, hell. Had Danny's mother really made a habit of asking Danny what was wrong with him when he couldn't perform up to his brother's standards? Didn't she know how special children with Down syndrome were?

"I want you to listen to me, Danny." Jack waited until the boy looked at him. "Nothing is wrong with you. You're good and kind and fun to be around. I wouldn't change a single thing about you. And neither would Tara or Carrie."

Danny caught his breath on a sob. Jack reached over and hugged him. Danny held tight.

"I don't want to hear any more about what you can't do," Jack said. "I want you to start showing what you can do."

After a long moment, Danny's hold on Jack lessened. He ruffled Danny's hair, then stood up and extended a hand to the boy. He pulled him to a standing position. They walked side by side to the playground, with Jack unable to think of anything else to say.

Once they arrived, Danny sat down on a swing a distance away from the other children. He scuffed his foot in the sand but didn't swing.

Tara got up from the park bench where she'd been watching the children and came to stand beside Jack. "What was all that about?"

Jack told her as succinctly as possible, unable to keep the disgust out of his voice. "Can you believe a mother would do that to her own flesh and blood?"

Tara shook her head, her expression troubled.

"There's lots of ignorance surrounding mental disabilities. Danny's mother might just be uneducated."

"You're being too kind." Jack bit off the words. "I wish I could give her a piece of my mind."

"It's better you give Danny your support," she said.

"Yeah, but I don't think I got through to him." Jack gestured to where Danny still sat motionless on the swing. His sadness arrowed straight to his heart.

Tara braced a hand on Jack's shoulder. Without warning, she brought her head close to his and kissed him on the lips. The contact was short but unutterably sweet.

"What was that for?" he asked in surprise.

"For trying," she said. "And for caring."

The wind was playing havoc with her hair again, blowing the errant strands into her face. He brushed them back, wishing she wasn't wearing sunglasses so he could see her eyes. It was time, he thought, to lighten the mood and make a move.

"Would you see through me if I capitalized on this warm feeling you seem to have for me right now by inviting you to my place for dinner tonight?" he asked.

Her lips curved into a gorgeous smile. "Only if you tried to get me into bed when I got there."

He grimaced. "You got me. That's exactly what I planned to do. Forgive me?"

"After how you just handled things with Danny," she said, reaching up to touch his cheek, "I'd forgive you anything."

CARRIE LET THE SURF WASH over her bare feet early on Friday evening, barely able to believe that she was enjoying the warm, wet feel of the salt water. If someone had told her even three weeks ago that she'd go on a boat tour and a walk along the beach the same day, she wouldn't have believed it.

But then three weeks ago, she hadn't met Gustavo.

"Yes, ma'am," he said from where he walked alongside her. "I once ran across the University of Maryland campus wearing nothing but sneakers and a smile."

"You're pulling my leg," she said, laughing.

It seemed as if she'd been laughing all day. Maybe all week. And why not? She'd been ridiculously lucky the night they played bingo, winning two jackpots that gave her enough money to pay for Danny's second week of camp. Then earlier today, when they'd chaperoned the field trip to Chincoteague together, they'd had such a good time that Carrie had readily accepted when he'd invited her and Danny to dinner.

She'd also said yes when he asked her to take an

after-dinner stroll on the beach. Danny and Susie had stayed behind with a neighbor who'd dropped by unexpectedly and offered to watch them.

"Oh, yes, I did," he said. "This was the dead of winter. At one point I went down on some icy pavement and slid on my butt about ten yards. It was so cold I couldn't even feel it."

She laughed at the word picture he'd painted. "Why would you do a fool thing like that? The streaking craze was long over by then."

"I told you," he said. "My roommate dared me."

"So if I dared you to strip to your birthday suit right now, you'd do it," she challenged.

"Damn straight."

He grabbed the hemline of his shirt and tugged it over his head.

"Hold on a minute!" Carrie shouted. "I didn't dare you. It was a hypothetical."

One of his hands was already at the waistband of his shorts. He grinned at her, looking better bare chested than he did with his shirt on, impressive for a man in his late forties. He had good muscle definition, a flat abdomen and just the right amount of chest hair.

"You didn't make that clear," he said.

Behind him the sun was low in the sky, casting red-and-gold streaks over the water. It covered him in a soft glow, highlighting his almost-black hair and the long nose that gave his handsome features a Latin cast. She couldn't say for sure what looked better, the sunset or the man. She almost protested when he tugged his shirt back on.

Time to focus on the sunset, she thought.

"It's been so long since I was at the beach this time of night that I forgot how darn pretty it was," Carrie said.

"I love coming down here," Gustavo said. "Whoever buys my grandma's B and B and gets it up and running again should advertise that the beach is in the backyard."

A tall sandy embankment rose on one side of the narrow strip of beach, with the B and B and neighboring houses set well back from the cliff. Steep wooden staircases leading to those houses dotted the beach at regular intervals.

Small seabirds soared parallel to the waves, waiting until the water receded to snatch crustaceans exposed by the surf.

"Then don't sell it," she said. "I know you closed the house to guests, but the business is already in place. You could hire somebody to fix up the house and help you out."

"That's an idea," Gustavo said. "Got anybody in mind?"

Me, Carrie thought. Just as quickly, she rejected the idea. She already feared she was spending too much time with Gustavo. What kind of message would it send if she finagled it so she saw him every single day?

"Hey, you don't have a job right now, do you?" Gustavo asked, almost as though he'd read her mind. He didn't wait for her answer. "If I do decide to keep the place and reopen it, would you be interested?"

"No," she said quickly.

"Why not? You like to cook, right? And I'd have no problem with you bringing Danny to work with you. He'll be going to the same school as Susie and me. I told you I have a teaching job that starts in the fall. Once classes start, he can even catch rides with us."

Carrie shook her head. "It's a bad idea."

"What if I offer you double what you made at your last job?" he asked.

"Now, why would you do that?" Carrie asked.

"Camp's over and I like seeing you every day. Susie does, too. It'd be great if you were the female influence in her life. And who knows?" He nudged her gently with his elbow. "If you spend more time with me, I might grow on you."

Thanks to the cash prizes at bingo, she no longer had to worry about finding the money for camp. However, she needed to come up with money to pay her bills. She felt certain she could help make the B and B a success and that she'd love everything about managing it. But she couldn't take advantage of him, not when he was such a great guy.

"I'm not gonna date you, Gustavo," she said.

"That's odd," he said, "because we're already dating. What did you think dinner Wednesday night was all about?"

"Two people getting together." She repeated his words back to him.

"That's the definition of a date," he said. "The only reason I didn't take you somewhere fancier is because I didn't want to freak you out."

No way would she tell him about how she'd changed from her sexy black dress when she'd spotted him out the window. Or confess she'd been initially disappointed when he suggested bingo after dinner, because she'd envisioned him taking her for a nightcap to someplace elegant with candles on the tables.

"We're together now and this isn't a date," she said.

"It's almost a date," Gustavo said. "Why do you think I picked up that seafood paella from Lucia's Restaurant for dinner?"

"Because I told you how it's so good I can hardly stand it?"

"Yes," he said. "And that neighbor who stopped by and offered to stay with Susie and Danny while we took a walk? That was no coincidence. I asked her to do that."

"Why'd you go and do that?" she asked.

"Why not?" He stopped walking and took her hand so she had to stop, too. "I like you, Carrie. A lot. I think you feel the same way about me."

With the sun dipping lower on the horizon so it looked partially submerged in the cool gray-blue water of the bay, the colors of the sunset had intensified to create a fiery sky. The deserted beach setting couldn't have been more romantic.

The reality, though, was that Carrie hadn't been in the market for romance in three decades.

She slowly lifted her eyes to his, expecting the memory of her late husband to intrude, the way it always did when a man showed interest in her.

She saw only the strong planes and angles that made up Gustavo's handsome face and the desire in his eyes.

Dear heavens, she wanted him to kiss her.

As though reading her mind, he tugged on her hand to bring her closer. Then he dipped his head so he was the only one she saw. His lips descended, getting closer....

"No," she said, turning her head and pulling her hand out of his at the last second. She took a few staggering steps backward. "I can't."

He quickly masked his obvious disappointment. "Then I'll be patient. I'm not asking you to forget about Scott, just that you make room for me."

"It's not Scott." She could barely believe her own

words, but it was true. The husband whose memory she'd held on to so tightly wasn't the reason she couldn't be with Gustavo. "There are things you don't know about me, things you wouldn't like."

"Nothing you say could change how I feel about you," he said.

Water splashed at her ankles while her feet sank into the sand. The tide was coming in, but she didn't move. "Trust me on this."

"I can't," he said. "I know you're a good person, Carrie."

"Would a good person have enrolled her foster son in a camp when she didn't have the money to pay for it?" she asked. "I even tricked poor Tara into volunteering because I thought maybe then I could get you to forget about the tuition."

"You never asked me to do that," he said.

She couldn't explain why she'd been reluctant to put him in that uncomfortable position.

"Didn't you notice how late I was paying for the second week of camp?" she asked. "If not for those bingo jackpots, I wouldn't have had the money."

"That's not so terrible," he said. "You wanted the camp experience for Danny. You did it for him."

"That's another thing," Carrie said. "You think I became a foster mother because I saw children in need. It was the other way 'round. After Tara went to college, I needed people around who needed me. Being alone plum terrified me."

"You're being too hard on yourself," Gustavo said. "Whatever your motives, look at all the children you've helped. It's no crime to need people in our lives."

She shook her head, her stomach twisting at the effort of holding back her deepest, darkest secret. "You're not getting it. There's something else, something I can't tell you. Something I should never have done."

He took both her hands this time. "Try me."

Could she break the silence she'd kept all these years and confess her biggest transgression, especially because it involved Tara? Could she ever move forward with her life if she didn't?

He gently squeezed her hands, gazing at her with his remarkable green eyes. "I dare you to tell me."

She took a breath of the salty air, released it on the breeze and told him the terrible thing she'd done.

CHAPTER FOURTEEN

TARA WAS HUMMING ON Saturday morning, something she almost never did. Recognizing the tune, she wrapped her arms around herself and smiled.

Earlier this week at camp she'd led the children in a rousing version of "If You're Happy and You Know It." Right about now she felt like clapping her hands, stamping her feet and shouting aloud all at the same time.

Spending last night with the sexiest man on the planet could do that to a girl. Okay, perhaps that was an exaggeration. She'd never been out of the United States and had barely left Virginia. Still, she couldn't imagine a sexier man.

She'd stopped resisting Jack after watching the interplay between him and Danny at the dock. The passionate way he'd defended the child had warmed her through and through. It had suddenly seemed silly to keep him at arm's length because of Hayley Cooper, a little girl who in all probability had no connection to her whatsoever.

So she'd given in to her heart and invited him home with her last night after her busy shift at

O'Malley's. This morning he'd rewarded her by awakening her in the most pleasurable way possible.

Her body still tingled from the aftermath of making love to him. Deciding to believe she was Tara Greer unless proven otherwise had been a very wise move. It had been inevitable, too. Fighting her growing attraction to Jack was too hard.

She dug around in her kitchen cabinets until she found a coffeemaker her mother had insisted she take when she'd bought a new one. Tara hadn't really wanted it but now was glad she'd accepted it along with some packets of coffee. She didn't drink the stuff, but Jack did.

He stuck his head out of her bedroom. He was dressed only in his boxer shorts, his hair was a mess and he needed a shave. She thought he looked terrific. If he asked, she'd tumble back into bed with him in a second.

"I'm gonna take a shower, if that's all right," he said.

"Sure. I'm putting on coffee. Want me to make breakfast?"

"Thanks, but I'll grab one of those muffins I saw on your counter on the way out," he said. "I need to get in some solid work on my shoulder."

"How's the rehab going?" she asked.

"It's going," he said. "A few more weeks and I'll be ready to throw some pitches."

She thought of what Art Goodnight had said about Jack never pitching in the majors again. She should talk to him about that. However, now wasn't the time to bring it up.

"Any idea of what you'd like to do later?" Jack asked.

"Not yet," Tara said. "How about you?"

"As long as we do something together, I'll be happy." He winked at her, then disappeared into the bedroom.

She smiled to herself. She felt the same way. While she was putting a blueberry muffin on a plate and pouring herself a glass of milk, she heard the shower start to run.

As good a time as any to check email.

With the glass of milk cradled in one hand and the plate in the other, she padded across the room to the computer sitting atop the rolltop desk that had once been her mother's. Maybe she'd ask Jack to help her strip off the original finish this weekend. The materials they'd bought at the hardware store were still in her garage.

She sat down in the desk chair and arranged her food and drink to be easily reachable. She pressed the button that booted up the computer, bit into her muffin and waited while she chewed. She washed the bite of muffin down with a swig of milk and waited some more.

She'd forgotten how long the old computer took

to get up and running. She might as well double-check to make sure the desk drawers were completely empty in case she got around to refinishing the rolltop in the next few days.

Her mother had done a fair job cleaning out the top two drawers, aside from a few loose paper clips. The bottom drawer, however, was half filled with assorted desk supplies. Tara went to the kitchen for a plastic grocery bag. When she returned to the desk, the icons on her computer screen had finally appeared. She positioned the mouse over her email icon and clicked. And waited. It'd be another few moments before her computer could access the internet.

She started taking things out of the drawer and dumping them into the bag. Scissors. A stapler. Tape. A couple of tablets and some sheets of loose-leaf paper. The drawer was empty in no time except for something stuck to the bottom of it.

It looked like the back of a photo.

Very carefully Tara peeled the item loose. From the texture, she could tell she was right. It was a photo. She flipped it over.

The face of the woman from her nightmares stared back at her. Her lips curved upward, but her eyes were cold. Tara heard herself gasp. Her hand flew to her mouth. Why did her mother have a photo of the awful woman?

The woman wasn't alone in the photo. She

stood behind a small girl about three years old who could have been Tara. Brown bangs fell into the girl's eyes similar to the bangs Hayley Cooper had sported in the website photo.

What did it mean?

It meant the woman was real.

Tara tore her eyes from the woman staring back at her from the photo paper. Her gaze landed on her email inbox and a subject line that read "DNA results."

The email had been sent late yesterday from the company she'd paid extra for expedited results. All this time she'd been in bed with Jack, it had been waiting for her.

Her heart hammering so hard she heard blood rushing in her ears, Tara reached for the mouse. Her index finger hovered over the button. Then she clicked.

The text of the email appeared, the first sentence jumping out at her.

Jane Doe is excluded as the biological mother of Tara Greer.

Because Tara hadn't provided a name to go along with the hair sample, in actuality Jane Doe was Carrie Greer.

Who was not her mother.

Not her mother. Not her mother. Not her mother.

The surreal words echoed in Tara's brain, making her entire life a lie.

"Mmm. This looks good." Jack was in the kitchen, opening the package with the blueberry muffins. "Hope you don't mind, but I'm gonna pass on the coffee."

She heard him talking, but the only words that computed were the ones she'd just read.

"Tara?" Jack came toward her, a muffin in one hand. "Everything all right?"

He got increasingly closer, almost near enough to see the computer screen. She quickly closed her email program.

"Everything's fine," she said, the words sounding like a lie even to her own ears.

He cocked his head. "Are you sure?"

Things had never been less okay in her life. Again she yearned to confide in him, but she couldn't, not until she figured out what to do—maybe not ever. She'd been a fool to give in to how she felt about him and dismiss the mounting evidence that she was Hayley, even if it was circumstantial.

She forced herself to smile. "I'm sure."

"What's that in your hand?" he asked.

She'd forgotten she was holding the photo. She crumpled it into her fist. "It's nothing. Just some trash from the desk."

He watched her with narrowed eyes, seeming about to say something else.

"Don't you need to get going?" she asked.

"Yeah, right." He leaned down and planted a soft kiss on her mouth, then straightened. "See you later."

He was almost to the front door when he stopped and turned around. "I almost forgot to tell you. We've got plans for tonight, after all."

It took everything Tara had to focus on what he'd said. Plans. For tonight. "We do?" she asked.

"Remember those calls I was getting last night that I let go to voice mail?" he asked.

She dredged up the memory and nodded. He'd said the calls were from one of his sisters.

"I just checked my messages," he said. "My sister's in Virginia Beach. She'll be at my place late this afternoon. I thought the three of us could go to dinner together."

Tara gulped back her panic. She needed to ask the question, although she already knew the answer. "Which sister?"

"Maria," he said.

The private investigator who'd been hired to find Hayley Cooper, the little girl Tara now knew she used to be.

JACK HAD THOUGHT OF ALMOST everything to make the first meeting between Tara and his sister go well. He'd made reservations at a classy restaurant by the water. He'd requested a table by the window with a view of the sunset. He'd gotten himself and Maria to the restaurant on time.

The one thing he hadn't done was insist on picking up Tara.

"Are you sure you told her the right time?" Maria asked, twirling the stem of her wineglass. "She's already fifteen minutes late."

"I'm sure." He'd called Tara with the plans a few hours ago, although they'd talked only a minute before she had to ring off.

"Did you check to see if she left you a message?" Maria asked.

Jack hadn't heard his cell phone go off, but he pulled it out of his pocket to double-check. "No messages."

Their waiter, a gentleman with slate-gray hair, gave another pass by their table. He was as elegant as the restaurant, a new place with a black-and-silver color scheme that took advantage of excellent views of the bay. It was nearly full, mostly with older customers who looked as if they were on vacation, the kind of people who had expendable income.

"We're still waiting for one more person," Jack told the waiter. To Maria, he said, "Let's give her five more minutes. If Tara's not here by then, I'll call her."

Maria had striking coloring. Pale skin, long black hair and blue eyes that were the definition of piercing.

"You really want me to meet her." It was a statement, not a question. "Why is that? You can't have known her long."

"It doesn't take long to know you like someone," Jack said.

"How much do you like her?" Maria asked. "Enough that you have things to talk about when you're not in bed together?"

Jack kneaded the spot between his eyes. "You're not shy about asking me anything, are you?"

"Why should I be?" she asked. "I'm your sister. I love you."

He might as well answer or she'd find another way to wheedle the information from him. "I enjoy Tara's company, okay? Everybody does. She's really plugged in to her community."

Maria broke eye contact with him so he no longer felt like an insect under a microscope. She leaned back in her chair, "Bully for you, then. Summer flings can be a lot of fun."

"Did I say it was a fling?' he asked before he could stop himself. Who knew what Maria would make of that question?

"You said she has roots here," Maria said. "You can't be thinking of staying much longer."

The text tone on his cell phone buzzed, saving

him from answering. He wasn't sure how he'd respond, anyway. He'd been living day by day, thinking only of working toward the goal of getting his arm healthy. He checked the display screen.

"It's from Tara," he told Maria.

He pressed a key and the text appeared. Sorry. Can't make it tonight.

"What's wrong?" Maria asked.

He realized he was frowning. "Tara won't be joining us."

"Why not?'

He didn't have the foggiest idea. Her text had offered no explanation. "Something came up," he said vaguely.

"Then let's get the waiter over here. I'm starving." Maria said, raising a hand to signal him.

She ordered seafood and ate with gusto when the food came, deflecting his attempts to get to the bottom of the reason for her visit.

"Okay, enough," he said after she'd eaten every bite of her meal and the waiter had brought her a piece of key lime pie. "I want to know what you're really doing here."

"I told you," Maria said. "I was in Virginia Beach running down a lead on a case."

"The Hayley Cooper case?"

She shook her head. "I'm afraid that one won't ever be solved. The trail's too cold. This case was workmen's compensation fraud."

He frowned. "Why did the client call you and not someone local?"

"I went to college with the owner of the business," she said. "I'm the only private eye he knows."

"*You* know other private eyes. Why not just refer your friend to someone else?" He groaned as the answer struck him. "It was because of me, wasn't it? You wanted an excuse to come here and check up on me."

"Not entirely." She put a forkful of pie into her mouth and closed her eyes in apparent bliss. She chewed before answering. "I also wanted an excuse to come to the beach for a few days."

"Then you admit you're checking up on me?"

"I prefer to think of it as providing moral support," she said, waving a fork at him. "I know how tough these shoulder problems have been on you."

"I'm working through them," he said. "Getting stronger every day."

"I meant mentally," Maria said. "It can't be easy to face up to the fact that you'll never pitch in the majors again."

He felt his spine stiffen. "That's an opinion, not a fact."

"Shared by everybody but you," she said.

He looked out at the water. Clouds obscured the sinking sun, ruining what should have been a great sunset.

"I'm the only one who's attached to my shoulder," he pointed out. "Can we change the subject?"

"Okay," she said. "When are you coming back to Kentucky?"

When my shoulder's where I want it to be, he thought. *When I'm ready to contact a major league club to say I've bucked the odds. When I can tear myself away from Tara.*

"I haven't decided," he said.

"Because of that woman, Tara? Is she why you're sticking around?" In typical Maria fashion, she didn't give him time to answer. "How did you meet her, anyway?"

"She's the physical education teacher who looks like the age progression of Hayley Cooper," he said.

Maria snapped her thumb and the third finger of her right hand together before pointing at him.

"Maybe she is Hayley," she said, eyes dancing. "Maybe she didn't want to meet me because she thought I might figure it out."

"Good try, but Tara isn't Hayley Cooper," Jack said. "I'm friends with Tara's mother. Carrie's such a good person that she's the foster mother to a special-needs child."

"Oh, well," Maria said, spearing another piece of pie. "You can't blame a P.I. for trying."

He didn't. Considering Tara hadn't provided a reason for standing them up, Maria's joking guess was as good as any.

TARA KEPT HER HANDS A shoulder's width apart on the paddle and stroked on the right side of the kayak Sunday morning, rotating her torso as she pulled the paddle alongside the boat. She snapped the blade out of the water and repeated the motion on the polyethylene boat's left side, exactly as she'd been doing for the past two hours.

Her arm muscles ached with the effort to keep the twelve-foot kayak moving at speed through the shallow water of the tidal creek, and her lungs strained. The conditions, light wind and virtually no tidal current, would have made for smooth and easy paddling if she hadn't been traveling much faster than normal and passing every other kayaker she saw.

Usually all it took to clear her mind was a leisurely look around at the scenery. Shorebirds resting on the marsh grass that stuck out of the water in tufts. Fish leaping from the water before disappearing again into the depths. Sun shining out of a crystalline blue sky.

The stunning vista hadn't worked today, less than twenty-four hours since she'd discovered her entire life was a lie.

Today, when her brain felt as if it might explode, her goal was to become too tired to think.

She'd spent yesterday in a daze, driving aimlessly for a few hours before hiking through a state park in the heat of the day, replaying scenes from her childhood, wondering how she hadn't noticed any warning signs.

When darkness fell she'd been no closer to figuring out anything, least of all how to handle the information that she'd been abducted from a shopping mall in Kentucky. She'd parked her car in the elementary school lot, kept off her porch light and switched off her phones.

She didn't want anyone to know she was home. Not the mother who wasn't really her mother. And not Jack, who had expected her to show up at that restaurant to meet his sister, the private investigator who was searching for her.

Jack, whom she'd stood up with a terse text message that bordered on rude.

She groaned. Her plan wasn't working. Vigorous kayaking wasn't going to provide a respite from all that was wrong in her world.

She pulled the paddle from the water and let the kayak glide while she caught her breath. A light wind was at her back, propelling the kayak forward without any effort from her.

She'd been paying so little attention to her surroundings that she was surprised to see she was approaching the public access spot where she'd put the kayak into the water.

The tiny parking lot, populated with an assortment of cars with boat trailers and roof racks, became visible. So did a tall, dark-haired man leaning against the truck bed of a white pickup truck.

Tara released a long jagged breath. It wasn't just any man. It was Jack.

What was he doing here? How had he found her?

Even as the questions whirled through her head, she knew the answers didn't matter. What mattered was protecting the woman who'd been her mother for twenty-eight years. Tara wouldn't let anything bad happen to Carrie Greer, no matter what she'd done.

She wondered why it had taken her almost an entire day to figure that out when the conclusion had been inevitable all along.

The only way to protect Carrie, however, was to drive Jack away. If he hadn't been close to his family, she might be able to risk it. But he lived in the same town as his parents, and his sisters didn't let many days pass before one of them called him. Maria had even driven to Shell Beach to check up on him.

No, being around Jack was much too risky. She took a breath that sounded like a sob and schooled her features into a mask.

She didn't know whether she could do this.

She had to do this.

She steered the kayak to the public access ramp while Jack straightened from the truck and walked down to meet her. Earlier the ramp had been teeming with activity, but for the moment nobody else was around. When the water was shallow enough, she stepped out of the boat to drag it onto dry land.

"Let me give you a hand with that," Jack said.

"Thanks," she said, trying not to soak in the sight of him. His pale yellow T-shirt and khaki shorts called attention to how his tan had deepened since he'd started renting the beach house. Even in the loose-fitting casual clothes, it was obvious what great shape he was in. He dragged the kayak onto the cement slab, his mouth twisting in what looked like pain. His shoulder, she thought.

He lifted her kayak and carried it to her car, strapping it to the roof as though he'd done it a hundred times before. The only sign that he might be hurting was a tightness around his mouth. Or maybe the strain was there for another reason.

He didn't seem inclined to open the conversation so she did. "How long were you waiting for me?"

"A half hour or so," he said. "I watched half a dozen other kayakers come and go."

"How did you know I was here?" She asked another of those questions that paled in importance to the real issue, partly to stall until she gathered her courage to do what had to be done.

"We talked about going kayaking together, remember?" he asked.

That was right. He'd made short shrift of her concern that kayaking would be hard on his shoulder. So she'd intended to borrow a kayak from a friend and show him the ropes. But that was before she found out she was Hayley Cooper.

She had a terrible premonition that for the rest of her life there'd be an invisible dividing line between before and after.

"I forgot about that," she said.

"I called this morning to remind you, but your phone went to voice mail," he said. "I couldn't reach you last night, either. I tried after my sister and I got back from dinner."

"Is your sister still here?" She fought to keep the worry out of her voice.

"She headed back to Kentucky early this morning," he said.

Some of the tension left her shoulders. He was watching her carefully. "Mind telling me why you didn't want to meet her?"

This was the question she'd both anticipated and dreaded. If she was going to keep her mother safe, it was imperative that she be believable.

"Oh, come on, Jack." She made herself sound chastising, the way she sometimes spoke to a physical education student who'd disappointed her.

"Just because we slept together a few times doesn't mean I need to meet your family."

His mouth actually dropped open. She was glad his eyes were covered by dark shades, because she didn't want to see more evidence that her words were hurting him.

"It's like you said when you walked me to the hardware store," she continued in the same detached voice. "It's not like there could ever be anything serious between us."

"That was before." He didn't elaborate. He didn't need to. He meant that was before they'd slept together and discovered their feelings ran deep.

But this was after she'd discovered who she really was.

"Nothing's changed, Jack," she lied. "I'm still staying here in Wawpaney and you're still leaving. Speaking of leaving, I should go."

"Wait a minute. Sit with me awhile." He indicated a large flat rock that overlooked the salt marsh. "Make me understand where this is coming from."

The more time she spent in his presence, the more her facade was crumbling. Yet she couldn't leave, not until she'd done a better job of driving him away.

She preceded him to the rock and sat down, gazing out at a great blue heron at the marsh's edge.

She'd never seen the majestic birds in pairs, only alone. As she would soon be.

"It's like this, Jack." She watched the heron and not him. It flapped its wings and flew off into the bright blue sky. "It's inevitable that our relationship is going to end. I say we end it now."

"What if I told you I'm willing to do what it takes to make things work between us?" he asked.

Her heart leaped with hope. Just as quickly, it plummeted. She couldn't let herself soften toward him, no matter the emotional cost.

"I'm supposed to accept this, from a guy who's spent the last few years lying to himself?" she asked.

He frowned. "What am I lying to myself about?"

"Your shoulder, Jack." She needed to be blunt, no matter how much it pained her. "I see you wincing. I know it hurts more than you admit, yet you keep insisting you're going to pitch in the majors again."

"I am," he said.

"See? That's exactly what I'm talking about," she said. "Everybody but you knows that isn't going to happen. Your family. The doctor back in Kentucky. The specialist vacationing on Tangier."

"Art Goodnight said—"

"He said you're delusional if you think you'll pitch in the majors again," she interrupted harshly. "That's what he told me."

"Art said that?" Jack looked and sounded stunned. He shook his head. "Then obviously he isn't the best person for me to be working with."

"Nobody is, Jack," she said. "Face facts. Not only about your baseball career, about us."

His hand shot out and captured her chin so she had to look at him. He carefully took off her sunglasses and laid them on the rock beside them.

"Who are you to tell me to face facts?" He laughed wryly. "You won't even admit you're falling in love with me."

She shook her head. That couldn't be true. She wouldn't let it be.

"Let's try an experiment, then." He flipped up his sunglasses so they perched on top of his head. Before she could even think about moving away, his mouth came down on hers.

Despite the heat behind his words, his lips were soft and gentle, coaxing instead of demanding. She should pull away from him, she thought, but she couldn't muster the strength, not when a warm tide seemed to be flowing through her body. Because she couldn't help herself, she kissed him back, her lips clinging to his even when he drew back.

"That kiss proves you have feelings for me." He didn't sound smug. He sounded relieved.

She didn't have the luxury of surrendering to her emotions. If she failed to drive him away, it could spell doom for her mother. She called upon her resolve, praying she could get through the next few minutes without Jack realizing she was feeding him lies.

"All it proves," she said slowly and succinctly, "is that I'm physically attracted to you."

His hand dropped from her shoulder. His eyes filled with pain.

"Accept that it's over between us, Jack," she said. "I have."

She got up from the rock and moved away from him toward her car before he could say anything else. She didn't dare look back. She couldn't afford to let him see the tears she felt slipping down her face.

CHAPTER FIFTEEN

A PROMISE WAS A PROMISE, Jack thought later that Sunday afternoon as he rapped on the screen door of Carrie Greer's house.

He wasn't about to break his to Danny just because Tara had dumped him. He took a deep breath. The pain of it was so raw, it felt as if he'd swallowed something with jagged edges.

Tara hadn't even let him down easily or kept alive the possibility they could be friends. If he hadn't heard her with his own ears, he'd never have believed she had the capacity to be so cruel.

Evidently she wasn't the woman he'd thought she was. That was no consolation. He still wanted her. He probably always would.

He stood, waiting. The kitten Danny had adopted pranced into the foyer on dainty feet, not stopping until she peered up at him from the opposite side of the screen door.

"Meow!" It wasn't an entirely happy sound, more plaintive than not.

"What? You're not having a good day, either?" he asked the cat. "Join the club."

He heard the murmur of voices coming from the back of the house. "Hello," he called.

No reply.

The kitten scratched at the door, her claws gaining her no traction as she tried to make the climb.

"Get back," he told the cat, opening the door slowly so he didn't hurt her. He came inside, picking up the soft animal. She immediately snuggled against his chest. She was awfully young to be separated from her mother. She was probably missing her.

"Hello," he called again.

Again, no response. He followed the voices through the house to the family room.

"Am not!" Danny cried. His fisted hands were balanced on his hips and his face was turning red, a marked contrast to the smiley face on his red T-shirt.

"Are, too!" Susie shouted in a singsong voice, twirling the skirt of her casual summer dress, sounding more smug than angry.

"Stop shouting, children." Mrs. Jorgenson was the third person in the room. She stood between the children like a referee, wringing her hands and looking every one of her eighty-plus years. She appeared to be even more upset than Danny. "How many times do I have to tell you that?"

Jack cleared his throat to draw attention to himself and stepped into the room. "Hey, how's it going? The door was open so I let myself in. I hope you don't mind."

"We don't mind at all," Mrs. Jorgenson said in an overly cheerful voice. "Look who's here, children. It's Jack."

She was making an obvious attempt at misdirection, something Jack had used to effect with his magic tricks. The problem was, Danny wasn't even looking at her.

"Am not!" Danny shouted again, stamping one of his sneaker-clad feet for emphasis.

Jack closed the distance between him and the child. For once, the boy didn't seem in the mood for a hug. "What's this all about, Danny?"

"Susie called me a scaredy c-cat." Danny thrust out his lower lip. "I'm not a scaredy c-cat!"

The kitten hid its face against Jack's chest. The irony, he thought.

He turned to Susie, stooping to get on eye level with her. "Why'd you call Danny that, Susie?"

"Because I'm gonna take swimming lessons and he's afraid to," Susie said.

Her statement was on the money. Jack remembered Carrie telling him she'd been forced to discontinue Danny's lessons earlier this summer after he refused to submerge so much as a toe in the water.

"Tell her I can do anything I want to, Jack!" Danny parroted back the message that Jack had tried to drill into him after the field trip, the one Jack thought had fallen on deaf ears.

"That's right," Jack said. "If Danny gets it into his mind to learn how to swim, he'll learn how to swim."

"Tell her how special I am, Jack," Danny commanded.

Jack hid a smile. "You're both special," he said. "And it sounds like you're both going to take those swimming lessons."

"I am," Danny said. He stuck out his tongue at Susie. "So there."

She, too, stuck out her tongue, wagging her head and making a funny face. Danny laughed. Susie joined in. Mrs. Jorgenson did, too. Soon all four of them were chuckling.

"This calls for milk and cookies," Mrs. Jorgenson said, obviously relieved. She bustled off to the kitchen while the children cheered.

The kitten had relaxed as soon as the children stopped shouting at each other. Jack put her down, pulled a CD out of his back pocket and held it out to the boy. "This is for you, Danny. It's the book *Misty of Chincoteague* on audio tape. That means somebody will play it for you. I told you I'd find it."

"Thanks!" Danny said, snatching it out of his hand.

"I want to listen, too!" Susie said.

"Maybe you can listen to it together." Out of the corner of his eyes Jack saw Mrs. Jorgenson motioning to them. "Right now, though, let's have the milk and cookies."

While the children settled themselves at the kitchen table, Jack snatched a cookie and hung back with Mrs. Jorgenson.

"Thank you for breaking up that argument." She had a nice way about her, with kind eyes and a face softened by age. "You're wonderful with the children, you know."

"It's trial and error," Jack said.

"You seem like an expert to me. I was never so glad to see anybody when you walked into the living room."

"I'm just glad I could help." Jack bit into the cookie, savoring the gooey chocolate center. "This is great, Mrs. Jorgenson." He raised his voice. "Aren't these cookies delicious, kids?"

"Delicious," Susie repeated.

"Mmm-hmm." Danny nodded but kept on chewing with obvious enjoyment. Jack remembered that he had a sweet tooth.

"Don't forget to drink your milk," Mrs. Jorgenson called. "Especially you, Danny. Carrie says it's healthy for you."

"I've been meaning to ask," Jack said, once again talking only to Mrs. Jorgenson. "Where is Carrie?"

"I think she's at Tara's." Mrs. Jorgenson frowned. "Or maybe she's trying to find Tara. I wasn't real clear on that. Gus went with her. Don't you think they make a lovely couple?"

"They do," Jack agreed.

"You and Tara make a lovely couple, too." Mrs. Jorgenson's eyes twinkled, unaware that even the mention of Tara was like a thorn in Jack's side. "She told me the other day that she's sweet on you."

Shock rippled through him. "She did? When was this?"

"Oh, let's see. It must have been Wednesday. Yes, it was Wednesday. I confess, I did ask her about you. I've seen you around and Carrie mentioned that she thought Tara was falling for you."

Then why had Tara blown him off with as much gusto as hurricane-force winds over the Atlantic Ocean?

It didn't make sense that she'd gone from hot to ice-cold in four short days simply because he'd invited her to meet his sister. If Jack hadn't known better, he'd think Maria might have been onto something when she joked that maybe Tara was Hayley Cooper.

But of course she wasn't. Tara had convinced Jack of that right away. He cast his mind back to their first meeting. She'd matched the photo of Hayley except for the shade of her brown hair, yet it now occurred to him that Tara could easily have added the reddish highlights. She also could have been lying when she said she'd seen photos of herself as a baby.

His gaze fell on one of the family photos on a side table of a smiling, cherubic baby in the arms of a young Carrie. The baby's hair was blond, but that didn't mean anything. Lots of kids started out blond before their hair darkened.

"See that photo over there?" He pointed to the one in question. "Do you know if that baby is Tara?"

"Oh, no, that's Sunny," Mrs. Jorgenson said. "You can tell because she had a tiny mole above the left side of her mouth. I never met her, but Carrie mentioned it once."

Now that she'd pointed out the mole, Jack could see it. He surveyed the rest of the photos. There were several of Sunny with Carrie's late husband and a number of Sunny by herself. As a baby, a toddler and a very small girl.

"Where are the photos of Tara?" he asked.

"I believe there are some in the hall," she said with a delighted smile. "I bet you'd like to see them."

"I would," he said.

She led the way to the foyer, leaning on her cane as she walked. The walls were lined with more photos. Mrs. Jorgenson indicated three of them.

"There's one of Carrie and Tara. And there's a photo of Tara by herself. And there she is in her high school graduation photo."

Tara was about eight or nine in the first photo, much older in the others. Nowhere was there a photo of Tara as a baby or young child. Also absent were any photos of Tara with her father or with Sunny. Didn't parents always photograph their children together? A shiver ran through him.

"Is something wrong, Jack?" Mrs. Jorgenson was regarding him with a pinched brow.

He turned up the corners of his mouth as his mind worked. Could it be possible? "I was thinking I'd love to see what Tara looked like when she was really young. Do you know if there's a picture like that around here?"

"Not here in the house, no." Mrs. Jorgenson smiled brightly. "But I have one. If you keep an eye on Danny and Susie, I'll go across the street and get it."

Normally Jack would have refused because of Mrs. Jorgenson's mobility issues, but these were not normal circumstances.

"I'd love that," he said.

The next five minutes were interminable. He nodded at all the right places, but only half listened to Danny's chatter about how he and Carrie were going to start spending a lot more time at the B and B.

Mrs. Jorgenson finally rejoined them, waving a photo. "I think it's sweet that you want to see what Tara used to look like. I ran across this photo just the other day when my daughter was visiting. It brought back such memories."

Jack clutched at his pant leg so he wouldn't rip the photo from her hand.

"I took this the week Tara and Carrie moved here in 1984," she said. "I invited them to my daughter's high school graduation party. Wait till you see what Tara did."

She presented the photo to him with a flourish. In it, a little girl stood beside a cake marred by a hand-shaped crater. Her right hand was covered in chocolate crumbs and golden-brown bangs fell into her eyes.

He held back a gasp.

The girl was a ringer for the three-year-old Hayley Cooper he'd seen pictured on the missing-persons website.

"Wasn't Tara precious?" Mrs. Jorgenson asked. "Even with that cake all over her?"

Jack nodded mutely while his mind churned. If Tara was Hayley, it made sense that she wouldn't want to meet his sister. It was logical that she'd dump him to keep her secret safe.

But maybe his memory was playing tricks on him. Jack couldn't be absolutely sure the photos were of the same girl until he compared them side by side.

"Can I have this photo for a couple days?" Jack asked. "I promise I'll give it back to you."

"Oh, yes!" Mrs. Jorgenson winked at him. "I think you must be sweet on Tara, too."

Shortly afterward, Jack invented an excuse about why he needed to leave. He drove straight to his beach house, booted up his computer and navigated to the missing-persons website.

He clicked through until he had the photo of Hayley Cooper as a three-year-old on his screen. He looked down at the photo of Tara at the birthday party and then up at the one of Hayley.

The breath left his body.

There was no question. They were the same child.

JACK WAS LEANING AGAINST the outside of the fitness club when Tara left the building on Sunday evening.

Even though she'd spent her spinning class with an uneasy feeling in the pit of her stomach, his presence came as a surprise.

Jack straightened to his full height, managing to look impressive even in faded jeans and a T-shirt. A rush of joy shot through her. She determinedly tamped it down. Jack's very presence meant she hadn't done enough to drive him away.

But how could she summon the nerve to alienate him a second time when her first attempt had been so hard on her heart?

"Hello, Tara," he said, stepping from the shadows into the light of a streetlamp. He was unsmiling, his handsome face more serious than she'd ever seen it.

Her heart felt as if it would jump out of her chest. Had he figured out her secret?

She nodded in acknowledgment, not trusting herself to speak.

"Do you have a minute?" He pointed across the street to a city park that came alive in the daylight but looked forlorn in the darkness. "There's a bench over there where we can sit and talk."

She swallowed, shoring up her defenses against him. "I don't have anything to say to you."

"Then do me the courtesy of listening," he said. "You need to hear this."

She couldn't refuse him, not when he asked like that. She nodded. With a sweep of his hand he indicated that she should precede him. The side street where the fitness club was located got a fair amount of traffic during the day, but quieted down at night. It was deserted now, the only person in sight a lone man walking his spirited cocker spaniel.

"Beautiful night," the man remarked, as if there could be no dissenting opinion.

Then again, the man couldn't see the storm gathering inside Tara. She walked to the nearest bench on shaky legs she couldn't blame on her recent spinning class and sank onto it. Clasping her hands together, she tried to look composed.

He sat down beside her, withdrew a piece of paper from his back pocket and unfolded it. Without speaking, he handed it to her.

Darkness had already fallen, but the night was moonlit and the bench was under a streetlamp, providing ample light for Tara to clearly see the image on the piece of paper. Dread crept up on her with icy fingers.

She tamped down her panic. "That's the picture of Hayley Cooper from the website."

"It is," he said.

Without another word he handed her something else—a photo this time. With her heart in her throat, she gazed down at what was indisputably the same little girl. This one was at a graduation party, her hand covered in chocolate cake.

She felt her body sway. The rush of blood in her ears sounded loud enough that it drowned out the sound of the cocker spaniel. She tried to muster the words to convince him she wasn't Hayley. They wouldn't come. It would be pointless, anyway.

Lengthy moments passed.

"How long have you known?" he finally asked, his voice soft.

She closed her eyes, wishing she'd never heard of Hayley. But then she'd never have met Jack.

"Since Saturday morning." She wouldn't tell him about the DNA evidence, not when she didn't know what he'd do with the information.

"You didn't want to meet Maria because you were afraid she'd put it together." It was a statement, not a question. "My guess is that's why you broke up with me, too."

"My mother…" She stopped, unsure how to finish the statement. She wasn't even sure if she should be referring to Carrie Greer as her mother.

"Have you talked to her about this?" he asked.

"No." She'd been dodging Carrie's phone calls and visits, not ready to face her.

"You must have suspected who you were, even before Saturday," he said. "Why didn't you just ask her?"

Tara didn't have to think about the answer. "I didn't suspect before you came to town, not really, although maybe I should have. Carrie's loving and kind. But all my life I've been dreaming of this cruel woman who yells at me and shakes me. If that woman is my real mother, I guess I didn't want to know."

He nodded slowly, as though he could relate. And maybe he could. Earlier this morning she'd accused Jack of not wanting to face the truth about his shoulder injury.

She took a ragged breath. "All those things I said to you this morning—"

"We don't have to talk about that now," he interrupted. "You have something more important to do."

She didn't pretend to misunderstand him, although she could barely breathe at the prospect. "I have to talk to my mother."

She'd done it again. She'd called Carrie her mother.

"Would you like me to go with you?" he asked.

She shook her head. "This is something I have to do for myself. I do have a favor to ask, though."

"Name it," he said.

"Don't do anything until I talk to her." She held her breath as she waited for his answer. She was asking a lot of him. He knew of a terrible crime that had been committed, one his sister was trying to solve.

"You've got it," he said.

CARRIE STARED AT THE images on the television screen, aware that the actors were speaking, but not processing their dialogue. She'd switched on the program after Gustavo and Susie had left and she'd put Danny to bed, because she was afraid to be alone with her thoughts.

The distraction wasn't working.

Canned laughter erupted from the television.

Carrie couldn't even say for sure which sitcom was playing.

She felt a tear drip down her face and then another and another. For twenty-eight years she'd managed to be happy and not think about what she'd done. Now that she'd admitted her transgression to Gustavo, she could think of nothing else.

Somehow she needed to make things right with Tara. However, Tara was avoiding her, almost as though her daughter was aware of Carrie's misdeed and deemed it unforgivable.

More tears fell until Carrie was crying in earnest.

What if, once she knew the whole truth, Tara never forgave her?

"Mom? What's wrong?"

As though Carrie had conjured her up, Tara stood by her recliner in her workout clothes. She must have come from one of her exercise classes.

Carrie composed herself and wiped at the tears on her face with her hand. "Don't mind me. Everything's just fine."

Tara didn't look convinced. "The door was open. I called, but didn't get an answer."

"I must not have heard you over that darn TV." Carrie switched it off, plunging the room into silence. She tried to smile and didn't succeed. "I've been trying to track you down since yesterday."

"I know." Tara seemed about to say something else, then lapsed into an uncharacteristic silence.

The first few months Tara had lived with Carrie, she'd been shy and withdrawn. That hadn't lasted long. Once Tara became accustomed to her new situation, she'd blossomed. By the first or second grade, Tara had had trouble with the concept of not speaking until she was called upon. Carrie even used to have to shush her in church.

Carrie took a deep breath, trying to fortify herself with courage. It was in short supply. However, she had to do this. "I have something I need to get off my chest."

"Me, first." Tara narrowed her eyes and set her features, a determined look Carrie had seen hundreds of times during Tara's childhood. She perched on the edge of the sturdy coffee table directly across from Carrie. "I know you're not my mother."

Carrie closed her eyes. She felt her lips tremble. She hadn't envisioned the moment unfolding this way. She was supposed to break the news to Tara.

"How?" she asked, her throat feeling parched.

"I didn't tell you the whole story about how I met Jack," she said. "His sister Maria's a private investigator."

Carrie's heart constricted. Even though she knew about Jack's sister, she'd convinced herself she had nothing to worry about. This was her worst nightmare come to life. She'd never imagined anybody would come looking for Tara.

"Hayley Cooper's mother hired her," Tara said, answering Carrie's unspoken question.

The statement didn't compute. "Who's Hayley Cooper?"

Tara's mouth twisted. "I am."

Carrie shook her head. "No. Your name was Tina Freeman."

"Freeman? Isn't that your maiden name?"

"That's right." Carrie nodded. Her shoulders rose and fell with her deep breath. "I'm not your mama. I'm your aunt."

"I don't understand," Tara said.

Carrie leaned forward, desperate to tell her side of the story now that she was finally coming clean. "You've heard me talk about my sister, Jenny, right?"

"The one who overdosed when I was a kid?"

"Yes. What you don't know is I tracked down Jenny after Scott and Sunny died. We hadn't talked in years, but I could barely deal with the grief." Carrie remembered how vulnerable she'd been, how desperate she was for support. "I begged her to come visit me. When she did, she had you with her."

Tara shook her head, as though the story didn't add up. It was a lot to take in. Carrie needed to tell Tara the rest for it to make sense.

"Jenny and I were so out of touch, I no idea she had a child. Jenny said she didn't know who your daddy was." Carrie almost smiled, recalling the way her heart had swelled when Tara came into her life. "You were such a sweet, quiet little girl. I fell in love at first sight."

Tara was still shaking her head. "You thought your sister was my mother?"

"Jenny *was* your mother," Carrie said. "But she was sick, an addict. She was high when she showed up with you. She really didn't understand what she was doing—as a mother—and she knew it." Carrie cleared her throat. "I never did see her alive again."

Tara's face had gone deathly pale. She reached into the athletic bag she had with her, pulled out a photograph that looked as if it had been crumpled and handed it to Carrie.

"I found this in the rolltop desk," Tara said. "Is that woman your sister, Jenny?"

"Yes," Carrie said. "That's Jenny."

Tara covered her face with both hands. "Oh, no."

"I know it's a lot to take in," Carrie said, aching as much as Tara, "but there's more. Understand, I already loved you. I was so darn afraid someone would take you away from me that, well, I didn't do things by the letter."

Tara took her hands from her face. "What does that mean?"

This was the worst part, perhaps the unforgivable part. She had to tell Tara, though. She had to tell her everything.

"I started calling you Tara and moved with you here to Wawpaney because it's off the beaten track. I changed your age, too. From three to four." Carrie took a deep breath. Unshed tears pricked at the backs of her eyes. "I did it so I could use Sunny's birth certificate to get a social security number for you. Her given name was Tara. I know it was terrible. But we never did call her Tara, always Sunny. Please believe me that I never tried to pretend you were her. I knew she was gone. But you were alive."

"So you thought for all these years that I was your niece?" Tara asked, an odd note in her voice. "You've actually never heard of Hayley Cooper?"

A chill ran from Carrie's head to her feet. Tara had mentioned that name when the conversation began. "Why do you keep asking me about her?"

Tara didn't answer for a long while. Carrie could hear the tick of the wall clock and the beat of her racing heart.

"Hayley Cooper was abducted from a shopping mall in Kentucky when she was three years old," Tara said. "I'm pretty sure your sister abducted her. I'm Hayley Cooper."

TARA LEANED BACK IN THE uncomfortable plastic chair on the screen porch of Jack's beach house, gazing out at the beautiful morning.

The bright sun shone out of a cloudless azure sky and the gentle waves of the Chesapeake Bay lapped at the shore. Gulls soared through the air and the wind gently whistled.

Everything seemed perfectly in order—ironic considering that for Tara nothing would ever be the same again.

After she'd phoned Jack last night and told him the whole story, she'd slept in the bedroom that had been hers as a child. Carrie had been so upset once they'd pieced together what must have happened that Tara hadn't wanted to leave her. Carrie was especially distraught that her sister had mistreated Tara and caused those years of nightmares.

It had been difficult leaving Carrie this morning, too, but Tara had something she needed to say to Jack. Something that couldn't wait.

She spotted him in the distance slowing from a run to a walk, and a wave of intense feeling swept through her. He balanced his hands on his hips, his head slightly bowed. She imagined he was catching his breath.

She loved the way he moved, with the casual grace of an athlete. His injured shoulder, however, seemed to dip. He walked a bit longer. When he was roughly even with the house, he stripped off his shirt, bent and slipped off his shoes and socks. Then he turned and headed into the bay, diving into the water when it was waist-deep.

His dark head emerged in seconds. She expected him to cut through the water with powerful strokes, but he immediately headed for shore. Again it seemed to her that he was holding one of his shoulders lower than the other.

He picked up his shirt and shoes and headed through the sand to the house, his steps faltering when he was almost to the porch. He raised a hand in greeting. Her heartbeat accelerated, emotion rising in her like high tide. She waved back and waited.

"Hey," he said, talking as he came through the screen door. "I didn't expect to see you here. I was about to take a shower and go to your house."

He reached for a beach towel that was draped over the second plastic chair and dried off. Her throat was dry, she wasn't sure whether it was from nerves or how very good he looked. She cleared it.

"I came to apologize in person," she said.

He paused in the act of drying his hair. "You don't have anything to be sorry for."

"Yes, I do," she said. "I said some terrible things to you."

"Not so terrible," he said. "Some of them, like what you said about me never pitching in the majors again, were true."

She scooted forward in the chair. "What? I thought you didn't accept that. Did something happen to change your mind?"

"You happened," he said.

Tara felt sick to her stomach. She couldn't bear to be the one to wreck his dreams. "What if I was wrong?"

"You're not wrong," he said. "I threw some pitches yesterday afternoon. I'm not close to the level I once was. I have to accept that I never will be."

"I'm sorry." She shook her head. "I'm sorry about so many things."

"You've been under a lot of stress," he said.

"Not as much stress as my mother is under now." Tara took a ragged breath. Their phone conversation last night had been brief, focusing on what had happened in the past and not the consequences that would result in the future. "What did your sister say when you told her you'd found Hayley?"

He cocked his head. "I didn't tell my sister."

"You mean you haven't told your sister *yet*." She'd requested he wait to take action until she'd spoken to her mother, and that time had passed.

"I meant I'm not going to tell her at all," he said. "Your aunt was the truly guilty party and she's dead."

He was right. Jenny Freeman had abducted Tara and treated her cruelly, although they'd never know why. "While your mom shouldn't have done what she did," Jack continued, "from what you told me, she really thought you were her niece."

"But…but…" Tara stopped, trying to get her thoughts in order. "But you can help your sister solve the case."

"My sister isn't my priority." Jack took a step closer to her. She raised her gaze and saw the softness in his eyes. "You are."

"Those other things I said…" Her voice trailed off. It hurt to think about the harsh words she'd fired at him.

"You didn't mean them," he said.

Her heart swelled at his readiness to believe the best of her. It had been the same when they first met—he'd been willing to overlook how coolly she treated him because he saw beneath the surface to who she really was. He truly was a most remarkable man. A courageous one, too. If he could accept he'd never again pitch in the majors, she could face the truth of how she felt about him.

"You're right," she said. "I didn't mean what I said about us."

He extended a hand. The gesture seemed symbolic, as though he were asking her to grasp all he had to offer. She placed a hand in his and let him draw her to her feet.

"This might be crazy because we haven't known each other long, but I've never been so sure of anything in my life." She took a deep breath and a leap of hope. "I love you, Jack DiMarco."

"If you're crazy, then so am I." He put his hands

on each side of her face and gazed deeply into her eyes. "It doesn't matter to me if you call yourself Tara or Hayley. I love the woman you are."

He bent his head and she raised herself to meet him halfway. It felt as if more than their mouths were merging, maybe their very souls. A lot of issues still needed to be resolved between them, but resolve them they would. The argument she'd used to drive him away, that he'd never stay on the Eastern Shore and she'd never leave, didn't hold water anymore. They loved each other. They'd make it work.

She wasn't sure how long they kissed. It could have been minutes. It could have been hours. When they broke apart, however, she was sure of more than how she felt about Jack.

It seemed as though the cloud that had been distorting her thoughts had lifted. In the circle of Jack's arms, she felt empowered to do the right thing.

"If I get in touch with Hayley Cooper's family," she asked, "do you think my mother will be arrested?"

He thought a few moments. "She did falsify documents to get you a social security number, but I can't imagine she'd go to jail over that."

"She might, though."

"It's possible," he conceded. "Did you ask Carrie what she wanted to do?"

"She's a mother. She's sick over the pain she caused Hayley's mother, no matter how inadvertent. She doesn't want her to continue to suffer." Tara paused. "Neither do I."

"Sounds like you've already made your decision," he said.

"I have," she said. "Then I should warn you the road ahead will be bumpy."

"Say the word and I'll travel the road with you."

"That is what I want. You have to do what's right for you, though. I'll understand if you have to go back to Kentucky." She paused, reaching a decision she never thought she'd make. "But if you do, count on me coming with you."

His eyes went wide. "What? You'd leave the Eastern Shore? You'd leave your mother?"

She nodded, supremely sure of one thing. She needed to be where Jack was. "You and Mary Dee have been right all along. Carrie is much stronger than I thought she was. She can get along without me, but I don't think I can live without you."

His hold on her tightened. "You won't have to. I'd rather we didn't live in Kentucky, though. I like it here."

Joy leaped inside her at the prospect of making a home with Jack in the place she already loved. She tried not to get ahead of herself. "What would you do here?"

"You're not the only one who changed the direction of my life. Danny did, too."

"Danny?

"You know how I told him during that field trip to Chincoteague that he was special, that he didn't have to be afraid to try new things?"

She nodded.

His mouth broke into a wide smile. "He listened to me, Tara. He's giving the swimming lessons another try."

She smiled at him and touched his cheek. "You're good with kids like Danny."

"I believe that's true," he said. "I want to go back to school and get a degree so I can work with mentally challenged children."

"Sounds good to me. Who knows? Here on the Eastern Shore you might find you're good at a lot of things." She paused. "I can think of one already."

"Oh, yeah?" he asked. "What's that?"

She smiled at the man she'd come to love in so short a time, the man who was helping her discover the woman she was supposed to be.

"This," she said before she sweetly placed her mouth on his.

EPILOGUE

One year later

TARA STEPPED OUT OF JACK'S pickup truck and took his arm, cutting a glance at him. He wore dark gray pants and a lighter gray shirt that looked fantastic with his dark coloring.

"Are you going to tell me what the surprise is or do I have to guess?" She smoothed the skirt of her flirty red dress, one of the purchases she'd made after discovering red was Jack's favorite color. She was no longer adding reddish highlights to her hair, though. Once again it was golden-brown through and through.

"Neither," he said with a teasing tone. "What do you not understand about the word *surprise?*"

They were approaching the waterfront seafood restaurant where almost exactly one year ago Tara had stood up Jack and his sister Maria. Was that it? Was Maria back in town determined the three of them have dinner together? Tara had met Maria a few times but always in Kentucky.

"Is Maria in there?" she asked.

"You might as well stop guessing, because I'm not telling you anything," he warned.

If he hadn't mentioned the surprise, Tara would have been content to spend the evening at either his place or hers. She didn't need fancy dinners and nights on the town to keep her happy. All she needed was Jack. She still marveled that she never would have met him if she hadn't been abducted.

"Okay, okay," she said. "I suppose I can wait another minute to find out."

That was about how long it took for a hostess to lead them past diners enjoying meals at candlelit tables that overlooked the bay to a far corner of the restaurant. A long table had been set up, and it was full of people. Tara stopped dead, hardly able to believe her eyes.

At one end of the table, her mother and Gus sat across from Mary Dee and her husband. The other end was filled with Coopers. Celia, her biological mother. Frank, her dad. Sydney, the sister who looked so much like her. Sydney's husband and two children were even present.

Everybody was smiling and waving. Tara felt the corners of her own mouth turn up. She and Jack had visited her "other family" three or four times. Up to this point, however, the Coopers had resisted coming to Virginia.

Though a warm person in every other regard, Celia was not favorably disposed toward Carrie

Greer. Celia claimed her beloved daughter Hayley might have been found much sooner if Carrie hadn't spirited her away to Virginia under another name.

Thankfully Tara had been able to convince Celia not to make it her mission to see that Carrie was convicted of a felony. Because the Virginia statute dealing with fraudulent use of a birth certificate had some wiggle room, Carrie had been charged only with a misdemeanor.

"How did you get both of my mothers here together?" Tara asked Jack under her breath.

"It wasn't easy," he whispered back.

"Are Celia and Frank staying at the B and B?" she asked. Her mother had done wonders with the place since she and Gus had reopened it nearly a year ago. Tara often wondered why she and Danny didn't just move in with him. Carrie, however, claimed she and Gus were taking things slowly.

"Sydney and her family are staying there," he said. "Celia was adamant that she and Frank get another hotel."

"It's still the best surprise ever," she said, smiling up at him and kissing him.

Somebody at the table hooted. Tara was pretty sure it was Mary Dee.

"Come join us," Mary Dee called. "Plenty of time for that later."

Never enough time, Tara thought.

She slipped her hand in Jack's and together they approached the table, greeting each person in turn with warm hugs. Tara's cheeks were damp with happy tears when she finished.

"I was just telling Jack what a wonderful surprise this is," Tara said to the group. "But what's the occasion?"

"I was hoping," Jack said, drawing out each word, "it could be an engagement party."

Tara covered her mouth with her hands, happiness bubbling inside her. It spilled over as Jack withdrew a small black velvet box from the back pocket of his slacks. Getting down on one knee, Jack opened the box, displaying a ruby surrounded by tiny twinkling diamonds.

"Tara Hayley Greer Cooper," he said, merging the name she used with the one that should have been hers. "Will you marry me?"

"Yes!" she shouted.

Jack rose to his feet and gathered her into his arms for a promise-sealing kiss while her old family and new one cheered together.

* * * * *

LARGER-PRINT BOOKS!
GET 2 FREE LARGER-PRINT NOVELS PLUS
2 FREE GIFTS!

Harlequin®

Super Romance®

Exciting, emotional, unexpected!

YES! Please send me 2 FREE LARGER-PRINT Harlequin® Superromance® novels and my 2 FREE gifts (gifts are worth about $10). After receiving them, if I don't wish to receive any more books, I can return the shipping statement marked "cancel." If I don't cancel, I will receive 6 brand-new novels every month and be billed just $5.44 per book in the U.S. or $5.99 per book in Canada. That's a saving of at least 16% off the cover price! It's quite a bargain! Shipping and handling is just 50¢ per book in the U.S. or 75¢ per book in Canada.* I understand that accepting the 2 free books and gifts places me under no obligation to buy anything. I can always return a shipment and cancel at any time. Even if I never buy another book, the two free books and gifts are mine to keep forever.

139/339 HDN FEFF

Name	(PLEASE PRINT)

Address	Apt. #

City	State/Prov.	Zip/Postal Code

Signature (if under 18, a parent or guardian must sign)

Mail to the **Reader Service:**
IN U.S.A.: P.O. Box 1867, Buffalo, NY 14240-1867
IN CANADA: P.O. Box 609, Fort Erie, Ontario L2A 5X3

Not valid for current subscribers to Harlequin Superromance Larger-Print books.

**Are you a current subscriber to Harlequin Superromance books
and want to receive the larger-print edition?
Call 1-800-873-8635 today or visit www.ReaderService.com.**

* Terms and prices subject to change without notice. Prices do not include applicable taxes. Sales tax applicable in N.Y. Canadian residents will be charged applicable taxes. Offer not valid in Quebec. This offer is limited to one order per household. All orders subject to credit approval. Credit or debit balances in a customer's account(s) may be offset by any other outstanding balance owed by or to the customer. Please allow 4 to 6 weeks for delivery. Offer available while quantities last.

Your Privacy—The Reader Service is committed to protecting your privacy. Our Privacy Policy is available online at www.ReaderService.com or upon request from the Reader Service.

We make a portion of our mailing list available to reputable third parties that offer products we believe may interest you. If you prefer that we not exchange your name with third parties, or if you wish to clarify or modify your communication preferences, please visit us at www.ReaderService.com/consumerchoice or write to us at Reader Service Preference Service, P.O. Box 9062, Buffalo, NY 14269. Include your complete name and address.

HSRLP11B

The series you love are now available in

LARGER PRINT!

The books are complete and unabridged—
printed in a larger type size to make it
easier on your eyes.

♦ Harlequin *Romance*

From the Heart, For the Heart

♦ Harlequin
INTRIGUE
BREATHTAKING ROMANTIC SUSPENSE

♦ Harlequin *Presents*

Seduction and Passion Guaranteed!

♦ Harlequin *Super Romance*

Exciting, emotional, unexpected!

Try **LARGER PRINT** today!

Visit: www.ReaderService.com
Call: 1-800-873-8635

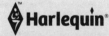

♦ Harlequin

A *Romance* FOR EVERY MOOD™

www.ReaderService.com

HLPDIR11